OVERKILL

OVERKILL

A FOLLY BEACH HALLOWEEN MYSTERY

BILL NOEL

ANGELICA CRUZ

Front cover photo and design by Bill Noel

Author photos and original map painting by Susan Noel.

ISBN: 978-1-958414-20-0

Enigma House Press

Goshen, Kentucky 40026

www.enigmahousepress.com

Other Folly Beach Mysteries by Bill Noel

Folly

The Pier

Washout

The Edge

The Marsh

Ghosts

Missing

Final Cut

First Light

Boneyard Beach

Silent Night

Dead Center

Discord

A Folly Beach Mystery COLLECTION

Dark Horse

Joy

A Folly Beach Mystery COLLECTION II

No Joke

Relic

A Folly Beach Mystery COLLECTION III

Faith

1

Mel leaned back in the chair, his leather bomber jacket, sleeves cut off at the shoulder, fall short of covering his stomach, and says, "How long's it been, Chris?"

"How long's what been?"

"Since the damned dinosaurs roamed the beach," he said and huffed. "What do you think I mean? How long since I've heard from you?"

"Couple of years."

Mel looked around the patio of Rita's, one of Folly Beach's most popular restaurants, snarled at an elderly man staring at him from a nearby table, turned back to me, stuffed a fry in his mouth, and mumbled, "You done turned homophobe in your old age and dumped your gay buddy?"

I chose not to remind him that he was only five years

younger than my near seventy years roaming this earth or that it'd been just as long since he'd contacted me. Instead, I said, "How's business?"

Mel Evans owns a marsh tour business based at the Folly View Marina, located over the bridge separating my home on Folly Beach, South Carolina, from the rest of the state.

He pushed his camouflaged fatigue cap with *Semper Fi* on the crown back on his bald head, and said, "Couldn't be better. There're more sniveling, flaming liberal, beer-drinking, self-centered, college deadbeats than ever giving me money."

If you were looking for a marsh tour where you could learn about the flora and fauna of the saltwater marsh bordering the north side of Folly, Mel would be the last person you'd call. Now, if you wanted to take a group on a moonlight ride to one of the sandbars in the area for an evening of beer drinking, partying, and basically hiding from the world and responsibilities, Mel's tour aboard a twenty-five-foot-long Carolina Skiff appropriately named Mad Mel's Magical Marsh Machine would be the way to go.

"No wonder you speak so highly of your college student customers," I said with more than a pinch of sarcasm.

"Smartass."

I smiled and was ready to ask about Caldwell Ramsey, Mel's significant other, when the phone rang. Charles Fowler, my best friend's name appeared on the screen.

"Guess who I'm having lunch with?" I said instead of a more traditional "Hi, Charles."

Traditional phone etiquette was near extinct among my friends. Charles and I had known Mel ten years, ever since he helped us through a situation that could've cost us our lives. It's hard to forget things like that.

"Guess what I just found?"

I should've started the conversation with "Hi, Charles."

"Mel Evans, and what'd you find?"

"A woman."

I laughed and said, "Congratulations. It's about time."

"A dead woman."

My laugh stuck in the back of my throat.

"Who, where?"

"Don't know who. I'm standing in the field beside Ninth Street West near where it turns toward the river and the Regatta Inn."

"You called the police?"

"They're on their way. Are you?"

I motioned our server for the check as I said, "Yes."

Since moving to Folly after retiring from a large health-care company in Kentucky some thirteen years ago, I, and yes, Charles, had somehow become involved in aiding the police solve several crimes. Neither of us had worked in law enforcement but Charles, who has an imagination far greater than anyone should possess, appointed himself a private detective.

The server brought the check. I fumbled getting money out of my wallet and paid. Mel leaned my direction, and said, "Charles found a dead chick?"

I nodded.

"Where?"

I told him.

"Let's go," Mel said and stood.

"You don't have to go."

"Hell I don't. Who's going to save your and Charles's sorry butts when you manage to get yourself in trouble? I should add, save you again."

My car was at the house, a couple of blocks from Rita's, so I said, "Why don't you wait here while I get the car?"

"I didn't go to college like you, so I'm not good at higher math, but I spent twenty years in the Marine's protecting you draft dodgers, and learned enough to know that my vehicle parked, what, thirty feet from where we're standing, is a hell of a lot closer than your house. I'm driving."

I make it a point to never argue with a 6'1", former Marine who looked like he could catch rattlesnakes bare-handed and bite their heads off without a second thought. I quickly made the thirty-foot trip to Mel's black, retro-styled Chevrolet Camaro, and barely had time to fasten the seatbelt before we were speeding out West Ashley Avenue toward Charles's location and who-knows-what else.

2

"Know where you're going?" I said as I gripped the door's armrest so tightly my knuckles were turning white.

Mel yanked the car into the oncoming lane as we passed a couple on a yellow golf cart going thirty-miles-per-hour slower than the Camaro.

"I'll fall back on my United States Marine Corps math and cypher that Ninth Street's the next numbered one past Eighth Street."

Our destination was near the Folly Beach County Park on the west end of the island. The Park was sandwiched between the Atlantic Ocean and the Folly River, and is favored by many visitors to the island since it offers accessible ramps to the beach and lifeguards. It was a great place to spend a day, but unfortunately, it wasn't our destination.

We'd already passed Eighth Street, so I gripped the armrest tighter anticipating an abrupt right turn.

Mel didn't disappoint. We skidded around the corner missing the STOP sign on Ninth Street by inches. Seconds later, it didn't take Mel's Marine training to figure out where Charles was. At the entrance to a parking lot reserved for Sunset Cay Marina, there must've been a half dozen police vehicles, two fire engines, and an ambulance. Most of the emergency vehicles were in the parking lot, but a gaggle of officials were gathered across the street beside a palmetto tree and an area of overgrown marsh grasses. Two members of the Folly Beach Department of Public Safety, more commonly known as cops, were stringing yellow crime scene tape around the edge of the road for at least fifty feet on either side of the gathering.

A police officer I didn't recognize motioned us to stop, glanced at me in the passenger's seat, then focused on Mel. "Sir, where're you headed?"

Before Mel could answer, I said, "The marina."

"Okay, park at the far end of the lot. Stay clear of what's happening over here." He waved his arm in the direction of the emergency vehicles like we wouldn't have known what to stay clear of.

Mel, probably feeling left out of the conversation said, "What's going on?"

"Police investigation, sir. Again, head to the far side of the parking lot."

And that's what we did. At least that was part of what

the officer had told us to do. The *stay clear of what's happening* part was not to be. While the officer was stopping a minivan and checking its destination, Mel and I crossed the street and approached the gathered emergency responders until we were spotted by another member of Folly's Department of Public Safety. Fortunately, it was someone I did know.

Allen Spencer joined the police force the year I arrived on Folly, and we'd shared countless conversations over the years. He was slightly shorter than Mel, and not nearly as trim as he'd been when we'd first met.

He stopped and blocked us from getting closer to the *police investigation*.

I smiled and said, "Hey, Allen, what's going on?"

"I suppose you and your friend," he glanced at Mel, "were here to take your yacht out for a spin and happened to arrive when all this was going on."

"Allen, you know Mel Evans?"

Mel reached out to shake the officer's hand.

They shook and Allen said, "Seen you around, but not recently. Good to see you again."

Mel nodded and said, "Likewise."

"Now, why're you here?"

Allen had known me way too long to believe what he'd said about us taking a spin on our yacht.

"You caught us. We received a call—"

Allen stuck his hand up, palm facing me, and said, "Let me guess. A call from Charles who said he found a body and told you to get out here so you could stick your nose where it don't belong."

I shrugged. "Partially true. Charles did call. He said something about a body but was so shaken that I didn't understand what he was talking about. He told us where he was and we thought we'd better make sure he's okay."

"I don't believe..., umm, never mind. He's over there talking to Detective Adair from the County Sheriff's Office."

Mel took a step back and said, "Crap."

Allen started to say something to Mel, but hesitated.

I knew what had irritated Mel. Five years ago, he had taken a group of students from the College of Charleston on one of his beer-guzzling excursions when one of his passengers was killed. Adair was the detective on the case and had accused Mel of being the murderer. Since Mel was standing beside me, it was obvious he wasn't the culprit, but it took Charles and me to solve the crime, much to the chagrin of Detective Adair.

I said, "Think Adair will be much longer with Charles? I'd like to get him out of here as soon as possible."

"I'll check. While I'm gone, don't try to sneak under the tape."

"You know I wouldn't do that."

"No I don't."

"Before you go, any idea what happened or who the victim is?"

"Nothing more than what I suspect Charles told you,"

Allen said before heading over to Detective Adair and Charles."

Mel watched Adair talking to the detective and said, "We going to stand here twiddling our thumbs, or get in there to find out what's going on?"

"I don't see an upside to sneaking among a bunch of law enforcement officers, especially knowing your history with Detective Adair. Besides, if there's anything to learn about the victim or what happened, Charles will've learned it."

"I keep forgetting he claims to be a private detective."

I wish I could forget it. History tells me I will not only be reminded of it several more times by Charles, but he will do more than remind me of his imaginary status.

Hopefully, we'll both live to tell people about it years from now.

3

While we were waiting for Charles, a couple of the first responders standing near the police tape kept glancing at us. Rather than having another official asking why we were here, I suggested we wait in the car. Mel said that was a great idea "since it's 117 degrees out here." I didn't waste words telling him that it was in the upper-70s, and he wouldn't have been so hot if he wasn't wearing a leather jacket, even if the sleeves had been removed.

It was another thirty minutes before I saw Charles looking for our vehicle, and then heading our way. He was leaning on his ever-present cane and moving slower than usual. I got out of the car to let him climb in the back seat, then asked if he was okay.

"No, far from it. You didn't see her. My legs are still wobbling."

I'd been with him a few times when he'd seen a murder victim. He'd remained calm and didn't appear outwardly traumatized by the gruesome sights. I also knew not to push for an explanation. He'd tell us when he was ready, and only then.

I said, "What happened?"

"I was delivering a package for Dude. Went to a couple staying at the Regatta Inn. Nice folks. They're from Vermont. Here for a week."

The Regatta Inn is a ten-room luxury B&B overlooking the Folly River and adjacent to the Sunset Cay Marina.

Mel interrupted with, "That damned, draft-dodging, hippy, druggy got you into this mess. Figures."

Despite what he'd said, Mel had known Dude Sloan, the owner of the surf shop that had Charles delivering packages, for decades, and they were good friends.

Before Mel elaborated on other less-flattering images of Dude or Charles told me if the couple from Vermont had pets and if so, their names and breed, plus countless other details about the couple neither Mel nor I cared about, I turned to face him in the back seat and said, "The body?"

He looked toward the group of first responders and said, "Was riding my bike back to town when I looked over and saw what I thought was a pile of colorful clothes plopped right down in the tall marsh grass." He shook his head. "I made the mistake of stopping. All I wanted to do was grab the pile of clothes and take it to the nearest trash bin. You know I hate trash thrown around. Anyway, the clothes were still attached to a woman." He hesitated. "Fellas, it was horrible. I didn't have to get close to know she was dead. That's when I called the police and you."

I waited for him to continue. Mel didn't wait and said, "COD?"

Charles said, "Huh?"

Mel took a deep breath, exhaled, then said, "Cause of death, what killed her?"

"I'm no expert, but think it was the hatchet or ax, don't know the difference, stuck in her back."

"That'd do it," Mel said.

The car's air conditioner was pumping out cold air as fast as it could but sweat ran down Charles's cheeks.

I said, "Any idea who she is?"

"No, but if she always dressed like she was, I figure I'd have seen her if she was from around here."

"Colorful clothes?"

"Yeah. Don't know what you call it, but she had on one of those long dresses that's layers of flimsy cloth. Red, blue, with gold around the edges. Like old-time dancers if you know what I mean. Oh yeah, she also had a red scarf wrapped around her head."

"Halloween's what, five, six weeks away?" I said. "Could it have been a Halloween costume?"

"Suppose so, but who dresses for Halloween in September?"

Mel said, "What about her shoes?"

"Guys, could we go where I can get something to drink?" Charles said and looked around like there'd be a concession stand in the field or in the parking lot.

I said, "Where's your bike?"

"Inside the yellow tape. I'll get it later if one of you brings me back."

"Sure," I said. "Where do you want to go?"

"Loggerhead's is closer than anywhere else."

Mel put the car in gear and said, "Your chauffeur will take you there. Fee and tip expected."

"Chris will buy you a beer," Charles generously offered.

"Cheap, but I'll take it."

Charles didn't say anything on the two-mile ride to Loggerhead's Beach Grill. There wasn't much time to since Mel drove slightly under the speed of sound on the way to the popular restaurant.

As we reached the top step to the deck, I said, "Charles, you okay sitting outside?"

"If it's in the shade. I'm cooler now than I was back you-know-where."

Ed, the restaurant's owner, greeted us and said he had a table in the shade along the railing overlooking the street. He then handed us off to Sarah, a college-age server, who led us to the table and asked what we wanted to drink. Charles said, "Water, lots of it." Mel said, "Water will never do," and ordered a Budweiser, and I stuck with water.

Sarah went for our drinks and Mel stared at Charles and

said, "Well?"

"Well what?"

An excellent question, I thought.

"Shoes."

Charles said, "What about shoes?"

"I asked about them back at the, well, murder site. Were they gold, high heel with a gold strap around the ankles?"

"Mel, I didn't stand there studying her feet. They could've been."

Mel nodded. "Probably a gypsy peasant dress, head wrap, gold-coin detailing, and traditional high-heel shoes."

Charles stared at Mel like he'd never seen him before and said, "How do you know all that?"

"Don't you ever go to the Diva Royale Drag Queen show in Charleston?" Mel raised both hands above his head. "Oh wait, I forget, you straight guys don't know how to have a good time. Anyway, a couple of the entertainers perform like they're gypsies, say they're nomadic Romani, and dress like you described plus the shoes."

"You saying the dead person is a drag queen?"

"Could be, but that's not what I'm saying. The dead guy or gal sounds like he or she was trying to look like a gypsy. That's all I'm saying."

Our drinks arrived and Charles took two gulps before responding, "All I'm saying is she or he was dead from a hatchet or an ax in the back. I don't know who it was, who put the hatchet or whatever it was there, or when it happened." He snapped his fingers. "Chris, why don't you call Cindy and see what she knows?"

Cindy LaMond was Folly's Director of Public Safety, shortened to police chief, and a good friend.

"Didn't see her. Was she there?"

"I didn't see her. Detective Adair in his starched-white shirt, navy blazer, and shoes so shiny you could see your reflection in them started interrogating me like I was the killer, so I didn't see much of anything during that."

Mel smacked his beer bottle on the table, stared at Charles, and said, "You know what Adair had on his feet but didn't notice if the dead person had gold shoes?"

"Charles," I said ignoring Mel's comment, "if Cindy wasn't there, I doubt she'd shed much light on what happened. Why don't I wait until tonight and call her?"

"I suppose. But don't forget, the sooner we know the who, what, and when, the sooner we'll be able to figure out who killed her. Yes, Mel, for now I'm sticking with it being a her."

I didn't care what Charles would be sticking with regarding the victim's gender, I was stuck on him saying we'll figure out who killed her.

Mel shook his head and sighed. "No offense, but that's a dumb-ass idea. You're going to get yourself killed one of these days. You're two old guys playing cop who know nothing about law enforcement. Dumb-ass idea."

Charles glared at him. "That wasn't what you thought a few years back when we pulled your bacon out of the fire. Kept you out of prison, as I recall."

Mel surprised me with a smile. "And I'm forever grateful. That's why I want to keep you two alive. Playing cop ain't a good recipe for living a long life."

I said, "First, I never said anything about catching anyone. Second, I'm sure Charles simply wants to know what happened, and not trying to catch a killer."

I wish I believed that.

4

The ringing phone interrupted my afternoon thinking about all that'd happened beginning with lunch with Mel. Cindy LaMond's name appeared on the screen.

"Good afternoon, Chief."

"You feeling okay?"

"Yes, why?"

"Oh, I don't know, it's been hours since Charles stumbled upon a body, and I hear nothing from you. Was about to do a welfare check on you two geezers."

"I'm touched."

"Don't be, just saving myself a surprise visit or call to add to my stress level."

"I'm insulted you'd think I would—"

"Save your breath. I've known you for what, a dozen

years, so this ain't our first rodeo. With all that mushy stuff out of the way, I wanted to let you know that the deceased was sent to Charleston for a complete autopsy. And don't ask, we don't know who she was."

"It was a female?"

Cindy said, "You saying Charles can't tell the difference between guys and gals?"

"Based on her attire, Mel mentioned the possibility the victim was a drag queen."

"Mel of Mad Mel's Magical Marsh Machine?"

"Yep."

"When did he become part of your phantom detective agency?"

I ignored the detective agency remark and said, "He was having lunch with me when Charles called."

"Did Charles seem okay after you picked him up?"

"You mean besides the shock of finding a body with a hatchet in its back?"

"Chris, it's not the first deceased person he's seen, crap, not even the tenth, but Detective Adair said your buddy appeared shaken."

"Adair was right."

"Take care of yourself and the nosy misfits you hang around with. Here's a novel suggestion, take a break and let the professionals handle this."

"Of course. Thanks for calling and keeping me on the straight and narrow."

"Smartass."

Before I replied, she was gone. I'm not sure if it's a good thing that the police chief knows me that well, but in the years living on my adopted island I've stumbled across more dead bodies than many small town coroners deal with. At least, this time it wasn't me who did the stumbling. This may've been the first time Charles was alone when he found a victim.

I dialed my best friend's number to see if he'd made it home after I'd dropped him at the crime scene to retrieve his bike. After four rings, I realized he wasn't going to answer and ended the call.

I leaned back in my recliner and rested my eyes, also known as taking a nap, when a sound jarred me awake. I looked at the clock to see that two hours had passed. Not seeing anything out of place that could have interrupted my slumber, I grabbed my windbreaker and headed next door to Bert's to pick up life sustaining necessities like Diet Cokes, Doritos, and Hershey's bars.

The short walk to the island's grocery revealed the source of the noise that disturbed my nap. A green, GMC pickup truck and a Jeep had tried to see which could be first through the intersection beside Bert's. They ended in a tie. Unfortunately, minor collisions are common on the small island. A husky man, probably in his early-50s, around 5'11" with a brown buzz-cut was examining the front bumper of his truck. The female driver of the Jeep was heading to retrieve two surfboards from the middle of the road. When she turned towards me, I realized it was Alyssa

Harp, a relatively new Folly transplant whose pastime was surfing.

"Let me help with that," I said, as I cautiously stepped into the street to grab one of the surfboards.

Alyssa smiled and said, "Thanks, Chris."

"You okay?"

"A little jostled. I forgot to strap the boards down. This'll teach me to be in a hurry."

The other driver walked over to where we were standing. "You injured?"

"No, I'm sorry," Alyssa said, "Wasn't paying attention. Are you hurt?"

The man smiled. "You admit it was your fault?"

"How could it not be?" Alyssa said as she looked at the man's truck. "I turned in front of you. Let me grab my insurance card and call the police." Alyssa started to walk to the passenger side of her vehicle.

"There's no need. The vehicles aren't that damaged, besides what does it say about me that I couldn't see and avoid a neon-yellow Jeep." The man laughed and extended his hand. "Jeffery Fuller."

"Alyssa Harp, and this is Chris, sorry forgot your last name."

I extended my hand to the gentleman. "Chris Landrum. Mr. Fuller. Alyssa, why don't we take this conversation to the parking lot."

After both vehicles were parked in Bert's side lot and out of the line of traffic, the damage assessed, and Alyssa and

Jeffery making small talk, I excused myself to continue shopping. With drinks and snacks in hand, I started back to my cottage when I noticed Mr. Fuller walking towards the market's entry.

"Mr. Fuller, did you get everything straightened out?"

"Please call me Jeffery. Yeah, no harm."

"Nice way to look at it."

"Life's too short to sweat the small stuff."

"I'm sure Alyssa is pleased her carelessness won't haunt her."

"She seems like a nice young lady. Known her long?"

"Not really, met her last Christmas. What brings you to Folly?"

"Work brought me, but the people here have made me want to call it home."

"It's a great place. What business are you in?"

"This and that, mainly construction, electrical, drywall, working on boats, you name it."

"Sounds like you're a handy person to have around."

He looked at the paper sack in my hand and said, "Don't want whatever's in there to melt or whatever, and I need to get some food. Nice meeting you."

"You, too."

5

Nothing puts me in a greater mood than being awakened by the ringing of the phone before the sun has risen. Incidentally, sarcasm is one of my less endearing traits.

I reached over and answered without bothering to look at the caller ID, to hear, "Where are you?"

"Morning, Charles."

"I know it's morning and who I am. What I don't know is where you are."

"Home, where should I be?"

"At the Dog enjoying breakfast with your friend."

"I'll be there shortly."

Rubbing my face to displace the remaining cobwebs, I'd finished getting ready and headed out the door. The sky was clear, the temperature cool, so I grabbed a light jacket and started walking six blocks to the Lost Dog Cafe. It was a few days away from October, so the roads were deserted with few visitors on the island, and certainly not this early in the morning. I wasn't surprised that many of the houses and most businesses were still dark. What did surprise me, several homes had Halloween decorations displayed, indicating fans of the holiday. I was never a big fan of Halloween and after last year with Charles and me finding a corpse in a haunted house, I had not changed my opinion.

Charles, wearing a black Wake Forest Demon Deacons sweatshirt, was parking his mode of transportation in the bike rack beside the parking area as I walked up.

"About time you got here," he said and looked at his bare wrist where most normal people wore a watch.

"Yes, I see you've been waiting hours. Inside or out?"

"These old bones are chilled from waiting on you."

Letting the comment pass, I said, "Inside it is."

Amy, one of the friendly servers, met us at the door and escorted us to a table near the back and took our drink order.

I said, "How're you doing, Charles?"

"Why?"

"Perhaps the shock you had."

"I'm still on yesterday time, haven't been to sleep. Close my eyes and see that woman." He rubbed the back of his neck while staring at the table.

"You seemed upset yesterday."

"Gee, I wonder why? It's not every day one finds a hatchet sticking out of someone's back."

"Sorry, I just meant—"

"I know, but you didn't see her."

Amy returned with our coffee and asked what we wanted to eat. After getting our order, she headed to the kitchen, leaving us to continue our unpleasant conversation.

"Chris, we've got to find out who killed that unfortunate woman. Have you talked to Cindy?"

"The police are capable of finding out what happened and yes, she called late yesterday."

"Why didn't you call me?" He sighed. "Never mind, what did she say?"

"Nothing we didn't already know. The young lady was killed, probably from the hatchet. They don't know who she was."

"Doesn't sound like the cops are solving it."

"That's not fair."

"I know, but I owe it to her to figure out what happened."

"You didn't even know the victim."

"I found her and can't stop thinking about her. Besides, it's what we do."

Amy brought our breakfast, and the rest of the meal was eaten in silence. By the time the check arrived Charles had regained his voice.

"Sad there's not going to be a haunted house this year."

"Oh yeah, I'm brokenhearted about that, since the one last year was so much fun."

"There should be something to do to get the community

into the holiday spirit. I heard a rumor about a masquerade party."

"Where did you hear that?"

"Making deliveries. Won't it be great? Getting dressed up in a costume, having fun guessing who everyone is. Then, letting them try to figure out who we are."

"Nope."

"It'll be fun."

"Nope."

He nodded and said, "You're right, we need to find a killer first."

Charles's logic at its finest.

"Nope."

"Scrooge."

"Wrong holiday."

"Whatever. I'm off to the surf shop to see if Dude has deliveries for me."

Before I could respond, Charles had hurried to the door and disappeared into the chilly morning. I took the final sip of coffee, paid Amy, then headed to the exit, when two men at the table near the door caught my attention. They were angry about something. They were in their thirties. One was muscular with a bald head and a brown goatee, the other with a slight build and long, brown hair. Before the door closed, the larger gentleman said, "Got what she deserved. She should've known better."

I'd turned on Center Street while staring at the sidewalk and thinking about the two strangers, when I looked up and faced a dog the size of a Volkswagen Beetle followed by a teenager who resembled the lead character in a vampire movie. Most people would cross the street to avoid the menacing duo. I'd known them nearly a year, so I kept walking their direction.

"Good morning, Desmond. How are you and Lugh?"

The seventeen-year-old gave me a look resembling a snarl, but I knew it was his friendly face, and said, "You know I don't do good, but Lugh is fine. He's still growing. If he gets any bigger, Roisin will be able to ride him."

"Speaking of your sister, how is she?"

"Her and mom are depressed. I guess I am too. Lugh and I are on our way to pick her up. She went to the marsh this morning with preacher man."

"It's good that she and Preacher Burl still go out and study nature in the marsh."

"You should stop by the house. Everyone would be happy to see you."

I smiled at the young man and said, "Everyone?"

"Well, not me. I see you now." Desmond held out his hand and I shook it and then patted the Irish Wolfhound's head.

"I'll stop by and bring Charles."

"Cool, heard the cane dude found a body yesterday. Were you with him?"

"No. Who told you about it?"

"I have a friend that lives on Ninth Street that told me."

"Interesting."

"Interesting that he told me, or that I have a friend?"

"Yes."

Desmond smirked, "That's why I like you." He turned and continued walking down the street with his dinosaur-size canine.

I continued home while thinking how I'd met Desmond and his family almost a year ago. The Stone family are practicing Wiccans and I'd never met anyone like them. Shortly after we'd met, tragedy struck the family when Desmond and Roisin's father was murdered. This Halloween season will be the first anniversary of his tragic death. I couldn't imagine how hard it would be for the family, including the morose Desmond, whom I knew to be nicer and kinder than he came across.

Chief LaMond's Ford F-150 pickup truck was pulling out of Bert's Market as I walked past the store. A quick blast from her siren stopping everyone nearby in their tracks.

I approached her lowered driver's side window to hear her say, "I love doing that. Are you and your misfits solving the murder?"

"Chief, I leave that to the professionals."

"Keep it that way," she said, then gunned the truck as she headed toward Center Street and I continued home.

6

’ve always been an early riser. When I had a full-time job, my alarm clock was seldom needed and not much has changed in retirement except my clothes are more comfortable. My suit and tie were replaced with khakis or shorts, polo shirts, boat shoes, and a Tilley hat. Today I’ve added my Nikon camera. Folly offers activities ranging from shark tooth hunting to surfing. Having done both, although my surfing experience ended after one failed attempt, I prefer remaining on land. Today’s motivation for getting outside early was a beautiful early morning blue sky and the hope of capturing some memorable images.

The walk down Center Street to the iconic Folly Beach Fishing Pier was a short journey. Then again, it doesn’t take long to get most places on the six-mile-long, half-mile-wide barrier island. The size makes it perfect for foot traffic, especially in the island's small center of commerce. Driving in summer traffic can seem more like being in a parking lot than on a street. During off-season, excessive traffic is not an issue.

I climbed the stairs leading to the pier and realized it felt like winter coming early regardless how beautiful the sky. The breeze off the Atlantic hit me with more force than I was accustomed to. I pulled my jacket tighter and scanned the horizon in search of the perfect photo opportunity, although even the seagulls seemed to give up on their quest for food and were perched on the roof of the Tides Hotel. I took the hint from my feathered friends and made my way to Roasted, the hotel's coffee shop.

I was surprised to see Preacher Burl Costello seated at one of the two small tables in the center of the room.

"Morning, Brother Chris."

"Preacher, what brings you out this morning?"

Burl was minister at First Light, Folly's newest house of worship, or more accurately, place of worship since most of its services are held on the beach near the Pier. Only inclement weather forces the services to meet in a storefront on Center Street.

"Sermon writing. I needed a change of scenery."

"I'll leave you to it."

"No need, please join me." He pointed to the chair on the opposite side of the table. "I'd rather have a cup of coffee with a friend."

"Don't suppose 'thou shall not procrastinate' is one of the commandments?"

He chuckled and said, "I am fortunate that it's not."

"Let me get a cup then I'll help you not break a commandment."

Penny, Roasted's manager, whose smile always was warm and friendly, stood behind the counter waiting on me to approach. A cup of coffee alone wouldn't do, so I ordered two cheese Danish. She handed me my change and said to let her know if we needed anything else.

"Since I interrupted your work, here's an offering." I set one of the pastries in front of Burl then took the seat across from him.

"Thank you but it's not necessary."

While my offering may not have been necessary, he grabbed one of the doughy delights before I could take it back. He took a bite, wiped crumbs off his mustache and said, "Heard Brother Charles made an unfortunate discovery."

"Afraid so."

"Any leads on the identity of the poor soul or what happened?"

"Those are questions for the authorities."

He smiled. "You act like I don't know you and Brother Charles."

"This time you're off," I said, hoping I wasn't lying to a man of the cloth. Changing the subject, I added, "How is Hope House doing?"

Hope House is a large house a generous member of First Light's flock, as Burl refers to his members, donated to be used as a boardinghouse for people who are unable to afford housing. Burl lives there offering spiritual and other forms of guidance to the residents.

"The soul of the house is strong for those who reside within its walls, but the structure's body is weak and always needs repairs."

"I'd offer to help but as you know, a crab with a hammer is handier than I'd be."

"Fortunately, I shan't be needing your or the crab's help. Do you know Sister Beth Powell?"

"No, who's she?"

"New member of my flock. She started attending services a couple of weeks ago, more important to this conversation, she's a plumber, so a blessing on multiple fronts."

"That is fortunate."

"Now if I can find a carpenter who needs a place to live, Hope House would be on the road to recovery."

"He's not a carpenter, but I saw Desmond and Lugh yesterday while they were on their way to meet you and Roisin. How is she doing?"

"Sister Roisin at twelve is still smarter than many adults with her clever and refreshing way of looking at the world."

"She's a surprising young lady."

"That she is," Burl said and glanced at his notebook on the table.

I smiled and said, "I've kept you long enough. I'll let you

get back to your sermon. I wouldn't want to deprive your flock of your inspiring words."

"Stop by Sunday so you can witness how well I inspired."

I smiled and nodded as I walked to the door. My attendance at First Light is spotty at best, but that doesn't stop the preacher from dropping not-so-subtle hints or simply asking me to attend.

The weather had taken a turn for the worse and I wasn't halfway home when the rain started. The only thing dry on me when I walked in the house was my camera I'd protected under my jacket. Perhaps I should start checking the forecast before heading out, but then again, retirement is about taking chances you didn't take during your other life, or so I told my soaked self.

The rain was determined to keep me in for the afternoon, so my thoughts turned to the woman who found herself with a hatchet in her back. I wondered if records were kept on how many people are killed by hatchets. It seems it would be a minuscule number and a harsh way to meet your end. Thoughts of unpleasant ways to die was fortunately interrupted by a knocking on the door. Opening it revealed Charles looking like a drowned rat.

He shook rainwater off his hat, and said, "Sorry, couldn't wait for you to meander over to my apartment."

"No, by all means, come drip on my floor. Let me get you a towel."

"Thanks."

"Trying to be Gene Kelly's stand in?"

"Chris, anyone ever mention you're a smart ass?"

"Might have heard it a time or two. Want a drink?"

"Sit down," he said and pointed at my recliner. "I'll get it."

He returned from the kitchen carrying a Coke and a Diet Coke.

He handed me the Diet Coke and said, "I think it's time for an enlightening conversation."

"What's the topic?"

"Gypsies."

"Interesting, and out there."

"Not far out there, considering I found one who had a run-in with a hatchet."

"Do you know if she was a Gypsy or simply wearing a Halloween costume?"

"Did you know there's a gypsy community not three hours from here? It's called Murphy Village and has the largest population of Irish Travelers in the country. They're gypsies, you know."

"I didn't know either of those facts, or I assume facts. How did you know about it?"

"I'm not only another handsome face, but an endless fount of information."

"No argument about that, the fount part. It still doesn't explain if she was a gypsy."

"That's one of the many things we need to figure out, the other is why she was killed, plus, of course, who did it."

"I'm guessing it'd be pointless to say for us to leave it to the authorities."

"Yep."

"So, Mr. Detective, where would you like to start?"

"No clue, but the rain's almost stopped and I'm a busy man, so I'm leaving so you can ponder our next move."

He grabbed his cane and Tilley and was out the door. In my many years, I've never met anyone quite like Charles, and would not change our friendship, even if it occasionally takes CliffsNotes to know what he's talking about.

7

The showers had tapered off before I decided that nothing in the house sounded appetizing for lunch, so I headed up East Ashley Avenue to Taco Boy. As I approached the restaurant, an inconsiderate driver pulled in front of me blocking my route. The window lowered revealing Folly's Director of Public Safety.

I moved closer and said, "Was I breaking any laws?"

Chief LaMond smiled and said, "Being a walking relic."

"I'm not aware of that law."

"Me either, but it fits. Actually, I have something that might interest you."

"I'm heading to Taco Boy, want to join me?"

"You buying?"

"How could I resist buying lunch for such a charming young lady?"

"True. I'll meet you there."

Cindy was waiting at the top of the stairs for me. Youth has its advantages, such as getting places quicker with fewer aches and pains. She was in her mid-fifties, 5'3", with curly dark hair, and a quick smile. The hostess asked if we had a table preference. I nodded toward Cindy who selected the corner table out of the flow of staff and diners. The server took our drink orders and left us to review the menu.

Cindy leaned back in her chair and said, "You getting ready for your favorite holiday?"

"If you mean Halloween, have you suffered a head injury or forgot who you're talking to?"

"Neither, just wanted to get your hackles up."

"You're cheery today."

"Working on being more people friendly."

"I repeat, are you suffering from a head injury, or is the mayor pushing again for you to play nice?"

"Let's change the subject. I have a meeting with the most honorable mayor this afternoon and don't want to ruin this nice lunch you are generously providing."

The server returned with our drinks and asked if we were ready to order. We each ordered a quesadilla, mine with grilled chicken, Cindy the carne asada. With our orders placed, silence filled the table, as Cindy looked around the room then focused on her drink.

She gazed around the room a second time, then again stared into her drink glass.

I said, "Is everything okay?"

"Yeah, I'm tired."

"Job keeping you up at night?"

"Not important. Figure you'd be more interested in the information I have."

That's the second time she'd mentioned it.

"Care to share?"

"Ruby Banes."

"Who's Ruby Banes?"

"Glad you asked, she's the dead, alleged gypsy Charles found."

"How did you make the ID so quickly? I heard there was no wallet at the scene. Was she in one of your missing persons' data bases?"

"You've been hanging out with Charles too long. His excessive and, I might add, often irritating questions have rubbed off on you."

"Ouch."

"You were correct that there was no wallet or purse at the scene, and I haven't been informed by Detective Adair if they got a hit on the fingerprints."

"So, you got her name from a Ouija board?"

"Nice spooky reference, but it was the living who gave us her name. Early this morning, one of our fine citizens came to the office to file a missing person's report. Our alert clerk showed the visitor a photo of the dead woman who then came close to barfing all over the room before identifying the deceased."

"Were they related?"

"Housemates. Trudy Miller identified the body."

"Don't believe I know either of them. They live here?"

"Ruby worked at Harris Teeter and shared a small two-bedroom apartment with Trudy near Lowlife Bar."

"That's not close to where Charles found her."

"True."

"Is Trudy a gypsy?"

"No, and it doesn't appear Ruby was either, at least not in the traditional sense. According to her housemate, it was just her persona, whatever that means."

"Isn't that odd?"

"Did you forget it's Folly?"

"She tell you anything helpful?"

"Not really. Claims she didn't know her well. Said they shared an apartment for convenience. In fact, Trudy didn't seem too upset but was worried since Ruby's scooter was at the building and her phone was in the room. Said it was unlike her housemate. She was more concerned about how she would pay rent without Ruby."

"Anything else?"

"Not really."

"Any information from the autopsy?"

"Sharp force trauma, aka the hatchet, but they're waiting on the toxicology report which will take several days before making it official."

"You think there might be other factors?"

"No, it's routine."

Our lunch arrived and our conversation turned to how

good the food was and how the weather had included more rain than usual. There were also stretches of silence, which are unusual for Cindy, but I didn't press. The check arrived. I reached for it as Cindy looked away then asked the server for tea to go. She told the server she needed all the caffeine she could get for her next meeting.

The server went for the tea, and I said, "You have an ID, but what about suspects?"

"You know you'll be the first person I tell when there are any."

"Really?"

"No, smart ass. In case you've forgotten, you're not on the city's payroll."

"Just making conversation."

"Yeah, right. Anyway, have a good afternoon and try and stay out of trouble."

"Me? You know I'm never in trouble."

"Smartass."

The server returned with Cindy's tea, and with a rare expression of gratitude, Cindy thanked me for lunch, before heading to potential verbal torture from the mayor. I was thankful I'm retired and no longer dealt will bureaucratic, let's say, bologna.

On the walk home, my mind returned to Ruby Banes. What could someone do to deserve a hatchet in the back. Also, she wasn't found near her home or place of work, so what was she doing on that side of the island, let alone with someone who wanted to end her life? I reached my front porch when another question came to mind. Why did I care?

As I was pondering questions with no answers, my phone rang. I was half expecting a robocall but saw Charles's name on the screen.

He opened the conversation with, "I'm sitting at Cal's. Its owner and I were wondering why you're not here."

"Is that an invitation?"

"Yes."

"Then, I'm on my way."

Rain was still in the forecast and parking shouldn't be a problem this time of year, so I drove the short distance to Cal's Country Bar and Burgers. Only a couple of cars were parked on the street in front of the bar and near Cal's vintage Cadillac Eldorado.

Walking through the doors wasn't exactly like walking into the fictional Cheers bar, but it still gave me the feeling of being at home, that is if home was an old, somewhat smelly bar and grill. Charles and Cal were sitting at the bar as the classic Wurlitzer jukebox played "Hey, Good Lookin'." I was certain the Hank Williams Sr.' classic wasn't referring to me, but it was nice to hear it anyway since I was a vintage country music fan.

Charles saw me, looked at his wrist, and shook his head.

Cal, stood, tipped his Stetson that's been on his head most of the last forty years, and said, "Hey pard, how are you?"

"Fine, and you?"

"On the good side of bad," Cal said and went behind the bar and grabbed another beer for Charles and a glass of wine for me.

Before moving to Folly and taking over the rundown bar, Cal, who was in his late seventies, had toured the south singing his brand of country music anywhere that'd have him.

I turned to Charles and said, "Been here long?"

"Made my last delivery for Dude. I hadn't seen Cal in a while, and thought you might be here, so here I am."

"Sounds like a full day. I had one myself."

"Which means?"

"Had lunch with Cindy."

"Well, what'd she say about the dead woman and who might have ruined her day?"

I thought about what Cindy had said about Charles and his endless questions and smiled to myself. My internal monologue must've gone on too long because Charles was tapping his beer bottle on the bar, while glaring at me.

I said, "The victim's Ruby Banes. Her attire was normal clothing for her, no indication she was a gypsy, and the cause of death was the hatchet. The police have no suspects."

"Was that so hard, keeping your best friend in the loop?"

"It was easier when you're not interrupting every ten-seconds."

"I'm trying to better myself. It also helped that I was taking a drink when you spouted all that."

Merle Haggard was singing "That's the Way Love Goes"

and Cal looked around the room to see if any customers needed anything. That didn't take long since there were only a handful of them. Seeing no one in need, he returned to his seat and said, "Charles tells me you two are playing cops again. Who're your suspects?"

I glared at Charles then turned to Cal, "We have no suspects. We're not the police, and this is none of our business."

Charles said, "To quote JFK, 'One person can make a difference, and everyone should try.'"

I said, "Charles, I'm certain Kennedy wasn't talking about us trying to find a murderer."

Laughter from across the room caught my attention, where I noticed the two men I'd seen arguing in the Dog. They appeared to have ironed out their differences. From the collection of empty beer bottles on the table, it looked like they'd been here a while.

"Charles, do you know those men?"

Charles followed my gaze. "Do you think I know everyone on this island?"

"Pretty much."

"Fair enough, yes, I know them, well, sort of."

"Who are they?"

"Who's the nosy one now?" He nodded like he'd smacked a game-winning home run. "But, to answer your question, the one with long, brown hair is Victor, and the one that looks like he could bench press the bar is Waylon. They work construction, seems they've known each other since Moses was a baby. Why?"

"Saw them the other morning at the Dog. I noticed because they were arguing. Where did you meet them?"

"I was making deliveries. They were unloading their pickup at a construction site on East Huron, Victor stopped me to ask about my 'rad ride' Schwinn and we talked. Let me introduce you." Charles started to stand.

"I don't want to disturb them."

Charles didn't get a chance regardless of my desires. They'd hopped up and headed to the exit before he could get out of his chair. Fortunately.

8

A knock on the door at six in the morning is seldom a good sign, so when I heard not a knock but a pounding on the door, I expected the worst. I set my coffee mug on the kitchen table and headed to the door with more than a tad of trepidation.

I was greeted by the glaring expression on the face of Mel Evans, again attired in his leather bomber jacket, woodland camo field pants, and his camouflaged fatigue cap.

He looked at my bare feet, shook his head, and said, "It's zero six hundred. What in hell are you doing in the middle of the day prancing around on those ugly, pasty-white feet."

I didn't think zero six hundred in Mel-speak was the middle of the day but knew pointing that out would be futile.

"Good morning. What brings you out so early this lovely morning?" I said with an emphasis on *so early*."

To be honest, I didn't know if the morning was lovely or not, since I hadn't taken time to look out the window since I got up twenty minutes ago.

"Go get your damned leather personnel carriers and let's get some chow."

"I would if I knew what leather personnel carriers were."

"Oh yeah, I keep forgetting you're a damned draft dodger. Get your boots, or whatever you plan to stick on your feet. Daylight's a burnin'."

If daylight burned itself out it happened yesterday since if I remembered correctly, sunrise wouldn't arrive for another hour. Mel didn't find himself at my door by accident, so rather than debate sunrise, leather personnel carriers, or why he felt 6:00 a.m. was the middle of the day, I asked if he wanted to step inside while I changed into something more appropriate for going to eat rather than lounging around the house. I'd also add deck shoes to my attire rather than boots. He stepped inside, looked around the living room like it was his first time there, and didn't utter another marine term insult while I changed clothes.

His next words were, "We're going to hoof it. Your chunky body needs to walk off some of that unsightly blubber, and my finely tuned, svelte body can benefit from the exercise."

Svelte was one of the last words I would've used about his ample body and one of the last words I would've expected out of Mel's mouth, but he was right about the walk doing each of us good. I told him to lead the way.

"What's going on?" I asked trying to hone into the reason

for his visit as we were nearing the Lost Dog Cafe, which I assumed to be our destination since it was the only restaurant that served breakfast in the direction we were headed. I was glad we walked since the Dog didn't open until 6:30, or whatever that's called in Mel's lexicon.

"Does something always have to be going on with you? Couldn't I want to have breakfast and share a table with a friend?"

Yes, I thought, but knew that wasn't the reason for his pre-sunrise arrival at my door.

"I was curious about why you arrived so early."

"No reason."

I suppose he would confide what the reason in *no reason* was once we reached the restaurant.

We were the first two customers in the door and the hostess, attempting to hide a yawn behind her hand, waved around the room and said, "Your choice."

I chose my favorite table along the back wall and Robin, apparently more awake than the other servers, was quick to the table with coffee for each of us. She said she'd give us a couple of minutes to decide what we wanted. I already knew, but Mel studied the menu like it was new to him.

He finally looked up and said, "Okay, I'm ready."

"Tell Robin, not me."

He waved his hand over his head, and fortunately for the sake of peace, Robin responded. We ordered and she headed to the pass-through window leading to the kitchen and put in our orders.

Mel tapped his fork on the table before saying, "Okay, what's going on with the dead chick?"

"How would I know?"

"Let's see, could be because you butt into every suspicious death within twelve miles of this spot. Could be because your best bud Charles doesn't only stick his nose into each death but throws his whole scrawny body into playing cop and dragging you along with him. Could be—"

I waved my hand in his face interrupting his next *could be*, and said, "Her name's Ruby Banes. She worked at Harris Teeter."

Mel smiled. "See, that wasn't hard, was it? What else?"

"You already know she was killed by a hatchet."

"And?"

"She lived in an apartment over here that she shared with Trudy something-or-other."

"Did this Trudy chick put the hatchet in her roomie's back?"

"Not that I'm aware. She was the one who told the police who the victim was since Ruby didn't have identification on her body."

Robin arrived with our food and a refill on our coffee interrupting Mel's interrogation. He took a couple of bites and said, "Nothing else?"

I shook my head.

Mel pointed his fork at me before saying, "Think I'm going to have to help you and your buddy catch the hatchet killer."

That was one of the last things I expected to hear from my friend, other than svelte, that is.

"Charles and I have no plans to, as you say, catch 'the hatchet killer,' so why do—"

He pointed his hand holding the mug at me, then took a sip of his refreshed coffee, set the mug on the table, and looked in it like he wondered what was in the mug, then said, "Lately, Caldwell and me are gaggle marching."

Caldwell Ramsey had been Mel's significant other for several years.

"What's gaggle marching?" I asked, thinking it was an excellent question.

"Sorry, I keep forgetting you hid under a rock so you wouldn't have to serve your country. Means marching out of step with your fellow soldiers."

"Who are you and Caldwell out of step with?"

He sighed then looked back in his mug. "Each other."

I'd met Caldwell and had spent several hours with him over the years. He's a concert promoter and a former college athlete. He and Mel are different in several ways, but I'd never detected any significant conflict or disagreements between the two.

"What do you mean by out of step?"

"You may not believe this, but I'm not the easiest person to get along with."

I absolutely believed that, but instead of agreeing, said, "You and Caldwell always appeared to get along, at least you did when I was around."

"Did don't mean do."

The scary thing is I understood what he meant.

"What changed?"

"Caldwell keeps saying we're growing apart. Ain't my fault; ain't his. Just happens, he says."

"I'm sorry to hear that. Are you still living together?"

"For now. His work's keeping him busier than ever. He's out of town a lot scouting talent to bring to Charleston and often works evenings, so we're not stuck looking at each other that much. Enough about me. What's our next move to catch the killer?"

"You think wanting to get involved is your way of avoiding whatever's going on with you and Caldwell?"

He glared at me. "Hell no. Can't you see that you two amateurs need help, and I don't even want to mention the incompetent cops who can't figure out where the best place is to get donuts?"

As if on cue, one of Mel's incompetent cops, Allen Spencer, entered the restaurant, saw Mel and me and headed our way.

"Chris, Mel, right?"

Mel nodded as he gave Allen a sheepish look like he thought Allen had heard his comment about incompetent cops.

"Want to join us?" I asked and pointed to the chair beside Mel.

"Would love to, but don't have time. Wanted to get some good coffee before heading to a meeting at City Hall. Don't tell boss lady, but the coffee in our office tastes like sh..., umm, let's just say, tastes horrible."

"Your secret's good with me," I said, and added, "You have donuts at your meetings?"

Mel gave me a nasty look. Allen gave me a look resembling confusion.

I said, "Never mind. Perhaps another time."

Allen said he'd look forward to it then headed to the counter to order coffee.

"Suppose you thought that comment about donuts was funny," Mel said as he watched Allen head to the exit.

"Don't know what you're talking about."

"Smartass."

"Takes one to know one," I said and chuckled.

Mel rolled his eyes. "So?"

"So what?"

"What's out next step to catching the killer?"

"All we know about the victim is her name, where she worked, her roommate's name, where she lived, and cause of death. How do you think there's any possibility that we, as in you, Charles, and I, could help identify the killer?"

"I grew up in a small town outside Palm Desert, California. In case you can't figure out by the word desert in the name of the city, my knowledge of things like the ocean, the marsh, sharks, and those damned little no-see-ums wasn't learned near where I lived. Know how I learned about them?"

"How?"

"Same way you and your detective buddy catch killers. You ask questions, you watch and listen to people, you think about how someone could pull off killing someone, and then you do some stupid, really stupid things. You stumble into nearly getting yourself killed and low and behold, the killer is caught. If you can do all that, so can I." He looked at his watch, looked around the room, and added, "Gotta go. Where's the waitress when you need her?"

"I'll get the check if you need to go."

He pushed his chair back from the table, started to stand, hesitated, then said, "Thanks for listening to all that crap about me and Caldwell."

"I'm sorry to—"

"Also, thanks for letting me help you and your buddy catch the person who did in that chick," he said as he headed out the door.

Robin reappeared and asked if I wanted more coffee.

"You serve bourbon this time of morning?" I said, sighed, and said, "Never mind. Yes, more coffee would be great."

Mel may have denied it, but it appeared obvious that his desire to get involved was a distraction from whatever was going on between him and his partner. What wasn't as obvious was why I wanted to get involved. Granted, Charles and I had somehow managed to help the police solve a few crimes, but most of the time, the victim was someone we knew or someone one of our friends knew. In other words, there was something connecting us to the victim. Granted, Charles found Ms. Banes's body, so there was a connection, however remote. Was that reason enough to get involved? And, as my arthritic fingers, weakening knees, and occasional aches and pains in various other parts of my body reminded me, I was nearly seventy years old. Wasn't that too old, far too old, to be interfering in police business, too old to possibly be risking my life and the lives of my friends?

The answer was a resounding yes. So, why was I sitting here thinking about it?

9

fter leaving the Dog, I made the short walk to the post office "excited" to see what junk mail I'd accumulated over the last few days. Folly doesn't have home delivery, so the only way to get mail is to visit the small building less than a block off Center Street. After living here for years, I still wasn't clear why home delivery wasn't available. The United States Postal Service has never asked my opinion or explained the strange policy, so I simply put it in the *it is what it is* category.

My pondering the uniqueness of the local branch of the post office while flipping through my auto insurance renewal notice and seven pieces of junk mail was interrupted by a familiar voice calling my name from across the small parking lot.

"Morning, Virgil," I said as he headed toward me exhibiting an ear-to-ear smile.

Virgil Debonnet was in his early forties, my height at 5'10", with slicked-back black hair. We'd met a few years ago and within seconds of meeting, he was telling me his life history, summarized by he was once wealthy, with him and his wife owning a large home overlooking the Battery in Charleston. Bad investments, bad drugs, and an overabundance of bad luck cost him his wife, his home, and his job as a stock market analyst. He now lives in a small, run-down apartment a few blocks from my cottage.

"Christopher, what brings you out this early in the morning?"

Finally, someone understood that it was early.

"Had breakfast with Mel Evens and went to the post office," I said as I deposited the junk mail in the trash. "What're you doing out?"

"Ah, thanks for asking. I was savoring the lovely morning's fall air, the beautiful blue sky, and the opportunity to run into and converse with wonderful people like you."

If not obvious from him comment, Virgil is one of the most positive people I've ever known. Despite his rapid decline in wealth, he remains cheerful, optimistic, and apparently content with life.

"You headed anywhere in particular?"

"I have an opening in my busy schedule. It seems that none of the residents in my apartment building have clogged sinks, toilets, or, well, anything else that gets clogged, all to say, I'm available to walk wherever you're headed."

Virgil earns rent money serving as an amateur plumber for his landlord.

"How about heading toward the beach?"

"Your wish is my command."

Our pleasant conversation turned darker as we approached the corner of Ashley Avenue and Center Street, the site of Folly's only traffic light, when he said, "Heard a rumor that Charles found a body on Ninth Street West. Any truth to it?"

"Afraid so."

"Holy moly, that boy's a murder magnet. I assume the person was murdered. Charles doesn't waste time finding bodies of folks who've died of natural causes."

"Yes, Ruby Banes was murdered. Someone put a hatchet in her back."

"Ruby Banes?"

I nodded.

"You're kidding."

"Afraid not. You know her?"

"A little. Talked to her a few times at Harris Teeter. As you know, my major means of transportation is a scooter the age of the Mayflower, so I don't often head far out of town."

I stopped in front of Rita's Seaside Grill and said, "What's your impression of her?"

"Nice lady; dressed strange. Whenever she saw me, she came over to talk. Not everybody does that, you know. I strike

some people as being homeless. Course I nearly was homeless, but anyway, that doesn't engender conversations with
strangers."

We crossed East Arctic Avenue and into the parking lot
for the Folly Pier when I stopped and said, "What did you
mean by her dressing strange?"

Virgil chuckled. "First time I saw her, I thought she
wanted to tell my fortune. Her outfit looked like those
fortunetellers in the circus or the ones who work out of
houses with a *Fortunetelling* sign in the window. Instead of
telling my fortune, she asked if she could help me with
anything."

"Know anything else about her?"

"Like who would've wanted to locate a hatchet in her
back?"

"You probably would've mentioned it if you knew that."

He nodded then said, "She didn't say. Did say she rode a
scooter, which grabbed my attention since that's my mode of
transportation. But back to her clothes; after she didn't offer
to tell my fortune, I asked if she was dressed up getting ready
for Halloween. She said no, but Halloween was her favorite
holiday. Said she knew that in an earlier life she was a
gypsy."

"What'd you say to that?"

"Didn't say anything, she smiled before saying, 'Pulling
your leg.'" Virgil slowly shook his head. "Know what she said
next?"

"What?"

"Her smile faded when she added, 'Or maybe not.'"

"Maybe not pulling your leg?"

"That's how I took it. Funny thing is after that first time I saw her, she never mentioned it again, but was always nice. I truly appreciated it."

Instead of climbing the stairs to the Pier, we moved under the deck in front of the Pier 101 Restaurant & Bar and the Gangplank Gift & Tackle Shop. I leaned against the railing and said, "Know anything else about her?"

Virgil was staring at a hawk perched on one of the pier's crossbars, then turned to me and said, "Spooky looking, isn't it?"

"I suppose."

"What was that question again?"

"Do you know anything else about Ruby?"

"Not really. But it's a shame something that bad happened to someone that nice."

"Do you know Trudy Miller?"

"No, who's that?"

"Ruby shared an apartment with her."

"Do you know anything else about her?"

"Not really."

"Could she have killed Ruby?"

"No reason to think so, but it's possible."

Virgil removed his ever-present sunglasses, wiped them with the bottom of his untucked, long-sleeve, white dress shirt, returned the glasses to his face, and said, "Charles has told me the constabulary always looks at the spouse first as the killer. Of course, that's if the dead person was married. Anyway, a housemate is like a spouse."

"Again, it's possible."

"Possible enough for the police to be looking at it, don't you think?"

"Yes."

"If they're not, you ought to let Chief LaMond know our theory?"

Our theory, I thought and said, "I'm sure she's already thought about it, but if I see her, I'll mention it."

"Good. Going to the Halloween masquerade party?"

Our conversation about the murder had ended.

"Charles mentioned something about a masquerade party, but that's all I know."

"It's going to be a blast. Happening in mid-October so it doesn't interfere with all the other Halloween events in the area. Will be in the large meeting room at the Tides."

"Think everyone will be wearing costumes?" I said, knowing if the answer was yes, I wouldn't be there.

"Christopher, when I was rich, I went to a couple of masquerade balls in some of those big old swanky private club buildings in downtown Charleston. My friend, they were *nanty narking.*

Virgil's ex-wife had majored in English, but as he'd told me, she didn't major in the kind of degree that was helpful to normal people. She had an emphasis on Victorian era language. In addition to him telling me several times that she claimed that poverty wasn't in her genes, which was the reason she left him, he'd occasionally throw out a Victorian phrase he'd unfortunately learned from her.

"Is that a Victorian phrase?"

"You're wiser as each day passes. Yes, it means the attendees were having great fun at the events. Oh, the memories. Some of those old rich folks wore costumes that cost more than some new cars, and only wore them once. Lordy, they couldn't be caught dead wearing the same attire to more than one party." He shook his head. "I must admit. I did the same thing." He shook his head again. "The good old days." He patted me on the back and added, "Will you be at Folly's version of a masquerade ball, or whatever it's billed as?"

"I don't believe so."

"Don't worry, you won't have to spend a new car's amount of money on a costume. I'm certain the costumes of most locals won't be that extravagant. Take me for example. My costume budget is, umm, well, just under seven dollars. A trip to Goodwill will accommodate my needs. Or so I hope."

"That's not the issue. I don't like costume parties. I've avoided them since I was in elementary school."

"I'm so sorry. Were you traumatized by something that happened at one of them?"

I laughed. "No, it's nothing like that. I simply don't like the idea of dressing up like someone or something else. It's great for many people. I'm certain you'll have a fantastic time. It's simply not me."

"If you say so. Anyway, I've slipped off the track of our

important discussion. Allow me to ask what you, Charles, and I are doing to catch the killer?"

Maybe talking about the masquerade party wasn't that bad.

"I have confidence that the proper law enforcement officials will get to the bottom of the murder and bring the guilty party to justice. I don't think we have anything to offer that'll assist them."

"Christopher, you're talking to your good buddy Virgil. I don't know what it is, but if I did, I'd say the Victorian word for bull crap."

10

With what seemed like a rainy fall, after awakening later than my usual time, I was pleased to see beams of sunshine peeking through the gaps in my blinds. After hopping out of bed, I realized that getting out of bed wouldn't be described using that word by anyone born after Ronald Reagan was President. My aging body padded to the kitchen, then realized that more food could be found inside a propane tank than in the room my refrigerator called home. With that depressing thought, I headed next door to Bert's for coffee and nutritious powdered sugar donuts.

I didn't get all the way through the store's double-door entry when Denise, one of its long-term, helpful employees, said, "Morning Chris, how are you today?"

"Great, and you?"

"How could I be better, working at the best place in the best city anywhere?"

"That's terrific."

She smiled and went back to stocking items near the register.

I headed to the complementary coffee urn, drew a cup, then made my way to the pastry area, where I grabbed a pack of mini donuts, before heading to the checkout counter. Jeffery Fuller was placing a jug of chocolate milk and a bag of donuts on the counter.

He saw me looking at his goodies and said, "Hi, Chris. That's right, isn't it?"

"Yes, good memory."

"I notice you're admiring my breakfast of champions. I get all my sugars early in the morning and sweat them out all day."

"Don't recall seeing you here this early."

"First time. I usually get my grub for the next morning at Harris Teeter after work. That way I can get up and go straight to work. I haven't been off island in a couple of days, so Bert's it is."

"You live on Folly?"

"Yeah, near Eleventh Street East."

"Don't let me keep you from work. Have a good day."

"Thanks."

After leaving Bert's, I went across the street and down Second Street East towards the beach where I saw Jeffery sitting on the tailgate of his pickup in a small gravel-covered lot eating his "breakfast of champions."

Seeing me, he smiled and waved me over. "Want to join me?"

I couldn't think of a reason to turn down the offer. The beach wasn't going anywhere, and the tailgate presented a place to sit, eat, drink, and to get to know more about another resident. "Sounds good."

"Heading anywhere special?"

"A walk on the beach to enjoy the nice weather."

"The weather here is okay but not like where I grew up in Southern California. Regardless, I like it here."

"Why'd you leave California?"

"Wanderlust, I suppose. I needed a change so went from one side of the country to the other trying my luck at different jobs." He looked toward the Atlantic then continued, "Stayed here because the work and the people are nice. You from here?"

"Kentucky but retired here."

"You plan on staying in South Carolina?"

"Folly is my home, you?"

"Was planning on staying awhile but never can tell when the nomadic life will call me."

"You were saying you usually get breakfast at Harris Teeter?"

"Yes, after work I would head over and get groceries since they carry my favorite brand of a couple of items that I can't get here. Why?"

"Do you know Ruby Banes?"

"Who's that?"

"She was the night manager at the store."

"Was?"

"She was killed a few days ago. I figured you might have known her."

"That's terrible. What happened, a car accident?"

"Sadly no, she was murdered."

"Oh. Why would I know her?"

"I thought since you shop at Harris Teeter in the evening you might have met her."

"I may have seen her but I'm not sure."

"I heard she often wore clothes that reminded some people of a gypsy. Remember anyone like that?"

"Don't believe so."

"I understand. So far, I haven't run into anyone who knew her."

He chuckled. "You sound more like a reporter than a retiree?"

"No. My friend found her body and it's been on my mind."

"Is your friend okay?"

"He will be. I need to get moving or I'll decide to go home instead of walking on the beach."

"I better get going before I find myself without a job. Thanks for the company."

Walking to the beach, it struck me how sad it was that someone could die, and it goes unnoticed. Well, that's not entirely true since her roommate was missing her enough to go to the police. What about anyone else? And, why such a violent death? Seeing the Atlantic brought me out of the depressing thoughts, as I stopped and savored the beautiful sight and sounds in front of me. My conversation with Jeffery played in my head. This was home, I might've been born and lived in Kentucky for most of my life, but this little barrier island is where I belong. For that I am thankful.

11

I extended my walk on West Arctic Avenue past last years haunted house. I shuttered thinking how that turned into a nightmare for Charles and me, and people wonder why I don't like Halloween. Then again, I disliked the holiday long before stumbling across the extra corpse in the holiday attraction and came seconds away from being added to the body count. The former haunted house is now a renovated residence, no haunting involved.

As I passed Loggerhead's, located adjacent to the former haunted house, I noticed one of Folly's finest carrying a to-go bag and heading to her cruiser.

"Officer Bishop, good afternoon."

Trula Bishop's head jerked in my direction, before she said, "Mr. Chris, you startled me. I didn't see you there."

"Aren't police officers always aware of their surroundings?"

She smiled and nodded. "Should be but sometimes the anticipation of lunch distracts."

"The chief keeping you so busy you can't eat in?"

"Not really," she said and shrugged. "Just strange circumstances."

"Ghost and goblins causing issues so early in October."

"I wish. That'd make more sense."

"What's going on?"

"Might as well tell you, knowing how you and Charles nose into everything."

"I wouldn't say that."

She smiled. "You don't have to, but I would. It's about the victim Charles found."

"Ruby Banes?"

"That proves my point," she said and set the to-go bag in the cruiser. "The coroner called a little while ago. She was poisoned."

"Poisoned? I thought her death was caused by the hatchet."

"That's what he said. They have to wait longer for the full tox report but could detect poison."

"Overkill?"

"Seems like it," she said before being interrupted by the radio on her hip asking for assistance near the Folly Beach County Park. Something about a smashed car window. "Duty calls."

"Be safe."

"You too."

The public safety officer got in her cruiser and headed toward West Ashley Avenue and the county park while I headed the opposite direction toward my cottage. In front of the Tides Hotel, I saw the chief's pickup truck pulling out of the parking lot behind Rita's. She saw me, stopped, and motioned me over.

"Know what I just learned?" she said as I approached.

"Ruby Banes was poisoned."

She gave me a look that could've either been awe or irritation, before saying, "How do you know?"

"Just talked to Officer Bishop. Sorry to steal your thunder."

"Okay, Mr. Know it All, did she tell you the official cause of death is still the hatchet?"

"No. How do they know?"

"Poison was in her system, but the large amount of blood we found at the body indicated her heart was beating when she was axed. Then there was something about the poison not making it all the way through her system."

"How was that determined?"

"Ever seen M.D. behind my name?"

"No."

"Then how in hell do you think this Tennessee mountain gal knows all that medical crap?"

I ignored that and said, "Someone really wanted her dead."

"Or more than one someone?" she said and put her right hand in front of my face, palm facing me. "That's a rhetorical question, not an invitation for you and your misfits to find a killer."

I nodded. "Or killers."

"Goodbye, Mr. Landrum," she said before driving off, leaving me pondering the possibility of two killers. Or would that be one killer and one attempted killer?

Instead of continuing home, I climbed the stairs leading to the Pier to sit on one of the chairs overlooking the beach and called Charles. It was time to let him know what I'd learned instead of telling him later and receiving a clump of grief for not sharing sooner.

Two rings later, he answered with, "Talking about you. Meet us for lunch. Planet Follywood." The phone went dead.

I smiled while shaking my head, thinking my friend has no idea what phone etiquette means, but then again, I'm not sure I would recognize him if he used it. I also realized I had no idea who *us* included.

It didn't take long to walk the three blocks to the restaurant where I saw Charles leaning on his cane and talking to Virgil. The mystery of who I would be having lunch with was solved. If all mysteries were as easy to solve.

"Virgil, seeing you twice in two days has to be a record," I said and shook his hand.

I nodded to Charles as I skipped shaking his hand.

"You missed out," Charles said. "Virgil was telling me he knew the recently departed Ruby Banes."

I didn't tell him Virgil had already shared that with me. Instead, I said, "I found out some things a little while ago that might be of interest."

Charles turned to Virgil. "Told you he's been holding out on me. What kind of good friend does that?"

Virgil said, "I'm guessing the same kind who talks behind one's back."

"Are we going in or what?" Charles said, apparently not wanting to continue down the road Virgil's comment had headed.

Planet Follywood, on the corner of West Erie Avenue and Center Street, is the quintessential beach bar and restaurant with beach scenes painted on the walls, posters of long-gone events competing with beer posters on windows and walls, along with other mementos of the good old days displayed. Of course, like most eating and drinking establishments on Folly, it has the ubiquitous television monitors. The activity doesn't pick up until later in the day, so being a little after 1:00 p.m. in October, our threesome brought the occupancy up to seven, not including the bartender who told us to sit wherever we liked, and she would be out to get our order.

Tour guide Charles led us to a booth in the corner near the window with a view of Center Street. Virgil and Charles sat on the same side of the booth giving me extra space opposite them. The bartender came over and introduced herself as Lana and asked what she could get "three handsome gentlemen" to drink. Charles and I ordered a Coke and Diet

Coke, Virgil went for something harder, a Firefly Sweet Tea Vodka. Lana smiled said she would give us a few minutes to look over the menu while she got our drinks.

I said, "Firefly Sweet Tea Vodka sounds interesting. I've never heard of it."

"It would appear that you don't have my sophisticated palette." Virgil said, laughed, and tipped his imaginary hat.

Charles said, "Firefly Distillery is in North Charleston."

That knowledge was no surprise to me since it came from the ultimate trivia collector and regurgitator.

I said, "You been there?"

"Nope," Charles said. "I just don't live under a rock like you do."

I remembered Mel had accused me of the same thing. Maybe there's some truth to it.

"Funny, but my under-rock living knows more about the death of Ruby than my sophisticated palette and GPS friends."

Lana arrived with our drinks and asked if we needed more time or knew what we wanted from the kitchen. I ordered the Dagwood Club, Charles went with Lil' Planets, and Vigil ordered the Colonel Sanders. Lana told us she would get them out ASAP or as quick as the grill would allow, laughed at her joke, and headed to the kitchen.

Virgil said, "Ordered the Colonel Sanders as an homage to your home state."

"Thanks."

"Enough," Charles said, "tell us what you know before we die of old age."

"You're mighty feisty today," Virgil said, "I'm sure Chris is waiting for the appropriate time."

I said, "Poison."

One word and you could have heard a pin drop. Virgil and Charles stared at me.

Charles broke the silence with, "Poison is not what I saw sticking out of that woman's back."

"No, but according to the coroner poison was in her system."

"Who told you?"

"Officer Bishop then I saw Cindy right before I called you and she added more."

"I'm not into murders like you two, but that seems odd to poison then bury a hatchet in someone."

Charles said, "You ever heard of someone poisoning and hacking someone to death? No, I bet. It's just—"

Virgil interrupted with, "My ex being an English major would say it was symbolism."

"Is that the same as done to send a message to someone?"

Virgil said, "Maybe."

"Gee, that explains it." Charles rubbed his head while looking perplexed.

"Charles, it's like in all those novels you read. Symbolism could be for the reader and not for a character in the book. Sending a message could be for someone else, like a warning per se."

"All fine in theory, but that woman I found wasn't in a book but in a field and five feet in front of me."

"Sorry, I wasn't making light of it."

Lana broke the tension with our lunch, and the next twenty minutes were spent eating and talking about how good the food was. When the plates were empty, Lana cleared the table and asked if we needed anything else, and if it was separate checks. I said one check and we were done. As we waited on her return, I returned to our previous conversation.

"Cindy said something in passing about it possibly being two killers because of the two actions, poisoning and stabbing."

Virgil took a sip of his exotic drink then said, "Two killers makes more sense than one. Now I'm not the great detective like you Charles, even you, Chris, but aren't guys more likely to smack someone in the back with a sharp object rather than gals doing it?" He snapped his fingers. "Woah, haven't I heard that women prefer killing people with poison more than men do?"

Charles patted Virgil on the back and said, "Excellent points, Detective in Waiting. I think we have our first big clue to solving the crime."

Virgil beamed like Charles had awarded him the Presidential Medal of Freedom.

I said, "I'm certain the police are considering all alternatives, including that one."

"Maybe," Charles said. "But our record of success is

better than the police, so it's time to put our detective skills in overdrive." He hit the table with his open hand.

I sighed.

12

Barb closed her used bookstore on Center Street early after I called to invite her to spend some time with me in downtown Charleston. I suspect her decision was influenced by me saying our trip would include supper at Husk, one of the city's outstanding restaurants. Barb and I have dated since she'd moved to Folly from Pennsylvania four years ago. With her being the sole employee of the bookstore, we seldom found time to enjoy the unmatched beauty of the historic homes and buildings in The Holy City, as Charleston is dubbed.

She was waiting for me in front of her store. Her hazel eyes and captivating smile reinforced my decision to suggest today's activities. Barb was nearly my age but looks years younger.

She slid in the passenger seat, leaned over, kissed my cheek, and said, "Okay, what's the deal?"

I pulled into the line of traffic before saying, "What do you mean?"

"The invitation to go to Charleston; supper at Husk."

"The weather forecast predicted a perfect day, so I thought spending part of it with a wonderful, lovely lady would be a treat for me, and hopefully pleasant for you."

She tapped me on the leg and said, "I'll accept that answer for now, but reserve cross examination for later."

"Fair enough," I said to the former defense attorney. We were passing Harris Teeter on Folly Road and I said, "Did you hear about the woman whose body was found off Ninth Street West the other day?"

"Is talking about a murder how you plan to make this afternoon pleasant?"

"No, sorry. It's just that she worked at Harris Teeter."

Barb sighed. "Yes, I heard about it, and I also heard she was found by one Charles Fowler, I believe a friend of yours."

"True. He was making a delivery for Dude and noticed what he thought was a pile of clothing. You know how he hates trash, so he stopped to pick it up. You can imagine how traumatized he was to find a body."

She glared at me. "Please don't tell me he, and as a byproduct, you, are getting involved in trying to find out what happened and who is guilty of the crime."

"That's not the plan," I said and focused on driving.

We'd crossed the James Island Expressway leading from

Folly Road to Lockwood Drive and maneuvered our way to the parking garage facing Queen Street and across from our supper destination. I suggested we probably didn't want to eat for a couple of hours and asked what Barb wanted to do. She narrowed the choices to walking up King Street, Charleston's premiere shopping venue, or walking South of Broad where some of the most beautiful homes and gardens in the United States are located. Barb said King Street would be her choice of the two in case I wanted to buy her a present. Most anything for sale on King Street would be less expensive than any house South of Broad, so I agreed with her decision.

I began to think it would be a long trip up King Street since she wanted to go into the Preservation Society of Charleston, the first retail space we came to. It clearly wasn't Barb's first time in the store since she pointed out that every-thing they sold was made in Charleston with the exception of many of the books and pecans that came from a couple of hours away. Charles would have gobbled up that nugget of trivia, but he would never hear it from me, mainly because I'd have forgotten it before I got much farther up the street.

When Barb picked up a Burls & Steel Chef's Knife with an eight-inch blade and asked if I liked the hand-crafted, colorful, maple handle, I had a flashback to standing beside the police tape near where Charles found the body. I didn't share my reaction with her but agreed the knife was beauti-ful. Barb then chuckled and asked when was the last time I used a kitchen utensil. I acted insulted and reminded her that I was adept at using a table knife when making a peanut butter sandwich. She laughed and apologized for not remembering that I was an experienced culinarian.

Fortunately, Barb didn't spend as much time in stores in the next few blocks as she had in the Preservation Society's retail outlet. I did have a good time listening to her critique both paintings and sculptures displayed in the windows of the art galleries along King Street.

We'd walked almost to where Marion Square dominated one side of King Street when she said, "Now that you've assured me that you are a master culinarian, shall we go into Williams Sonoma so you can get some more tools of the trade? I'll buy you a milk frother."

I thanked her for her generous offer but failed to mention that I had no idea what a milk frother was. I remembered flashing back to the day on West Ninth Street when I saw the knife at the Preservation Society store, and suspected Williams Sonoma had many more knives and possibly even a hatchet for sale.

I thanked her again for her generous, although most likely facetious, offer and suggested we should head back down the street toward Husk.

"I thought you were never going to suggest it. I'm starved."

Barb's metabolism would be the envy of many people including yours truly. She's rail thin but never avoids eating anything she wants.

By the time we reached Queen Street and made the half-block walk to our destination, Barb said I might have to carry her up the two steps to the entry to the stately, two-story restaurant since she was on the verge of starvation. I told her I had faith she could make it without my help. She did but huffed like they were the most difficult two steps she'd ever climbed.

Sunset was approaching, so it was too cool to sit in the courtyard and we were shown to a table beside a window overlooking Queen Street and were quickly approached by a server who introduced himself as Jason and asking if we wanted something from the bar. We each said a glass of wine, and Jason headed off to get our drinks.

"Thank you for inviting me," Barb said. "I love my bookstore, but occasionally think I'm missing out on the world when I'm stuck there most hours, most days."

Jason returned with our drinks and told us that if the food doesn't come from the South, it's not permitted in the restaurant, and that the menu changes regularly so even if we'd been in before, most likely there are new items available for our dining pleasure. We told him that wouldn't be a problem since this was our first visit. He said, "Welcome. I'll give you a few minutes to peruse the menu."

He left and Barb leaned in my direction and said, "Think that's the first time I've heard the word peruse since my high school Latin teacher spent an entire lesson on its origin."

"What's its origin?"

"I didn't say I remembered it, just that it was talked about way too long. Now, shall we peruse the menu?"

We enjoyed a couple more sips of wine before Jason returned to see if we were ready to order. Barb went with the Cornmeal Fried Catfish, and I took a less adventurous path and the Woodfired Half Chicken. Jason said those were excellent choices and headed to the kitchen.

I watched him go and said, "Wonder if he ever says someone's choice sucks?"

Barb smacked my arm with an unladylike gesture.

A sip later, she said, "I'll probably regret this, but did you learn anything else about the woman's murder or possible suspects?"

"A couple more things, and here's the strangest. At first, everyone thought the cause of death was a hatchet in her back."

"That's what I heard. Wasn't it?"

"Actually, it was, but the coroner found poison in her system."

"You saying she was stabbed and poisoned?"

I nodded.

"That's overkill, don't you think?"

"Therein lies the mystery."

"In addition to the identity of the person who killed her?"

"True."

"How did they determine the poison wasn't the cause of death and the decedent wasn't, umm, hatcheted postmortem?

"The poison hadn't made it through her system enough

to cause her death. They think she was still alive when the hatchet was inserted."

"Do the police have a theory why the killer used two potentially fatal methods?"

"If they do, they're not saying."

Jason arrived with our food and Barb focused on eating, reminding me that she'd said she was starving.

Roughly ten minutes into our meal, Barb said, "Do you, Charles, or any of your other friends have a theory about the poison and hatchet?"

"Not really," I said then added, "I'm curious. On the way over, you were adamant about me not getting involved in the murder, and now you're asking me about it. Why?"

"I'm keenly aware that during my first year on Folly, you and some of your friends saved my life. In fact, you risked yours to do it. What would've happened if someone had convinced you before then that you shouldn't stick your nose into police business? We wouldn't be having this fantastic meal tonight." She took a bite of her catfish, a sip of water, put her hand on mine, and said, "Do I wish you wouldn't get involved? Absolutely. Do I know it would be futile to try to keep you from getting involved? Probably. With that said, let me ask that you do one thing."

"Of course."

"Please be careful. I sort of like evenings like this; like spending time with you. Okay?"

"I'll try."

"Good, now on a more pleasant topic, have you heard about the Halloween masquerade party at the Tides?"

I could argue that that's not a more pleasant topic but didn't.

"I heard something about it."

"Do you know if this is the first time one's been held on Folly? I don't think there have been any since I've been there."

"I don't recall any."

"I went to a couple of them in Pennsylvania and had a great time. Want to go?"

"I'm not a fan of masquerade parties, so I'll probably opt out. Sorry."

"Hmm, we'll see."

That means I'll be going, I thought.

13

The morning began by brewing a pot of coffee, looking around the kitchen to see if by some miracle there was something to eat, then sitting at my underused kitchen table. Staring in my cup, I began to think about how enjoyable it was spending time with Barb in Charleston and regretted not having more time with her. When I had Landrum Gallery in the same retail space that now houses Barb's Books, I often wondered why I'd chosen to spend seven days a week of my retirement tied down to the business. Now, after closing the gallery because of its time constraints and because it was losing more money than I could sustain much longer, I had unlimited time to do whatever I wanted to do, and Barb was the one handcuffed to the same facility and her business. The main differences, I suppose, are that she truly enjoys the day-to-day activities of owning the store, plus, unlike my venture into retail, Barb's Books is successful.

She'd mentioned a couple of times about hiring a part-time employee to free her so she could spend more time getting to know the area, spending more time with her half-brother Dude Sloan, and hopefully more time with me. I looked forward to that happening. Until then, I needed to find more opportunities to encourage her to do things with me.

A few sips later, my thoughts turned darker when I recalled how Barb had accepted my involvement in seeking the identity of Ruby Banes's murderer. She wasn't excited about me getting involved but knew that most likely I'd get sucked into it. Did she know me better than I would've guessed?

Barb wasn't the only person who leapt to the conclusion that I'd get embroiled in the investigation, for lack of a better word. Mel Evans immediately said that I would, as had Virgil. Folly's Director of Public Safety assumed I would somehow get involved enough to warn me against sticking my nose where it didn't belong. And Charles with his imaginary detective agency was already looking for suspects and assumed I was with him in the quest.

While I would say it was up to the law enforcement officials to solve the murder, and concede that they had the resources and responsibility to determine whoever was responsible, what harm would there be for me to see what I could do to assist them? Don't I owe it to my best friend to support his effort to learn who was responsible? After all, he found the victim and I knew he would never be able to walk away from his conviction to solve the crime.

Who am I fooling? I'll never find a cure for cancer, broker peace among warring nations, or eradicate climate change, but supporting my friends and feeling a sense of accomplishment by helping others are within my reach. Yes, if history is any indicator, there could be danger involved, but there's also danger trying to cross Center Street in heavy traffic, and while I know I shouldn't, I've done that many times.

I also realized that even if I wanted to assist the police, I had no idea where to begin. To my knowledge, the police haven't identified any suspects and other than Virgil who'd met her briefly, I haven't met anyone who knew Ruby. Adding to no suspects, what's the deal with the combination of poison plus a fatal hatchet wound? Could there be something to Virgil's theory that there were two people involved in the murder, one female and one male? Yes, I've heard that women prefer poison as a murder weapon, and men would lean toward a blow by a sharp implement, but what does that tell me? Little if anything, I'm afraid.

Asking myself questions while receiving an inadequate number of answers revealed one thing. I was hungry. The one question I knew the answer to was, did I have anything in the house to eat? That answer was no, so I headed next door to Bert's to find the solution to the problem of something to eat.

I approached the pastry case, my go-to spot for breakfast, and noticed Allen Spencer in front of me and staring at large cinnamon rolls on the top shelf.

I said, "Having trouble making a decision?"

"Oh, hi, Chris. Think I was standing here falling asleep."

"Are those rolls that boring?"

"It's not the rolls," he said as he grabbed one, put it in a small paper bag, and stepped out of my way. "I'm exhausted."

"Too much surfing and lifting weights?" I said, knowing those were his hobbies.

"I wish. Remember when we first met?"

I nodded. "Yeah, we both had recently arrived on Folly."

"And I was thin. Somewhere along the way, I stopped weight training and haven't surfed that much the last few years." He patted his stomach a second time. "This is what happens."

Instead of feeling guilty for taking a Danish which would add to my waist, I said, "Aging will do that to us."

Allen moved to the side of the room and said, "Remember that time when you saw me running after that shoplifter on Center Street?"

"And he tripped on the sidewalk and landed face first in front of the Crab Shack," I said and laughed as I followed Allen out of the path of customers.

Allen joined me laughing. "That's the one. Today I couldn't catch a ninety-five-year-old with a broken leg."

"You're not that bad. If the pastry wasn't putting you to sleep, what was?"

"The last two weeks, I've worked a bunch of double shifts."

"Isn't that rare this time of year?"

"Normally it is, but we've had two officers out sick and more things going on than I've experienced in the fall. There's been a series of burglaries in vacation rentals, two bad wrecks in three nights on Folly Road, that hit-and-run out near Sol Legare Road, and the body found off Ninth Street West."

"Does sound like you've been busy."

He nodded and said, "That doesn't even count last night right before I was ending a double when I had to break up a fight at Chico Feo between Jose Pardo and some guy whose name I can't remember."

"Who's Jose Pardo?"

Allen put his hand in front of his mouth, yawned, and said, "Teaches Spanish at a school on James Island, likes surfing, lives near his work, has a master's degree in Spanish, in his mid-thirties."

"You got all that from breaking up a fight?"

Allen chuckled. "No, I'd met him before. He's dating Alyssa Harp and I ran into them a couple of times at Woody's Pizza and Alyssa introduced us. Anyway, last night was no big deal, so I let them go after they promised to go separate directions."

"While I've got you, can I ask something?"

"As long as it's an easy question."

I smiled and said, "The question is easy. Not sure about the answer. Are there any theories about why Ruby Banes was struck with a hatchet and poisoned?"

"I don't know what the Sheriff's Office is thinking, since, as you know, they tell us lowly small-town cops squat. I know Chief LaMond's perplexed. She's asking everyone from the coroner to strangers on the street their theories about why the two methods."

"Strangers on the street?"

"Not really. I simply meant she's asked several people."

"What's your theory?"

He shrugged before saying, "I suppose someone really wanted that woman dead."

"What about suspects?"

"If I said none, that'd be too many. We can't find many folks who even knew her. Her coworkers at the grocery said she seemed nice, was a little odd, but was good at her job."

"A little odd?"

"Mostly, I think because of her clothes. Nothing bad, you know, no reason to want her dead."

"What about the woman she was living with?"

"I didn't talk to her, but the chief said the person, name's Trudy Miller, told her they weren't close. Mainly lived together to afford the rent on their apartment. The chief did say Trudy didn't appear broken up by the death." He yawned again and added, "I'd like to talk more, but better get home before I fall asleep standing here. If you hear of any good suspects, let the chief know. She'll bitch and groan about you butting in but would appreciate it."

"I have confidence you all will figure it out and won't need my help."

"I wouldn't bet on it."

14

"**K**now what I've got a hankering for?" Charles said as way of introduction after I answered the phone in mid-afternoon.

"Why don't you tell me?"

"You're not going to guess?"

"Nope."

"You're no fun."

"What do you have a hankering for?"

"Thought it'd be nice to take a pleasant walk around town with my best friend."

"Why didn't you start with that?"

"Wanted to see if you could guess.?"

"I'll meet you in front of the library," I said and ended the call before he could. It felt good.

Ten minutes later, I saw Charles sitting on the bench in

front of the Folly Beach Branch of the Charleston County Public Library. He would've been hard to miss in his stoplight red University of Georgia sweatshirt.

He saw me approach and said, "What took you so long? You stop for a milkshake at Dolce Banana and a slice of pizza next door?"

"Don't forget the bucket of oysters I shoveled down after the pizza."

Charles sighed then said, "That's ridiculous."

"Good, then we agree about your reason for me taking so long. Where are we going?"

"Let's head over the bridge and let our feet tell us where to go next."

I resisted saying "That's ridiculous" and instead said, "Lead on."

He did and after more banter about things nearly as absurd as me eating a milkshake, pizza, and oysters on the way to meet him, we found ourselves across the Folly River and at the entrance to Mariner's Cay condos. The development is gated, but the gate only prevents non-authorized vehicles from entering but allows pedestrians to walk onto the property. No, we're not supposed to, but since I knew a few people living in the development, I didn't think we'd be in much trouble for enjoying the pleasant walk through the complex and to the marina on the edge of the property.

Charles picked a bench overlooking the marina and the back of his apartment building on the island side of the river.

"Well," Charles said, "how're we going to figure out who killed Ruby?"

I glanced over at him and said, "You're the detective. Isn't that a question you should be answering?"

"This is part of your training. How will you get to be as good as I am if you don't figure out stuff like this yourself?"

"In other words, you don't have a clue what to do next?"

He watched a man cleaning the deck of a sailboat anchored in the river and said, "Yep."

"Have you learned anything new about the victim?"

"Nope. Seems not many people knew her. In fact, nobody I've talked with knew her, and that includes busybody Loraine Beauchamp."

"Who's that?"

"Woman living in my building. Claims she knows every-thing about everybody."

"Does she?"

"Not really. Thinks I'm Clive."

"Then why'd you mention her?"

"I woke up at two this morning."

"What's that have to do with Loraine?"

"Nothing."

It was time for me to sit here and not open my mouth until Charles rewound his brain and started making sense—sense for Charles.

"Aren't you going to ask why I woke up in the middle of the night?"

"Nope."

"No wonder you're not as good a detective as I am."

"Why did you wake up at two this morning?"

"That's better. When I found Ruby out there in the high grass, it shook me a bunch, a big bunch. Can you believe I thought it was a pile of clothes someone dumped?"

"I understand why you thought that."

"I may not have seen it right. I didn't spend much time looking at the hatchet. No, may not have seen it right." He shook his head and looked down at the gravel at his feet.

"Help me understand. What did you see, or think you saw?"

"The hatchet had a wood handle, fourteen, maybe fifteen inches long. Anyway, on the handle, umm, you know how people burn stuff into wood like words or pictures?"

I nodded.

"Something was burnt into the handle." He hesitated and I wondered if he was going to continue. Finally, he said, "Like I said, I could be wrong, but it looked like a cat. It wasn't perfect and at that time the last thing I wanted to do was figure out what it was. Could've been a tiger for all I know. You know what I thought when I woke up in the middle of the night?"

"What?"

"It was a black cat. Don't witches always have black cats? Haven't black cats always been associated with death?"

"How do you know it was supposed to be a black cat? It was burnt into the wood, so it would've been a black image."

"Like I said, I don't know."

"It's also possible it could've been the logo of the company that made the hatchet."

"It wasn't neat enough to be a logo. It was burnt into the wood later. I'm sure of it."

"Do you think someone burnt it into the handle to send a message about why he or she killed Ruby?"

"That's my middle of the night thinking. It's some kind of satanic thing. Devil worshiping stuff."

"That's possible but let me suggest something. Could it be because it's almost Halloween and you've been thinking about the masquerade party, and even possibly you're subconsciously thinking about the horrible experience you and I had last Halloween in the haunted house?"

"I don't know," he said, looked across the river, and whispered, "I don't know."

"How about—"

He interrupted with, "Let me tell you what I do know. I'm hungry. What time is it?"

"A little after five. Think you can eat this early?"

"Did you miss me saying I was hungry? I didn't have lunch."

"How about grabbing something at The Washout?"

"If you insist."

We headed back across the bridge to Folly and to The Washout, the first restaurant we came to on the island. We were the only people in the dining area on the covered patio; a handful of others were at the bar.

Samuel, a server that'd waited on me several times, was

quick to the table with menus and the question about what we wanted to drink. Charles said a beer, any kind; I said a Diet Coke and Samuel headed to the bar for our drinks.

"Charles, do you remember anything else about the hatchet or seeing anything on or near the body?"

"You sure know how to cheer up a person."

"Sorry. You don't want to talk about it?"

"No, umm, yes." He huffed. "I don't know."

"We don't have to, but if you ever do, you know I'll be glad to discuss it with you."

"I know."

Samuel returned with our drinks and asked if we wanted to order anything to eat.

Charles said a burger with American cheese and apparently I wasn't as hungry as my friend, so I went with a starter-size order of chicken fingers.

We ate mostly in silence. Charles appeared to not want to talk more about the death and I wasn't wanting to depress him more by bringing it up. I told him about Barb's and my trip to Charleston, to lighten the mood. Charles asked some benign questions about the evening and shared about his discussion last evening with another of his neighbors.

As I was paying for our meals, Charles pointed to the bar at the far end of the patio and said, "There's Victor and Waylon, let's go talk to them."

At first, I didn't remember who they were but then it came to me. They were the two guys I'd heard arguing in the Dog plus Charles and I had seen them at Cal's.

I didn't have to say yes or no since Charles was already halfway across the room on his way to talk, or most likely, interrogate them.

Charles put his arm around one of the men, looked at me, and said, "Chris, do you know Waylon and Victor?"

He knew I didn't, but when did the truth ever stop him from his reality?

"Don't believe so," I said and stuck out my hand.

The taller and clearly stronger of the two met my hand with his and said, "Hi, I'm Waylon Atwood, not to be confused with Waylon Jennings."

I smiled at what I assumed was a joke about him claiming he wasn't the county music great, the deceased country music great.

The shorter of the two also offered his hand and said, "I'm Victor Harlan."

Apparently, he didn't think I'd confuse him with anyone.

Waylon said, "Weren't you in Cal's the other night with Charles?"

I nodded.

"Thought so. I'm good at remembering faces."

"Guys," Charles said, "let us buy you another drink."

Which meant let Chris buy you a drink, I thought but simply smiled.

"Deal," Victor said, and waved the bartender over and ordered another beer for each of them.

After spending some of my money, I said, "You live on Folly?"

"Wish we did, but no," Waylon said. "We live in an RV over in the campground at the James Island County Park. Cramped but meets our needs."

"That's interesting," I said. "You work over here?"

"Here and over on Isle of Palms. Do construction. Work for different companies but for J & B Renovations when they have projects."

"Charles and I know John and Bri Rice, owners of J & B. Great people."

I chose not to mention that was the company that was renovating last year's haunted house so Charles and my contacts with John and Bri were awkward at times.

Charles said, "Did you know Ruby Banes?"

Waylon glanced at Victor then turned to Charles and said, "Yeah. Tragic what happened."

"How'd you know her?" Charles asked.

Waylon set his beer on the bar and leaned into Charles comfort zone before saying, "Why?"

"Curious. I've talked to several people and none of them knew her."

Waylon continued leaning close to Charles, and Victor said, "We talked with her a couple of times after work in Harris Teeter; well, it was after our work, but she was working since she was the night manager out there. We also saw her once in here, think it was one night after she got off work. Why does it matter if we knew her?"

"Any idea what might have happened to her or who

might have killed her?" Charles asked ignoring Waylon's question.

Waylon still hadn't moved back a decent distance from Charles, when he said, "Why are you asking?"

I said, "We were curious about what might have happened and since you're the only people we've met who knew her, figured you might have some ideas."

Waylon again glanced at Victor, took a sip of his drink the bartender set in front of him, and said, "Don't know for sure, but it seems like the person that killed her must've known her pretty good. Maybe a boyfriend or someone she worked with."

Charles said, "Why say that?"

Victor said, "We've done construction work out near where they found her body. If she lived where she said she did, that's nowhere near her apartment. She must've known the person for someone to take her out there. That's why I think it was someone who knew her more than to say 'Hi.' What do you think, Waylon?"

Waylon looked at me then turned his attention to Charles and said, "Yeah, had to be someone close to her."

Charles said, "Any idea who that might've been?"

"No," Waylon said. "We barely knew her so didn't know who her friends or family were. Victor, what do you think?"

"I agree with Waylon. We wouldn't know about suspects."

Waylon took two quick sips of his drink, motioned for the bartender to bring their portion of the check, then said, "Would love to talk more, guys, but we need to be going."

He paid for their drinks, thanked us for the additional beer, and hopped off the barstool.

Victor patted Charles on the back, said it was good talking with us, and followed Waylon off the patio.

Charles watched them go, made a check mark motion with his hand, and said, "Think I just started my suspect list."

"Victor and the non-singer Waylon?"

"Yep."

I said, "Because they were quick to blame the murder on someone who knew her well?"

"That combined with how many times they said they barely knew her."

"Charles, none of that says one or both of them killed her."

"That's why they're on my *suspect* list and not on a *they did it* list."

15

Thoughts of a day on the golf course, fishing, or going to a movie often dominate many retirees' mornings as they savor their first cup of coffee. So, instead of cream, why was I stirring into my coffee thoughts of murder, especially when it was the murder of someone I had never met?

I was saved from having to analyze, or perhaps psychoanalyze, that question when there was a knock on the front door. For the second time in recent days, I opened it to find Mel Evans staring at me dressed exactly as he had been on his earlier visit and wearing the frown that I'd become accustomed to.

He said, "Is this better?"

"Is what better?"

He tapped his forefinger on his watch and said, "Me

waiting until most of the day was gone before interrupting your beauty sleep?"

"What world do you live in where nine in the morning means most of the day is gone?"

"You going to quibble about time and my world, or you going to get your butt in gear and come with me to breakfast?"

"Since you asked so nicely, how could I turn you down?"

"My point, exactly."

Instead of prolonging our healthy, cheery dialogue, I told him to give me a couple of minutes and I'd meet him on the porch. While he wasn't ready to divulge it yet, there was more to his reason for appearing than to harass me.

It was unseasonably warm, so I suggested we walk to the Dog rather than taking either vehicle.

"It's warm out here because we've already wasted most of the day. Heats up late in the day, you know."

"You taking a group on a marsh tour today?" I asked, to change the subject.

"No, sir. Came over to piss you off."

I smiled. "You're a success."

We entered the Dog and were greeted by Amber, the server who had worked at the restaurant long before I'd arrived on Folly. She was also my favorite server on the island and for a while after I first arrived, we had dated. Fortunately, we'd remained friends.

"Glad to see you, Chris, and if I remember correctly, you too, Mel.

"Damned sure better remember me, woman."

As she led us to a table against the front wall, she said, "How could I forget someone as sweet, kind, and adorable as you."

"Coffee for both of us," I said to keep me from laughing at Amber's remark.

Less than a minute later, she returned with our coffee, then said, "You two going to the masquerade party?"

I said, "Don't think—"

"I am," Mel interrupted.

That surprised me since Mel struck me as someone who avoided social gatherings and groups where he couldn't be the center of attention.

I said, "You are?"

"We're here to eat not gab about stuff not on the menu. Amber, I'll have bacon, eggs, and two slices of toast with extra butter on it, and, umm, orange juice."

"Got it, and you, Chris? No, let me guess, French toast?"

I nodded and she headed to put in our orders.

"You a French toast addict?"

"Addict, no, but I am a fan."

"Hmm, how many times you come here and the server says French toast and you say no?"

"Not often."

"Sounds like that means never and that makes you an addict."

"Whatever. You really going to the masquerade party?"

"Didn't I say I was?"

"Yes."

"Then what part of that tiny three letter word didn't sink in?"

"Can't picture you in a costume," I said and was tempted to say what he almost always wore looked like a costume.

"You going to be there? You didn't answer when Amber asked."

"I would've if you'd let me finish my sentence."

"You going to be there?"

"Probably not."

"Then you won't get to see my costume. Your loss. Now, are we going to talk about the reason you wanted to meet or are you going to waste my time talking about a party?"

"Remind me what it was I wanted to meet about."

"The murder, duh."

I nodded. "Okay, you have any theories about who committed it?"

"Good question. No. Don't know who, but from my way of thinking it was someone who knew her good."

"How do you figure that?"

"From what I heard, she lived near here, yet she turned up dead way out by the end of the island."

"How does that say she knew the person well?"

"Just does."

"That helps. Others have said the same thing. Have you heard about the poison?"

"What poison?"

"In addition to the hatchet wound, she had poison in her system."

"Did it kill her?"

"No, the coroner thinks the wound in the back was the cause of death. The poison hadn't made its way through her system when her heart stopped."

"That could mean two people killed her. One a poisoner and the other a hatcheter."

"Could be."

"No, I got it," Mel said, "Since you mentioned poison, here's what happened. Some dude met her in a bar and got her liquored up. Then he slipped poison in her drink so he could get her out of the bar without her knowing what was going on. He took her out where Charles found her and smacked her in the back with the hatchet." He clapped his hands together and added, "There you go. Mel solves the case."

"Did I miss something in there about the name of the killer?"

"Hell, do I have to do everything? You and Charles can take it from there."

"Thanks for leaving something for us to do," I said, not hiding the sarcasm.

"You're welcome. What I can't figure out is why someone wanted her dead in the first place. Anyone got theories about that?"

"Not really. Charles said he thought he saw a cat, a black cat, burnt into the handle of the hatchet."

"Don't remember him saying that to us."

"He didn't. As you may recall, he was quite shaken when we picked him up. He said the image came to him the other morning."

"So, what's a black cat have to do with anything?"

Amber slipped our plates in front of us and left us to our discussion.

I poured syrup on my addiction and took a bite before saying, "Charles thinks the black cat means—"

"Don't think Caldwell and me are going to make it," Mel interrupted then took a bite of bacon.

Where'd that come from? Instead of asking, I said, "Mel, I'm sorry to hear that. I guess things have gotten worse since you mentioned you were having problems the other day."

"Worse, hmm, a lot worse. And know what? No matter what I try, I can't get through to him that I don't want it to end."

"I'm sorry," I repeated. "Do you think he understands how you feel?"

"You know I'm not a touchy-feely guy. I may lack some skill at communicating my feelings, but hell, we've lived together for years, so he must know how I am. Shouldn't he?"

"Sometimes it takes more than—"

"What in hell does a damned black cat burned into the hatchet's handle have to do with anything?"

I wonder why Mel thinks his communication skills might be lacking?

"He believes the cat could represent a satanic message."

"Does he know that doesn't make sense? I'd bet the woman never saw the hatchet, much less a burnt cat on its handle, so how would she have gotten the message?"

"That's a good point, but Charles thinks the cat was meant to communicate something to someone else."

He took a couple of bites of toast, washed it down with a gulp of orange juice, then took a bite of the eggs, before mumbling, "Who was the message for?"

"No clue."

"Then it's damned lucky that I'm taking time out of my busy schedule to help you two catch the killer, or killers. So, are you going to the party or not?"

"Probably not. I'm not a—"

"Did some scary clowns traumatize you when you were a kid?"

I shook my head. "No. I'm not a fan of dressing up like someone else."

"Okay, so what do you think I should do about Caldwell?"

"Do you think you've done a good job communicating how you truly feel, and also a good job listening to, and actually hearing his concerns?"

He looked at his empty plate, pulled his wallet out of his slacks, sighed, and finally said, "Probably not.... okay, not probably, no I haven't."

"Wouldn't that be a good place to start?"

He folded a ten and a five-dollar bill and placed them under his empty coffee mug, looked at me like he was going to say something, then cleared his throat, before saying, "You're damned lucky."

"Why?"

"Since I've been staying away from home more lately, the Caldwell situation, you know, I'll spend more time over here helping you and Charles catch the killer, or two killers, or whatever. Now that I told you how it happened, that damned killer is toast. Mark my words."

He stood, headed to the door, stopped, and turned back to me. "I'll try listening and letting you-know-who know my feelings."

I nodded to his back as he headed out the door.

16

Instead of heading home after my enlightening and at times confusing conversation with Mel, I swung down Center Street towards Barb's Books. It had been a couple of days since our trip to Charleston and I wanted to see how she was doing. Before I opened the door, I saw the small bookstore had been invaded by a group of middle-aged women all wearing the same style pink polo shirt. *Maddie's Manuscript Maidens* was embroidered on the back with a picture of a young woman sitting under a tree and reading a book. Not wanting to walk into that hornet's nest, my hand dropped from the door handle, and I backtracked to the previous storefront, First Light Church's foul weather sanctuary which also served as a home base for Preacher Burl.

I opened the unlocked door and looked around. The room wasn't large but could accommodate forty or so worshipers. There was a table on the right side where refreshments and coffee were made available prior to and after Sunday services and a repurposed high school lectern in the front that served as Burl's pulpit when he's honoring those present with his impassioned sermons. The one thing missing was the preacher, but before I turned to leave, he walked out of the storeroom in the back of the sanctuary.

He wiped his hands on his slacks, smiled, and said, "Brother Chris, I thought I heard the door. How are you this blessed morning?"

"According to Mel, it's closer to midnight."

"Huh?"

"Never mind. I'm doing well, and you?"

"Tidying up in case Sunday service must be moved inside, but I can use a break. How about a donut and coffee?"

"Thanks, but I just left the Dog."

"How was the French toast?"

I smiled at his assumption, his correct assumption, and said, "Excellent, as always."

Burl poured himself a cup and motioned to a couple of chairs near the table. I chose the one farthest from the food so he could be closer to the donuts in case they called his name as I knew they would. I'm not the only predictable person in the room.

"What's been keeping you occupied?" he asked as he reached for a donut.

"Enjoying retirement."

"Is investigating a murder on the list of things you're enjoying?"

"That's a job for the professionals."

"You know it's a sin to lie to a man of the cloth."

"Of course." I said and changed the subject, sort of, "I was wondering if you know Trudy Miller."

"Strange question, but yes, I've met Sister Trudy. Why."

"Curious. I asked since you know more Folly residents than most people. What's your impression of her?"

"Brother Chris, Peter was a fisherman in the Good Book, but you might have him beat with your fishing expedition."

"Preacher, I'm honored. Don't recall ever being compared to someone in the Bible. Trudy was housemates with Ruby, the murder victim. Chief LaMond said she didn't seem too brokenhearted with the death. Said she was more concerned about finding another person to share the rent."

"And the truth shall set you free." Burl said and laughed.

I couldn't help but smile.

He turned serious and said, "I met Sister Trudy one Saturday night at Bert's. I was there picking up refreshments for the next day's service when my attention was drawn to the sound of joyous laughter. It was Sister Trudy. I introduced myself and commented that I had not heard such cheerful laughter in years. We started up a conversation."

"Did she think that was a pickup line?" I said and poured myself a cup of coffee.

Burl chuckled and said, "She did give me a sideways glance, but figured this chubby fellow looked harmless.

We talked about thirty minutes. She was born and reared in West Virginia and moved here to fulfill her dream of living at the beach. She works in Charleston at Roper Hospital." Burl took another sip and added, "She seemed like a happy enough soul with her cheerful demeanor, but she's hiding something or trying to forget something."

"Why?"

"Preacher sense, I suppose. The cheerfulness seems to be a cover. I've seen it before. I invited her to attend our services so she could meet some of the locals."

"Has she attended?"

"No." He slowly shook his head. "She gave a strange response. Said she doesn't want to draw attention to herself; that no one needs to know her."

"That is strange."

"Before I could say anything else, she left me standing there. I haven't seen her since that evening."

"Some people want to keep to themselves. I suppose there's nothing too odd about that."

"You trying to convince me or yourself?" He took another bite of donut, sipped his coffee, and said, "Do you have inquiries about more of our citizens, or as you and Charles call them, suspects?"

"Now that you mention it, do you know two guys named Waylon and Victor?"

"Names don't ring a bell, who're they?"

"I've seen them around a few places and finally met them

with Charles. They seem nice enough but was curious to learn more about them."

Burl laughed, then said, "I find it hard to believe that you met them with Charles and only know their names. Was Charles off on his interrogation?"

"Not totally, we learned they live at the James Island County Park Campground and work construction on and around Folly."

"That's more like it. Are they suspects in Sister Ruby's murder?"

"Don't know. I heard them arguing over someone or something the day after the murder and they seem to know things about Ruby. I simply wanted to see if you knew them."

He stared at me and said, "Glad to see you are enjoying your senior years sitting on the front porch yelling at squirrels and not trying to catch a killer."

"Preacher, you're a—"

"Be careful, I don't have time to come up with a eulogy for you."

Our deteriorating conversation was interrupted by sounds of laugher and loud talk coming from Barb's Books.

"Sister Barb sounds like she is having a party. Weren't you invited?"

"I was about to go in until I saw the store overflowing with a group of women wearing pink polos."

"Must be *Maddie's Manuscript Maidens*."

"You know them?"

"A couple of my flock belong to the group. They're not

exactly maidens but who am I to argue about the age range of a maiden."

"Wise man."

"I didn't get this age choking on my foot. Anyway, they are a great collection of ladies, going around to local bookstores finding the perfect books for the club, and then spend the rest of the day at a restaurant talking about their finds."

"Sounds like you know a lot about them. You an honorary member?"

Burl took the last bite of his donut, wiped a crumb out of his mustache, then said, "I was in Blue Bicycle Books in Charleston when the group came in. Being an outgoing person, I started up a conversation."

"And I thought Charles had a monopoly on that."

"I'll take that as a compliment."

The laughter grew as more of the ladies walked past the door. I assumed they were headed to one of the local restaurants.

I said, "Some lucky restaurant is going to entertain quite a party for lunch."

"Speaking of party, are you going to the masquerade party at the Tides?"

"Don't think so."

"Brother Chris, think how enjoyable it would be for you and Barb to dress up and enjoy an evening of festive camaraderie."

"There you go, putting a positive spin on things. Will you be there?"

"Of course. It's going to be the biggest party this side of the marsh."

"Can't argue with that."

"Besides, it might give me some ideas for Hope House."

"Thinking of redecorating?"

"I want to throw a party on Halloween night. Since trick or treating is not permitted on Folly and there's no haunted house this year, the kids and adults need something entertaining."

"Don't you find it strange as a minister, that you'll be hosting a Halloween party?"

"Not at all, Halloween represents many things to many people. I want to provide a safe and fun party for those in the community who give so much to us at Hope House. I will expect you to attend, Brother Chris. No costume will be required, so you have no excuse not to be there."

I smiled. "You twisted my arm."

"Precisely," he said and sighed. "I need to get back to cleaning and I'm certain you would like to track down which restaurant the Maidens have commandeered so you can join them."

"My time will be better spent cleaning my own sanctuary."

I threw my cup in the trash and headed to the door, opened it, and cautiously looked up the sidewalk to see if any of the group was lingering nearby. Not seeing a single pink shirt, I assumed the group had found their afternoon hang out.

"Brother Chris, keep out of trouble. Guardian angels can only fly so fast."

"Always."

I looked at Barb's door but the closed sign on the door let me know she had ducked out to lunch or was in the back enjoying some peace and quiet. Instead of bothering her I headed home. With Burl asking me about the masquerade party it seems like the everyone on the island will be there. It wouldn't be that bad. But then again, I was still reluctant to put my name on the list of attendees.

17

The sound of heavy rain awakened me before dawn. I couldn't think of a good reason to get out of bed, so I didn't and listened to the rain pelting on the metal roof for twenty more minutes. The rain didn't let up, but my day was wasting and as Mel would say it's closer to supper than breakfast. Mr. Coffee would provide me with the caffeine I needed even if my refrigerator didn't offer breakfast. A search of the kitchen cabinets also proved useless unless I wanted a can of tomato soup for my morning meal.

A trip to Harris Teeter was now on my schedule for this afternoon, that is, if the rain subsided. As I sipped coffee and created a grocery list, I kept getting distracted thinking about the grocery's night manager who seemed to dance to her own beat. How is it that I lived in such a small community and couldn't find anyone who knew Ruby well, or even much about her? Beyond knowing where she worked, where she lived, that she dressed like a gypsy, and rode a scooter, that was all I'd managed to learn. I smiled thinking that I was sounding more and more like Charles.

The rest of the morning was spent cleaning and thumbing through a three-month-old photo magazine, which reminded me to make more outings with my camera in search of the perfect image. Noon rolled around and the weather gods deciding Folly needed more rain. I wasn't excited about opening the can of soup and definitely didn't want to spend another minute cleaning, so I grabbed my raincoat and Tilley and jogged to the car with lunch at Loggerhead's on my mind. I never would've considered trying to find a parking space at noon close to one of Folly's more popular restaurants but being October combined with the heavy rain gave me confidence that a parking space in the restaurant's small lot or nearby was awaiting my arrival.

I was rewarded with a vacant spot no more than thirty feet from the stairs leading to the entry. Thank you, fair-weather diners. Shelly, one of Loggerhead's long-term servers, was seated at the bar looking at her cell phone and patiently waiting for anyone to venture inside. I was the crowd.

She stood, grabbed a menu, and asked if I wanted inside or outside, then laughed.

"I'll go with inside."

"Excellent choice," she said with a straight face.

Given the choice of any table, I chose one near the back of the room.

After I was seated, she said, "What can I get you to drink?"

"Diet Coke will be fine, thanks."

Shelly scampered off to the bar, appearing happy to be waiting on someone, anyone. Tips in the off season can be few and far between.

Before she returned with my drink, four men entered, wiped water off their jackets, and sat at the bar. Shelly returned with my drink, and I jokingly asked if she could handle the crowd.

"It'll be a challenge," she said.

I ordered chicken tacos and she left to see what the new arrivals wanted.

I must have been daydreaming because the next thing I remembered was Shelly sliding my plate in front of me and asking if I wanted anything else. I said no and she headed to greet a couple who had arrived.

I took a bite and noticed one of the men at the bar looking at me. He then grabbed his beer and headed my direction. He appeared to be in his fifties with long, blond hair and an athletic build. I didn't recall seeing him before.

"Your name Chris?" he said as he stood close to the table and looked down at me.

"It is."

"Could I have a few minutes of your time?"

"Sure, have a seat Mr?"

"Mathers, Liam Mathers."

"Mr. Mathers, have we met?"

"Call me Liam. I was at the Lost Dog Cafe yesterday morning when I saw Mel Evans with you. After you left, I asked the waitress your name. I was going to speak to you then, but you left before I had a chance."

I smiled and said, "That sounds a little stalkerish."

Shelly, having seen Mr. Mathers at my table, returned and said, "Let me know if either of you need anything else."

I had a fleeing thought that I might need a witness to this strange man talking to me, but it quickly passed.

Liam watched Shelly go, and said, "Sorry, I guess that sounded strange. Let me start over. I work for the state studying ecology and the conditions of the marshes and other ecologically significant areas in the Lowcountry."

"That's interesting, but I'm not sure what that has to do with me."

"My job doesn't involve you. I had a run in with Mel, who people call Mad Mel for good reason. Anyway, we had a heated, I suppose you could call it debate about problems he's causing for the environment or giving him the benefit of the doubt, problems he's causing." He sighed. "I'm passionate about nature and what we can do to help instead of harming the environment. Mel threatened to do damage to my face if I brought the subject up again."

"That sounds like Mel, but what does that have to do with me?"

"It's my fault," he said in a calmer voice. "I approached

the situation poorly. I have a master's degree in environmental health sciences but should have added a minor in diplomacy instead of being, well, being the way I am."

"Many of us could use more diplomacy," I said to make him feel at ease.

"True," he said and smiled. "So, when I saw you and Mel talking, I thought that was my chance. In short, I wanted to apologize with you present so I wouldn't get my face rearranged in the process."

I found it humorous that anyone would think I could help with one of Mel's tantrums.

"It sounds like you're going out of your way to make things better between you and Mel. I'm guessing you're in the marsh often and perhaps concerned you might not make it out one of those times since you've insulted a determined and at times overbearing man?"

"That's quite perceptive. Were you in law enforcement?"

"No, but I have a few years, okay, more than a few years' experience observing human nature."

My phone rang before Liam responded. I don't often answer the phone when I'm talking with someone but, but seeing Charles's name on the screen, I answered on the third ring.

My friend said, "Got plans for later today?"

"No."

"You do now. I'll meet you at your house so we can discuss murder."

"That sounds like a fun discussion," I said with a hint of

sarcasm. "I'm at Loggerhead's if you want to join me for a late lunch?"

"I'm busy playing Charles's Delivery Service for Dude. Later will have to do. I'll bring snacks."

Before I told him that wouldn't be necessary, he'd ended the call.

My new acquaintance looked amused by the call he'd witnessed and said, "And I thought I was direct and to the point. I should get some pointers from whomever that was." He then chuckled as he tipped his beer towards the phone on the table.

"Direct and sometimes pointless, that's Charles's approach to phone calls."

He stared at me for a moment and finally said, "Wow, are you *the* Chris and Charles?"

"Never heard it put that way, but Charles is my best friend, why?"

"You're private detectives. I was talking to someone the other day about both of you and wanted to meet you."

"We're not detectives although Charles plays one in his mind. Who told you about us?"

"Beth Powell mentioned that you might be able to answer questions about an acquaintance of mine."

"That's strange since I don't know Ms. Powell."

"She doesn't know you either. Okay, let me clarify. Beth is helping Preacher Burl at Hope House with plumbing issues. There is a lot of tedious work in plumbing, and Beth and the preacher have a propensity for gab."

"Preacher Burl did mention one of his flock was helping there with the plumbing. That still doesn't explain why our names came up?"

"You'd have to ask them. I think it's something about how Charles would like Beth's cat, even though he's a dog person."

"Now, I'm more confused."

Thoughts of escaping this very weird conversation played in my head but since I have about twenty years on this athletic looking strange gentleman running was out of the question. My best option was to ride it out. Besides as strange as this was, Liam seemed like a nice guy.

"Think I'm confusing myself." He laughed so loud that a couple seated a few tables over pivoted toward us to see what was so funny. He continued, "Festus, Beth's cat, goes everywhere with her, walks on a leash, has the personality of a dog, and is bigger than many canines. The preacher brought up Charles then apparently your name came up."

"Who is the acquaintance we might know about?"

He took a sip of beer and said, "Ruby Banes."

"Ruby's a friend of yours?"

"We've talked a few times. She enjoyed spending her free time in nature, out at the marsh, or walking Boneyard Beach. One day, I was heading home from there when I saw her pushing her scooter, so I stopped and offered to help. It embarrassed her to tell me that she'd run out of gas. Anyway, that afternoon we went to lunch and had a pleasant conversation. She was a lovely lady." He looked down at the table then back at me. "I never saw her again."

"You seem to know more about Ruby than anyone I've talked to. I'm not sure how I can help."

He finished his beer and looked around for Shelly. She caught his gaze and he held up the empty bottle. She gave a thumbs-up indicating she got his message.

He turned to me and said, "I've heard several versions about what happened to her from folks out at the County Park where I like to swim. I wanted to find out what really happened. Was she stabbed? Are there suspects? How about motive?"

"I'm afraid those are questions for the authorities."

"I was hoping you could tell me something, that is, something I don't know."

"I wish I could help, but you know as much as I know. Why don't you talk to Chief LaMond? I'm sure she'd like to hear from someone who knew Ruby."

"I don't know what I could offer, but I might."

"She is a friend so if you'd like, I could set up a meeting with her."

"I don't think so but thanks for the offer. I've perplexed you enough for one day, but if we meet again, I'd like to chat further."

"Sounds good. It was nice meeting you."

He returned to the bar to pay his tab, then walked out of the building without looking back. I finished my tacos and motioned for the check.

Shelly returned to the table and said, "Want dessert?"

"No, just the check."

"Your friend took care of it."

That was so rare that I was tempted to ask her to photograph the paid check with her phone. Instead, I handed her a tip and headed into the rainy afternoon. Two groups were moving quickly up the ramp into the dryness of Loggerhead's as I walked to my car.

My grocery list that I'd left on the dashboard reminded me I still needed to go to Harris Teeter. The rain had eased slightly, so I might as well get one of my least enjoyable chores out of the way. There was little vehicle traffic on the streets and little foot traffic in the grocery. I didn't have to dodge shoppers, so I had more time to notice how decorated the store was for Halloween. I didn't recall it being this festive in previous years. It was adorned with ghosts, goblins, and witches' toys and decorations, and more pumpkins than you would find in a patch. And that wasn't even counting the candy displays at the end caps of several aisles.

My phone rang as I returned to the car. When I saw Charles's name on the Caller ID, I answered expecting to be yelled at, with him saying he was sitting on my porch and claiming he'd been sitting there for hours awaiting my arrival.

I started with, "You can't say I'm late. We never set a time."

"Uh, yeah, no, was calling to postpone our catch a killer meeting."

"Postpone, are you okay?"

"I'm fine, but it's been a long day. I'm not in the mood to go back out in the rain. Do you know who the killer is?"

"No."

"Then it would be an even longer day trying to help you figure that out."

"We can try again tomorrow."

"If you solve the who-done-it before then, call me."

Before I could tell Charles there would be no phone call, the line went dead. It's not often that my friend bails on me, especially since the meeting was his idea. Could it be a sign that he was maturing?

Nah.

18

I spent much of the afternoon thinking about my conversation with Liam then headed to Cal's for a late supper and hopefully some time to talk with the bar's owner. Center Street was more crowded with vacationers taking in the various shops, restaurants, and music venues than usual for this time of year. While it was far from the in-season crowds, it reflected the trend of extending the traditional vacation season into months longer than when I'd first arrived on the island. The added weeks of vacation season was a boon for local restaurants and shops, but an increasing nuisance for locals dealing with increased traffic, trash, and noise.

The bar greeted me with the aroma of stale beer and long-consumed hamburgers along with the sounds of

Skeeter Davis singing "The End of the World" from the jukebox on the corner of the small, elevated stage.

"Hey, pard," the 6'3", slim, bar's owner said as he stepped out from behind the bar and met me near the entry. In a room full of locals, Cal's rhinestone-studded white coat and Stetson stood out like a giraffe in a coterie of groundhogs.

"You've got a full house," I said as we shook hands.

He removed his Stetson, ran his fingers through his long, gray hair, and looked around the room before saying, "It's a welcomed sight to this old crooner. Seems there's a meeting going on at the Tides. Most of the folks in here have been bored all day listening to speakers drone on about something I didn't understand, at least that's what a couple of the guys told me." He returned his Stetson to his head and continued, "What brings you out?"

"Thought I'd grab a burger and sip on a glass of your finest red wine."

Cal glanced around the room one more time then at the bar at the side of the room and said, "Head on over to that empty barstool and I'll put in your order with our executive chef. I figure one of the tables will open up in a few minutes and you can grab it."

Cal's executive chef was his son, Cal Junior, or simply Junior as he preferred to be called.

After Cal took my food order into the small kitchen beside the bar, he poured me a glass of his *finest red wine* from a box on the backbar and set it in front of me.

He looked around the room again, I assumed to see if anyone needed anything, then turned to me. "Learn anything new about that gal that got herself killed the other night?"

"Not really. How about you?"

"A rumor here, a rumor there. Nothing I'd bet any of my hard-earned money on."

"Do you know Liam Mathers?"

"May if I saw him, but the name doesn't mean anything. Who's he?"

"Ran into him earlier. He's in his early 50s, about 5'9", athletic looking. Says he comes over and swims out at the County Park. Thought he may've come in here."

Junior inched his dad aside and set a plate with my burger on it in front of me, put his muscular arm around Cal, and said, "This old guy pestering you?"

"No more than usual," I said.

"If he does, let me know."

I assured Junior I would before he headed back to the kitchen.

Cal raised his hand and said, "Hold that thought. Guy over there has an itch for another Bud."

I wondered what thought I was holding as Cal grabbed a Budweiser and moved to the other end of the bar to scratch his customer's *itch*.

"Pard," Cal said as he returned, "I didn't just fall off a pumpkin wagon. You don't ask questions to hear words fall out of your mouth. What's the deal with this Liam fellow?"

Johnny Horton's "North to Alaska" was playing as I was

reminded once again about how bright and perceptive Cal was, regardless of his good-old-boy image.

"Nothing much, really. He had a run-in or two with Mel. Liam has a master's degree in environmental health sciences and thought Mel may be abusing the marsh with his, as you could say, not so environmentally friendly marsh tours."

"He's right, ain't he?"

I smiled. "Probably."

"Then what's the problem?"

"There's not really a problem. Thought it unusual for him to come up to me and start talking about Mel and mentioning that he'd heard Charles and I were private detectives."

"You think he may've been the person that killed the gal?" He pointed behind me. "Hold that thought. There's an empty table. Grab it and I'll clean it in a sec."

I slipped off the barstool, took my plate and drink, and moved to the vacant table. This time, I knew what thought I was holding.

A couple more customers entered and were looking around, I assumed for an empty table. I was glad Cal pointed me toward this one before it was taken.

Cal arrived carrying a glass of red wine and set it beside the one I hadn't finished. "Figured you'd want another," he said then took the chair opposite me. "I'm getting too old to be doing this. My union says I get as many breaks as I want."

Cal was his *union*, so he made the rules.

"What about this room full of customers?"

"Junior can take care of it. That's why I pay my kid his astronomical salary."

Cal's *kid* was knocking on his sixtieth birthday and his salary was far from astronomical, but he'd sold a chain of fried chicken restaurants in Arkansas before moving to Folly to be closer to his dad, the dad he'd never met until he arrived here a few years ago. He didn't depend on whatever Cal was paying him.

Cal leaned back in his chair, stared at me, and said, "Now stop changing the subject. You think that Liam guy killed her?"

"I have no idea. Thought it was curious how he approached me, a stranger, and started talking about the murdered woman and that Charles and I were detectives. Sounded like he was fishing for what I knew about the death."

"Who sounded like that?" the familiar voice of Charles said from behind me.

"Welcome, other half of the famous detective duo," Cal said as he tipped his Stetson to Charles who now had moved to the vacant chair beside me.

Charles tipped his Tilley to Cal and said, "Cal, did Chris tell you he invited me to join him in your fine drinking establishment?"

"Don't believe he did."

"Know why he didn't?"

"Why?"

"Because he didn't invite me."

I sighed and said, "Before you burst into tears, I didn't invite you because I didn't know I was coming until I was on my way. And, what about you being so tired you cancelled our meeting?"

"The rain stopped; a nap worked wonders." He nodded like that explained everything, then said, "Apology accepted. Now, who sounded like what?"

"You done lost me, "Cal said. "Let me get you a beer before you confuse me more." He pushed himself out of the chair and headed to the bar.

He'd lost me when he accepted a never-offered apology, so I ignored it, and said, "I was telling Cal that I'd talked with Liam Mathers and that it struck me as strange how he started talking about you and me being private detectives. He asked if—"

"Hold that thought," Charles said and hopped out of the chair and headed toward the front of the bar.

I was busy trying to figure out how many thoughts I was holding and what they were when Charles returned with his arm around Jeffery Fuller's shoulder.

"Chris, guess who I saw at that table behind you?"

I would've said the Easter Bunny to irritate my friend but didn't know how Jeffery would take it. Instead, I said, "Jeffery, good to see you."

"You too. Charles invited me to join you. Hope you don't mind."

"Not at all," I said as Jeffery moved to the chair Cal had vacated. "How do you know Charles?"

He smiled and said, "We go way back. Met him day before yesterday. Ran into him at the gas station."

"Yeah," Charles said. "Thought he looked familiar, so I went over to say howdy."

Jeffery laughed. "Not many strangers come up to me and say howdy."

I said, "Charles is far from being like other people, but he is strange."

Charles said, "Jeffery was telling me that he knew Ruby. That's quite a coincidence, isn't it?"

"Yes."

Cal interrupted when he set Charles's beer in front of him, pulled a chair from the next table, moved between Jeffery and Charles, and said, "Jeff, you know these two vagrants?"

"A fiddle, umm, little," he said.

A scratchy—scratchy from hundreds of plays on the jukebox—version of "End of the Story" played in the background.

Jeffery pointed over his shoulder in the direction of the music machine and said, "Guys, did you know that's sung by Cal here? This living legend had a monster hit with it in, what was that year again, Cal?"

"Sixty-two. Same year 'She's Got You' was a big hit for my good friend Patsy Cline. God bless her soul," he bowed his head as if in prayer.

"Ain't that amazing?" Jeffery said.

"It certainly is," I said like I'd heard it for the first

time, and not for, oh, let's see, the five-hundredth time from Cal.

Jeffery said, "Cal, didn't you say it was the number one hit in the country when it came out?"

Cal smiled. "Not quite that big, but it was number one in my hometown of Lubbock."

"One's one, ain't that bright, umm, right?" he said and clapped when the song ended.

I suspect the beer in front of Jeffery wasn't his number one tonight.

Charles leaned closer to Jeffery and said, "Now, what were you telling me about how well you knew Ruby?"

Talk of Cal's number one hit, be it in Lubbock or the universe, was getting in the way of Charles's interrogation of the newcomer to the table.

"Told you I didn't know her good. Talked to her in Harris Teeter a time or two and that's all."

"Oh, I figured since you said it was at night, she may not have been busy, and you had more time to talk."

"Sorry, but no. Cal, you got my check? Got to be at work early tomorrow."

Charles patted him on the back and said, "Don't worry about it. I'll get your drinks."

Jeffery headed to the exit, I took the last bite of supper, and Charles told Cal that I'd get Jeffery's check.

I finished the first glass of wine, took a sip out of the second one, and was thinking how much I enjoyed being here with good friends and enjoying the music.

Charles had other things on his mind as he said, "He did it."

"Who did what?" Cal said.

"Jeffery killed Ruby Banes."

"Pard, I ain't nearly the detective that you are. I missed whatever he said that told you he killed the gal."

I glanced at Charles then turned to the bar's owner. "Cal, don't feel bad. I also missed it." I turned back to Charles. "Care to enlighten us?"

"Clear as an ice cube," Charles said then leaned closer to Cal and me. "What did the boy do once I started asking how well he knew Ruby?"

"Said he talked to her a time or two," Cal said. "How's that say he killed her?"

"Cal, ole Cal, that doesn't say he did it."

"Pard, Jeffery had four beers tonight, and was acting a little confused. Now you've got me feeling like that, and I ain't had anything to drink. You ready to say what tells you he did it?"

"That man shot out of here like he had a bee up his butt."

Cal stroked his chin, nodded his head left then right, and said, "Didn't he say he had to be at work early? Wasn't that why he left?"

"That's what he said, not his real reason."

"And you figured that out because he was in a hurry to leave?"

"That's what detectives do, my friend."

I smiled and said, "Charles, you've got your phone, why

don't you call Chief LaMond and tell her about the confession you got out of Jeffery?"

"You making fun of me?"

Yes, I thought, but said, "Of course not."

"Good. Think we need to gather a little more evidence before turning it over to the police."

"You've got that right," Cal said. "You going to the masquerade party?"

Since Cal wasn't as good a detective as Charles, he was ready to change the subject.

Charles said, "Yes."

I said, "No. How about you?"

Cal said, "Got mixed feelings about it."

"What's that mean?" Charles asked.

"Figured since you were such a good detective, you'd already have that figured out."

"Now you're making fun of me."

"Yep," Cal said. "I'm pissed at the group putting it on. Never talked to me about having it in here."

"Cal," I said, "they're expecting a crowd. That's probably more than you could comfortably handle. The Tides has the largest meeting room on the island."

He sighed, waved his hand in the air, turned toward the bar, and said, "Yo, barkeep. How about a beer?"

Junior rolled his eyes, then grabbed a Budweiser out of the cooler and brought it to Cal, then headed to the table on the far side of the room to grab the empty bottles.

"I know I couldn't fit everyone in here, but they should've

asked me, so I could've told them that."

"You're right," Charles said.

"Anyway," Cal said, "Halloween ain't as much fun as it was when I was a youngster. Back in the '50s growing up in Texas, the holiday was wild. Probably too wild, to tell the truth."

Charles said, "What's that mean?"

"Now Lubbock ain't on the Mexican border, but lots of kids my age, and some a lot older, stole ideas from the Day of the Dead, a big Mexican holiday. It covers several days around Halloween. Real Mexicans take flowers to the cemetery and put them on graves of relatives buried there. There are also special foods, altars put near graves of loved ones, even parades."

"That doesn't sound like much of a Halloween," Charles said. "Is that all?"

Cal shook his head. "It's not really like a Halloween thing where ghosts and goblins and other things scare people but is more a celebration and way to remember those who are gone. We took it as another excuse to do bad stuff like burn piles of rags in front of people's houses or jump out from behind fences to scare horses and cattle." He laughed. "Some of us would go house to house and let the air out of car tires." He took a long draw on his beer. "Yes, sir, those were the good old days."

Charles said, "That's probably why trick-or-treating is outlawed on Folly."

I said, "It's more of a safety thing, so kids aren't running around after dark on our narrow streets."

"Or letting air out of tires," Charles said.

Our conversation didn't rise above that level for the next hour, but once again, allowed me to savor the atmosphere and friends before I headed out the door to the sweet piano sounds of Floyd Cramer's "Last Date."

19

The next morning began less eventful than recent beginnings. No former Marine pounded on the front door before insulting me and dragging me out before dawn. A distraught Charles wasn't wondering where I was. In a rare moment of introspection, I thought it was funny how seven decades of living on this revolving rock, I didn't recall having closer friends, friends who will drive me crazy and at the same time show me how important I am in their lives. I didn't know what I'd done to be so fortunate, but I'd take it.

The weather had finally offered a warm, dry day so I grabbed my camera, slung its strap over my shoulder, placed a Tilley on my head, and headed towards the Pier. The sky offered a perfect scene with rolling thunderheads offshore, so the blues, purples and backlit grays looked more like a painting than reality.

A dozen shots of the magnificent moving painting later, I focused on the shoreline where a few early-morning walkers were on the beach. One couple caught my eye as they headed towards the Pier. The woman's long red hair added to her soft complexion, and she was wearing a flowing green skirt with a flowery yellow blouse. Her companion happened to be a large Irish Wolfhound whose gray fur gave him a ghostly appearance. They both appeared as if they were stepping out of the past and into a new century. Something about how they almost flowed down the sand encouraged me to shoot a few images of the two before rushing down the ramp to the public access to greet Shannon Stone and Lugh as they were leaving the beach.

It had been a few months since I'd seen Shannon, and then it was only briefly in Bert's. I didn't have many opportunities to see her since she worked from home and spent a fair amount of time in Charleston, except when she was doting on her mini, carbon-copy daughter, Roisin, or wrangling her Ozzy Osbourne look-alike son, Desmond.

"Blessed be, what a surprise," she said, her Irish brogue had seemed to thicken since her husband's passing. Her emerald green eyes revealed true pleasure in seeing me.

"Morning, Shannon, and Lugh, of course."

Lugh's tail swung back and forth upon hearing his name.

Shannon motioned for her massive dog to heel which he did without protest, before she said, "Don't know which is more dangerous his tail or mouth. He clears every table in the house with that windshield wiper of a tail." She laughed and placed her hand on Lugh's head.

I smiled and asked how she'd been.

"October is hitting us hard," she said, looked at her left hand, and shook her head.

"I remember what Roisin said at Mike's service about death being another adventure. It still it must be difficult."

"Being Wiccan, we view life, death, and nature differently than most, but even with that understanding, there are times that are more of a challenge." Shannon waved both of her hands in front of her body as if brushing off a spiderweb. She offered a muted smile and added, "I would love for you and Charles to visit our home before Halloween."

"We'd be honored. I'll get with Charles and let you know when we're available."

"Until then, merry meet, merry part, and merry meet again."

I wasn't certain what to say to that, so I went with, "Okay."

She chuckled and said, "It's our way of saying nice to see you, take care, and hope to see you soon." She reached out and squeezed my hand. Lugh looked at her and whined as he looked toward Center Street.

She patted his head and said, "The impatient big baby knows we go to the Dog after our beach walk."

"I don't want to upset a hundred-fifty-pound baby, so I'll let you get on your way."

Shannon and Lugh headed to the Lost Dog Cafe and I

headed down West Arctic Avenue when I heard, "Chris, where have you been hiding?"

I turned to see Jay Vaughn walking in my direction from the Tides' parking lot. He had worked at the Tides since Noah was counting two by two. As the hotel's bellhop, concierge, greeter, public relations guru, and problem solver all wrapped into one cheerful personality, he was a true asset to the hotel as well as the city.

"Jay, I'm not hiding. See me standing in front of you?"

Jay shook my hand, and grabbed my arm, and offered his contagious smile. "Great to see you."

"You too. Is work keeping you busy?"

"Always, we have several conferences this week with boring speakers talking about who-knows-what, but the real shindig is our first annual masquerade party, the best Folly has ever seen."

I assumed it being the Tides' "first annual" contributed to it achieving such vaulted status. Instead of sharing that observation, I said, "Several have mentioned it."

He waved his hands over his head "Epic, that's what it'll be. There'll be a band from Charleston, food provided from not only our kitchen, but several local restaurants will be bringing samples of their fare. Rumors are the conference room decorations will put the Biltmore's Christmas to shame, but haunting, of course."

"I didn't realize it was going to be that big."

"Yours truly will be dressed as Riff Raff; you know from

The Rocky Horror Picture Show. I'll be looking spooky as I greet everyone who enters."

"Interesting," I said. Since horror movies or musicals weren't among my favorite movie genres, so I had no idea who or what Riff Raff was.

He put his arm around my shoulder and said, "You will be there, won't you? That's unless you and Charles are busy figuring out who did a Mercy Gold on that lady Charles found."

"Who is Mercy Gold and why is she a verb?"

He sighed and said, "Don't tell me you've never heard the ghost story of Mercy Gold?"

"No."

"I forgot you're not from here." He looked back at the hotel and continued, "It's my break so if you're not busy, I'll buy you a coffee and tell the story."

"Deal."

As I accompanied Jay to Roasted, I thought that running into a witch and now hearing a ghost story were two things that weren't on today's agenda. Could running into a headless horseman or zombies be far behind?

Penny took our orders. I stuck with coffee; Jay added a muffin to his coffee request and paid for both of us. Someone was seated at the two small tables in the center of the room, so we moved to the counter overlooking the Atlantic.

Jay took a sip, then said, "I'm on a break and not lunch so I'll give you the *Reader's Digest* version of Mercy Gold." He took a bite of muffin and another sip of coffee, then took a dramatic pause before starting the story. I waited and was almost ready to remind him it was just a break when he started. "Mercy was the daughter of Archibald Gold, a wealthy merchant in Charleston in 1674. That's even before you were born."

"Funny," I said to the fifty-plus-years-old youngster telling the story.

He laughed then continued, "Archibald was ruthless and basically not a nice man. Mercy was the exact opposite. She was a kind, giving person." Jay took a long drink of coffee and looked out on the ocean. This was getting to be like one of Charles's stories.

I said, "Okay, 1674 was four years after Charleston was founded."

"Very good, you do know some history."

I smiled and said, "Read it on a plaque at the Battery."

"One October night, Mercy went for a moonlit stroll along the tidal channel, or as we call it, the Stono River. She didn't return."

"Did she drown?"

"Nope, worse. When his daughter had not returned, Archibald sent a search party looking for her. They found Mercy with a hatchet in her back."

"A hatchet?" I said louder than I should have.

He nodded. "Like your murder victim."

"It's not my murder victim. So, who killed Mercy?"

"Did you know the Stono River was named after the Stono Indians, an extinct tribe?"

"No. What's that have to do with Mercy?"

"Stono Indians were still around Charleston in 1674. Archibald Gold told everyone that one of them killed his daughter. Mercy was found near the Indians' dwellings on the tidal channel and killed with a hatchet. It wasn't hard to convince everyone an Indian was responsible. The remaining Stono families were run out of the area and Archibald took over, in other words, stole their land."

"Jay, that's a sad story but I'm not seeing the ghost part."

"It's sadder than you know. Mercy wasn't killed by a Stono but was murdered by her father because of greed and hate. He had seen her walking with one of the young men of the tribe that night."

Jay looked at his watch. I was afraid he was getting ready to end his break before ending the story.

I said, "I'm still not seeing a ghost."

"The ghost story is what happens since that night. During October, if you walk along the Stono River at night there's a chance you'll see Mercy Gold walking along carrying a hatchet while looking for revenge. Others see Mercy Gold walking the bank looking for her love and asking those she meets if they've seen him."

"Have you seen her?"

"I'm not saying I believe, but I have no reason to be strolling along the Stono at night."

"Isn't it unusual that there are two different ways to see the, umm, ghost?"

"Something about what's in your heart determines which

Mercy you will see. There was even a little verse to go with the story."

"Continue."

"Mercy Gold looking for a soul. Mercy mercy upon our soul. Mercy Gold rest your soul."

Jay slowly shook his head and added, "I didn't grow up here but have heard that some parents tell their kids to recite it when they are out at night so Mercy will pass by without disturbing them."

"I don't believe in ghost stories, but it's a shame that two women met with the same fate."

"Chris, I'm not a detective, but using Mercy Gold's story, I'd look at those who are closest to, umm, what's her name?"

"Ruby Banes."

"Yeah, look to her family or people close to her for the killer." He once again glanced at his watch. "Anyway, I need to get back to work, and you need to find a killer."

I thanked him for the coffee and the story. Now, all I needed to do was find a killer using a 350-year-old clue.

I was passing Bert's when Cindy hollered at me from the store's entry, "You're harder to find than a June bug in a chicken coop."

"Sorry, am I under arrest?"

"No, but you should be. It'd keep you out of trouble."

"You know I'm a law-abiding citizen."

"I know no such thing. You're a nosy geezer who manages to get yourself in countless predicaments."

"If I was looking for insults, I'd call Mel. Other than harassing your fine citizens, what are you up to?"

"Grabbing a quick lunch and going to enjoy nature at the end of East Ashley. Might even take a walk out towards the lighthouse. Gotta keep this lithe body in shape, you know. Want to join me? I'll buy the food."

"Wow, the woman in charge buying me lunch in a brown paper sack. How could I refuse?"

"Smart ass. You want to go or not?"

"Of course."

With deli style sandwiches in hand and Cindy paying, a near historic moment, we headed to her truck.

Seeing her vehicle parked in my drive, I said, "You were looking for me?"

"Told you I was."

She drove in silence with the police radio crackling in the background. I was concerned about her since she looked tired but wasn't going to mention her appearance. I'd learned years ago to never tell to a woman how tired she looked, especially one toting a firearm.

I was about to break the silence when a maroon golf cart zipped through a stop sign on a cross street in front of us. Cindy hit the lights and siren and the cart's driver wisely pulled over. Cindy pulled alongside the offending vehicle, leaned my direction, lowered the passenger window, and told the driver he was driving a motor vehicle and was required to obey all rules of the road. Before the driver could say anything, Cindy raised the window, and we continued on our way.

Cindy stared at the road in front of us and said, "In law enforcement, that's called a teaching moment."

"Hmm, and I thought it was because you didn't want to interrupt lunch."

"That too," she said and smiled as we continued to the end of the road where she parked in the no-parking zone by the locked stanchions to the Lighthouse Inlet Heritage Preserve. No, I didn't share a "teaching moment" by telling her the definition of "No Parking."

"How did I rate this private lunch with Folly's finest?" I asked as she retrieved the bags off the back seat so we could start our in-cab picnic.

"I wanted to talk to you without prying ears nearby."

"About?"

"Aconitum."

"Gesundheit."

Cindy chuckled, shook her head, swallowed, and took a deep breath, before saying, "Aconitum, commonly called wolfsbane along with a collection of other unique names, is a poison. More specifically, it's the poison found in Ruby Banes."

"Wolfsbane sounds like something out of medieval times. Where would someone have gotten it?"

"People have been using wolfsbane for centuries, putting it on the tips of arrows, spears, and even harpoons. It's a wild-growing flowering plant that grows throughout a large part of North America."

"Wouldn't it be crazy to poison the edge of the hatchet that's deadly and quick enough by itself?"

"True. From what the coroner said, most likely she drank it. He found traces in Ruby's throat and esophagus."

"What would the symptoms be of someone poisoned with it?

"Don't know for sure. The coroner said something about lightheadedness, confusion, maybe fainting. I wasn't paying much attention since those things sound like what several of our fine residents experience every Saturday night."

I smiled. "True. Her being poisoned reminded me of something. Do you know Liam Mathers?"

"No. Please tell me he has a yard filled with wolfsbane and his favorite hobby is ax throwing, oh yeah, and he hated Ruby."

"Sorry. I've never been to his house and don't know his hobbies. I met him the other day but he did bring up the late Ms. Banes. He knew her and was asking what I knew about her murder."

"Jeez, even strangers know you're meddling in murders."

"Mathers has a degree in environmental sciences, meaning he would know about flora. Stuff like aconitum. Add to that, him approaching me asking what I knew about the victim. Doesn't that sound suspicious?"

She nodded. "Sounds like someone Detective Adair or I should have a chat with."

"Excellent plan. No wonder you're in charge. And, speaking of the murder, Charles remembered seeing a symbol on the hatchet's handle. Said it looked like a black cat. Did you see it?"

She sighed. "Yes, I saw it, as well as weird symbols on the reverse side of the handle."

"He didn't mention those."

"Charles wouldn't have seen it unless he was on the ground next to the deceased."

"What did the symbols look like?"

"I'll do you one better. How about pictures of the hatchet?"

She didn't wait for an answer. She grabbed her phone, scrolled through her photos, and handed me the device. The first image appeared to be a black cat or panther, while the markings on the other side of the handle looked like letters in an alphabet that I didn't recognize.

"Looks Greek to me."

Cindy laughed, "Great minds think alike, at least one great mind, and then there's yours. That's what I said when I saw it."

"Do you know what language it is?"

"Not a clue nor the meaning behind the cat-looking creature. It's not a logo I could find, and Detective Adair agreed. I'm almost afraid to ask, but do you have any ideas?"

"Charles was thinking satanic or occult with a black cat, also in stories witches often have black cats."

"You do realize those are fairy tales and ghost stories? I'm talking more in the realm in which we reside."

"Might be a long shot, but what if you ask Shannon Stone? Being Wiccan, she can tell you the difference between fact and fiction and any observations she may have."

"I haven't seen Shannon since releasing Mike's car after his death last year. I don't want to show up on her doorstep, or worse yet, call her to the station."

"I saw Shannon this morning. She invited Charles and me to her house before Halloween. If you send me those pictures, I can ask unofficially."

"Don't make me regret this but if you're simply asking a friend about the photos, how much trouble can you get into? If she tells you anything helpful, let me know. Please don't go on a satanic goose chase with Charles." She slowly shook her head and added, "Promise me, you'll simply ask and report back. Okay?"

"I promise," I said, speaking for myself. Charles is another matter.

Cindy's interest in taking a walk must have taken a back seat to heading back to town. I didn't argue with her decision.

20

As the sun peeked over the house across the street, and with a mug of coffee in hand, I decided to stay on the front porch and enjoy the mild October weather. The traffic was light and the drivers that passed didn't appear to be in a hurry to get to their destinations. The morning was as it should be in retirement, leisurely and uneventful.

The peaceful morning atmosphere was interrupted by the ringing of my phone with Charles's name on the screen.

"Morning, Charles."

"What about him?"

"What about who?'

"Who do you think? Liam."

"What are you talking about?"

"You're getting old. At Cal's you mentioned Liam and I told you to hold that thought."

"Didn't think you meant to hold it forever."

"Not forever, until now. So, what about Liam? Never mind, this isn't working. I'm on my way over." The phone went dead and so did my serene morning.

Charles arrived on his classic Schwinn, pulled into the driveway, and leaned the bike against the wall. He grabbed his cane and tipped his Tilley in my direction as he joined me on the porch and set a bag of mini donuts on the table beside me.

If I wasn't already awake, his gold sweatshirt with Kennesaw State Owls in black letters on the front would have awakened me.

Charles said, "Morning, fellow seeker of justice. Knew you wouldn't have anything here to eat."

"Seeker of justice?"

"You're always telling me we aren't detectives, so I'm debuting a new title."

"A rose by any other name."

"Too early to be quoting Shakespeare or a florist."

"Want something to drink?" I said, to change the subject.

"Yep. Stay seated, I'll get it. Need a refill?"

"I'm good," I said while wondering why he was being so accommodating.

Charles disappeared into the house, then rejoined me on the porch, while carrying a Coke.

He plopped down in the chair and said, "So what about this Liam fellow?"

"Liam Mathers, I'm assuming you don't know him?"

Charles shook his head as he opened the donuts and remained uncharacteristically silent.

"I was in Loggerheads, and he approached me wanting me to help him negotiate with Mel over a disagreement, also—"

"That's odd, why you?"

"That was the least odd thing he talked about. He said you and I were the detectives he'd heard about, then asked about Ruby's murder. He wanted to know if we knew what had happened, why it happened, and more."

"Our reputation is preceding us. We need to get business cards to help get clients."

Ignoring his comment, I took a sip of coffee and let him return to reality and not his imaginary detective agency, or seeker of justice agency.

"So Liam knew Ruby?"

"Yes, he claimed he talked to her a few times and once had lunch with her. Said she was a nice lady, and he wanted to know what had happened."

"Then why ask someone he doesn't know instead of going to the cops?"

"Told you it was odd. I even offered to go with him to see Cindy."

"What'd he say?"

"He turned me down, paid for my lunch, and left."

"Interesting. Sounds like Liam is wanting to hide something if he skedaddled after you mentioned going with him to the cops."

"You're right, and speaking of the police, I talked with Cindy yesterday about the symbols on the hatchet."

"The black cat? Told you it meant something."

"She also mentioned something that looks like writing on the side of the handle opposite the cat."

"I didn't see any writing. What'd it say?"

"Cindy sent me pictures," I said and grabbed my phone, scrolled to the images, and handed the device to Charles.

"What did Cindy think this weird writing was?"

"She doesn't know; same for the cat."

"It's clear as day, she wants us to find out what it means, and catch the killer."

"That's sort of correct. I suggested since you thought the cat might be satanic or dealing with witchcraft, we could ask Shannon Stone if she has ideas and if she has ever seen that type of lettering."

"About time the police figured out we're great detectives."

"Whatever."

"But wouldn't barging in on Shannon be bad, especially on the first anniversary of her husband's death?"

"I'm surprised you know the meaning of *barging in*."

"I'm not that bad."

"Right. Anyway, I saw Shannon yesterday and she invited us to stop by the house to visit. If you're available, I'll call and see if today is a good time."

"I think I can work it into my packed schedule."

I found Shannon's number and called. She answered and said she was thrilled that Charles and I could come over and for us to give her an hour before coming. She added that the kids should be there as well.

While we waited to head to Shannon's house, Charles rambled on about what costume he was going to wear to the masquerade party but couldn't settle on one idea. I was pleased that his list of costumes didn't have me being a horse's rear end to his front end. He also didn't ask what I was going as, so I didn't have to repeat that I didn't plan on attending.

The Stones lived a few blocks from my cottage, but Charles insisted we should take my car so we could get to a lunch destination quicker after meeting with the Stones than we could by walking. I didn't recall making luncheon plans.

I hadn't come to a complete stop in the driveway when Lugh lumbered off the porch and loped to the car. I put it in park and let Charles exit first. The massive Irish Wolfhound sped around the front of the car and came to a sudden halt in front of Charles. Lugh's entire body wagged as Charles began a conversation with one of his best friends, a conversation only they understood.

While they were "talking," I walked to the porch of the quaint cottage where a smiling Roisin was standing. Roisin Stone was the mini version of her mother and was growing up more with each passing week. Her red hair was pulled back in a ponytail fastened with a blue hair clip. She wore jeans and a maroon, long-sleeve, oversized T-shirt with what looked like a beaver on the front. She greeted me at the stairs with a hug.

"Mr. Chris, it's so good to see you."

"Same to you, Roisin. Be careful Charles doesn't try and steal that shirt. You know about his collection."

"I know, found it in Dad's closet and Mom said I could have it. The University of Minnesota is where he graduated,"

"Nice looking gopher." Charles arrived pointing to the shirt.

I said, "How do you know that?"

"It's the Golden Gopher of the University of Minnesota. Everyone knows that. I have one from there but not as nice as the one Roisin is modeling."

"Mr. Charles, you're silly, but I'm happy you're here, Mom will be serving tea and scones in the parlor." Roisin turned and led the way into the house followed by Lugh with Charles and me bringing up the rear. Once we were inside, Lugh plopped down by the door as if to guard the occupants.

Charles glanced around the room and said, "Your brother around?"

"Desmond was going to be joining us, but something came up," Roisin said, rolled her eyes, and added, "A girl."

"Desmond has a girlfriend?"

"Mr. Charles, no one is more shocked than Mom and me."

"I think Kelly, that's her name, is good for him. He's been a little less morose than usual." Shannon said as she entered the room carrying a silver serving tray with the tea and her homemade scones.

I smiled and said, "Allow me to help."

"I have this, please sit down. I guessed you both would like a scone with your tea."

Charles said, "Never turned down a scone from a beautiful lady."

"Charles, you flatter me."

Roisin helped her mom pour the tea while Shannon placed the scones on antique bone china located on the sideboard. The scene looked like Charles and I had stepped back in time with tapestries on the wall and Victorian furniture. I could swear that I was sitting in an old-world parlor instead of a cottage on Folly Beach.

Shannon gave us time to sip our tea before saying, "I'm so glad you both could come for a visit. I wanted to invite you earlier, but you know how life often gets in the way of our plans."

Charles said, "How have you been? Chris said he got to talk to you yesterday, but he doesn't tell me anything, you know."

Shannon smiled and handed Charles another scone. "We're doing as well as possible. Being the year anniversary brings back Mike's death in waves of emotions."

Roisin added, "I have planted several shrubs in the garden for Dad and every morning I walk along the beach and talk to him. He's a good listener."

"We each have our rituals to keep Mike involved in our

lives," Shannon said, "Now I can tell you are wanting to ask something, so out with it."

"You're a perceptive lady," I said and reached for my phone.

"Of course, after all, I am a witch." Her laugh filled the room and Lugh looked around to see what caused the laughter.

Roisin huffed and said, "Mom, we're not—"

"It was a joke, my little nymph. Chris and Charles know well what we are."

"I was hoping you would have some insights on these symbols," I said and handed Shannon my phone with the cat image on the screen.

Shannon looked at the picture, then turned the phone at an angle, to get a better view of the image, before saying, "It looks like a representation of Agnes Bowker's cat."

"Who's that?" Charles said as Shannon showed the picture to Roisin.

Shannon said, "In 1569, an English servant claimed to give birth to a cat. This looks like the old drawings of the feline. Frankly, I think people like using this image because it looks evil. Where did you get this?" She handed the phone back to me.

"I have another picture." I scrolled to the next picture and handed the phone back to Shannon.

She stared at the picture for a minute then turned to Roisin, showed her the phone, and nodded. Roisin quickly left the room. Charles looked at me with a confused look on his face.

I said, "Shannon, is something wrong?"

She smiled and said, "No, I sent Roisin to fetch a book so I can share something with you."

Roisin returned and carefully handed her mother a leather-bound book with yellowed pages that appeared well over a hundred-years-old. Shannon opened the book, turned through several pages and handed it to me. There were numerous symbols including some similar to the ones in the photo.

Shannon said, "It's called the Theban alphabet, has been around since the 16th century. It's a substitution cipher used by occultists and Wicca. It has only twenty-four or twenty-three characters instead of English's twenty-six."

"What's the word in the photo?" I said as I handed the book to Charles.

Shannon nodded slowly and said, "*Wraith*"

"*Wraith*, that doesn't sound good." Charles said, shook his head, and took another sip of tea.

"It's not. It can refer to a specter that is the exact image of a living person one sees before they die. Others say it's a product of spell casting dark and evil. Where did you get these photos?"

"Chief LaMond sent them to me, they are images from a hatchet's handle."

Shannon cringed and said, "The implement that killed that woman who worked at Harris Teeter?"

"Yes," I said. "I didn't like bringing things like this up but thought you might be able to help." I smiled and added, "and help you did. I will let the Chief know what you said, it might help with their investigation into her death."

"I'm glad we could help, but please tell the Chief the next time she needs help she can always call me. We are more than happy to aid the police."

"I'll let her know. She didn't want to bother you and I told her Charles and I were coming over to see you."

"She is a kind lady."

"Shannon, do you know anyone who works with dark spell casting or might have a hatchet like that?" Charles said as he placed his plate on the table and folded the linen napkin.

Roisin answered before her mother could, "Mr. Charles, we do not associate with people who have so much disregard for life."

"My little nymph, our friends mean no harm by their inquiries. It's a valid question since we did give them the answers they were seeking."

Roisin turned to Charles and added, "Never would we want to imply that you have so much disregard for life."

"I know."

We spent the next few minutes talking about more positive topics like Red Raven Herbs, Shannon's Internet business, and how Roisin enjoyed talking about nature with Preacher Burl.

I then said, "Shannon, thank you for a lovely time and the scones were better than I remembered."

"Our door is always open to you." Shannon stood and gave Charles and me a hug.

"I'll walk you out. Lugh will want to go for his beach walk," Roisin said and skipped to the door. Lugh stood and the four of us walked down the driveway toward my car. Charles patted the dog and shared his final words with Lugh before getting in the passenger seat. Roisin gave me a hug.

I said, "Take care of yourself, young lady."

"I should be telling you that since you are looking for a killer." She nodded and added, "Looking once again."

I watched the couple head down the road before I got behind the wheel. I looked at Charles who was tapping the top of his cane.

"What're you thinking?"

"I was right about the murderer being a satanist or some evil doer. You going to call Cindy and let her know?" Before I responded, he tapped his cane again and added, "Do you know if Liam has a wraith following him around?"

"I'll let Cindy know what Shannon said."

"Good. We can skip you buying me lunch. I filled up on scones and tea. I now need a siesta."

"You're mixing cultures, but I agree."

21

Barb called that afternoon, something she rarely did. After she began the conversation in a way I wasn't accustomed to from most of my friends, in other words, politely, she said, "You decided if you're going with me to the masquerade party?"

"I'm still thinking about it," I said, instead of no.

"You need to let me know soon, so if you aren't, I'll have time to accept the invitation from one of the many gentlemen who've invited me."

"I'll let you know in the next day or two," I said as I wondered if she was teasing about many invitations.

"Good. Have you talked with Dude lately?"

"Why? He ask you to go with him?"

"He told me he hadn't seen you in weeks. I think he's worried he's done something to make you mad."

"Did he say that?"

She laughed. "No, he said, 'Be confused by Christer's absence,' and I translated that to mean he was worried and that it'd been a while since he'd seen you."

Dude was prone to use one word when a normal people required a half-dozen or so to communicate the same thing.

"I'm impressed by your Dudespeak translation."

"Be fractional-sis talent," she said and laughed.

"I'll stop by and see him."

"Good. Gotta go, customer be awaitin'."

I smiled at the former attorney's efforts at Dudespeak, then decided now would be as good as any to visit Dude at the surf shop, spelled with all lowercase letters for reasons only know to Dude Sloan.

It was the surf shop's closing time, so I wondered if Dude would still be there. The business was on Center Street and Dude had owned it more than thirty years. The door was unlocked and the lights were on, so I took it as a good sign that the owner was there.

He wasn't in the front of the store, so I headed to his office in back.

"Dude, you here?"

He peeked his head around the door to his office. "Yo, Christer. Figured you moved to Nome, Alaska."

"Why?" I asked the seventy-year-old, 5'7", thin store owner whose appearance reminded me of a cross between Arlo Guthrie and Willie Nelson.

"Many moons since you be seen."

"Been here all along."

"Cool, then you be catchin' chick killer?"

I started to deny that when the phone rang with Cal's name appearing on the screen.

I held up a finger to let Dude know I'd better answer the phone since Cal seldom called.

Cal said, "Are you heading over here anytime soon?"

I hadn't been, but knew Cal wasn't asking to simply get a customer count.

"Thought about stopping by in a little while. Why?"

"Good. Tell you when you get here. Junior's off and I'm slammed, or I'd tell you now."

He'd ended the call before I could respond.

I turned to Dude who'd been leaning against the doorframe watching my fascinating phone conversation, and said, "What were you saying?"

"You be catchin' chick killer?"

"Afraid not. I didn't know her or anyone who knew her until recently. Besides, it's up to the police to catch the killer."

"Be hearin' that from you before, and before, and before. You'll catch him, unless it be her, then you be catchin' her."

That was longer than most of Dude's statements, but I understood what he'd said.

"Dude, I don't know enough about what happened to do anything about it. The police will catch him, or her."

"If you say so. Be country crooner on phone?"

"Yes, it was Cal," I said in case Dude knew some other country crooner it could've been.

Dude looked at his watch. "Be going to Cal's?"

"Yes."

"Need tag-along?"

"Want to go with me?"

He turned, grabbed a light jacket off the back of the office door, put it on over his short-sleeve tie-dyed shirt with a peace symbol on the front, locked the door, then walked toward the front of the store. He turned to me and said, "You comin'?"

I went out on a limb and interpreted that to mean he was going.

We walked the short two-and-a-half blocks to Cal's. More accurately, I walked and Dude skipped, less gracefully than Roisin had earlier, but still skipped. Cal was right about being slammed. The tables were occupied and every stool at the rustic bar was taken. The jukebox was playing Roger Miller singing about being "King of the Road," two men standing in the corner of the room were singing along, and Cal was weaving among the tables delivering beer to a table near the front of the room.

Dude looked around, patted his foot on the dark-green threadbare carpet, and said, "Feel like be honky-tonkin'."

I wouldn't have put it that way, but he was right. Cal's could easily have been in rural America during the 1940s.

Cal saw us from across the room and pointed one of the empty beer bottles in his hand at the end of the bar. I nudged Dude toward the designated spot.

Cal set the bottles on the corner of the bar and put his

lanky arm around Dude's shoulder. Adding his Stetson, Cal was a foot taller than Dude, but their combined weight would've been about average for one adult male.

"Dude buddy, great seeing you. How about a brew?"

Dude smiled. "Got martinis?"

Cal returned Dude's smile and said, "Got Buds."

"My number *dos* choice."

"Excellent choice, my friend," Cal said and headed behind the bar to get Dude's second choice. He didn't ask what I wanted.

Cal returned, handed Dude a bottle of Budweiser and a glass of red wine to me before saying, "Chris, you seen Liam?"

"Liam Mathers?"

"How many Liams do you know?"

Dude said, "Liam Neeson, the actor guy."

Cal rolled his eyes and turned to me and said, "Was talking to you, pard."

"Mathers is the only one I know," I said and took a sip of wine then added, "Why?"

Ferlin Husky was singing "Wings of a Dove" and a customer at the far end of the bar was waving for Cal's attention.

"Hold that question," he said and headed to meet the customer's need.

Dude watched him go and said, "Me know Liam Neeson from moving pictures plus Liam Mathers."

"How do you know Liam Mathers?"

"He be datin' Beth Powell?"

"How do you know Beth?"

"She be with Liam and bought surf wax. Paid with plastic. Saw name Beth Powell. She be Injun, Seminole."

"Did she tell you that?" I asked, wondering how that would've come up when paying for surf wax.

"She be like Jack's beansprout, so I said, 'You be beansprout tall chick.' She said, 'Six foot, tall for a Seminole.'"

"Is there anything you know about Liam other than he's dating Beth?"

"He be holding Festus, her cool cat. Festus not be Injun."

Cal returned before the conversation deteriorated further. He looked toward the door and mumbled something about never letting Junior have another day off as four more customers entered.

He continued looking at the increasing number of customers and said, "Liam came in to see if you were here since you were the last time he saw you."

"Cal, when did you meet Liam? Didn't you tell us the night Charles, Jeffery, you, and I were in here talking that you didn't know who he was?"

"Crowded that night, remember?"

I nodded.

"After you and Charles left, I asked Junior if he knew Liam. He said he not only knew him, but Liam was sitting right over in that corner sipping a beer." Cal pointed to a small table in the corner of the room. "Anyway, I went over to introduce myself and he said he saw us talking but didn't want to interrupt since we seemed to be in a deep conversation."

"I don't suppose he said anything about what happened to Ruby Banes?"

"Not a word."

"Okay, back to what you were saying about him asking about me."

"You weren't here, of course. I asked why he wanted to know, and he said he wanted to ask you something, think it was about the police, he was mumbling."

"Did he say anything else?"

"No, but he seemed irritated that you weren't here. Hope you don't mind, but I told him where you lived."

Great, Cal, I thought, *you gave my address to the person who Charles thinks killed Ruby.*

"That's okay, Cal," I said since the damage was done.

"Good. Sorry guys, I need to double-time it back to work. Have I told you lately how I'll never let Junior have another day off as long as I live?"

"Me heard," Dude said.

I nodded as Cal headed to the door to welcome more customers.

Dude took a sip of beer, nodded, and said, "Me hunchin' you think Liam offed chick?"

Dude is more perceptive and smarter than most people give him credit for.

"You could be right."

"So, how be provin' it?"

Excellent question, I thought, and said, "Dude, that's up to the police."

He looked at me, rolled his eyes, and said, "Yeah, right."

Told you he was perceptive.

We stood around a few more minutes, finished our drinks, listened to music, and realized Cal wouldn't have any more time to socialize with us before I suggested we call it a night. Dude agreed and we headed to the exit.

Before we reached the door, Cal waved for me. Dude and I stopped while Cal came over, thanked us for coming, and added, "Almost forgot something Liam said. I probably didn't hear it right, but it sounded like he said something about the person that killed Ruby."

I said, "Like he knew who it was?"

"Yes, umm. maybe. Sorry, customers call."

He headed back to his demanding customers. Dude watched him go and said, "That be clue."

As we left the bar, Patsy Cline summed it up with "Crazy."

22

My first thought as I rolled out of bed was what could Liam have wanted to talk to me about enough to go to Cal's to see if I was there? If Charles was right about him being the killer, I was afraid to think what he wanted, but on the other hand, I did offer to go with him to see Chief LaMond if he wanted to talk to her about what he knew about the murder victim. Finally, could Cal have been right about Liam possibly knowing the identity of the killer?

My second thought was why is my phone ringing at 7:00 a.m.? The answer to the person who was calling was revealed with Mel's name appearing on the screen. The why would have to wait a few more seconds.

"Good morning, Mel."

"Yes, it is a good day."

"What'd I do to deserve this early-morning call?"

"Haven't you figured out by now that it isn't that early, and you haven't done anything to earn such a cheerful call."

"I suppose if I wait long enough, you'll tell me why you called."

"I wanted to let you know I wouldn't be coming over for breakfast."

"Okay, was I expecting you?"

"Don't know. That's something you'd know the answer to. Why ask me?"

"I know you former leathernecks think this is the middle of the day, but as you've pointed out, we, as you call everyone who hasn't served in the military, draft dodgers think this is mighty early, so the only reason you called was to tell me you weren't coming for breakfast?"

"Affirmative, but while I've got you, what are you wearing to the masquerade party? It's just around the corner."

"Didn't I tell you I wasn't going?"

"Yes, but I figure that sweet bookstore lady you hang with has you changing your mind. So, what's your costume?"

"I don't know."

"See, you've changed your mind."

"What are you going as?"

"You'll have to wait until the party to find out. Got to go. Think Caldwell and me are going to have a confab over chow. I have to start writing down everything bad he does, so I don't forget any of it when he starts blaming me for everything that goes wrong."

The phone went dead.

Mel mentioning breakfast reminded me I didn't have anything in the house to pass for the first meal of the day. A quick trip to Bert's would resolve that dilemma.

The phone rang again before I made it to the front door. I smiled to myself, joking that it was Mel calling to tell me that in addition to not having breakfast with me, he wasn't coming for lunch.

I was wrong. It was Charles.

"Morning, what's up?"

"Calling to see what you're doing?"

"Let's see, I'm opening my front door, now walking onto the porch, and, oh crap, another drunk's sleeping it off on my step."

Unfortunately, living this close to Folly's bars, it's not the first time someone, let's say, overindulged in drink and didn't make it to wherever he was headed. At least, the overindulgers often walked rather than risking lives by driving to their destinations.

I pushed the screen door enough to squeeze through to awaken my uninvited guest, then stepped over the man's legs to get to a clearer view of his head. His face was resting against the concrete step, one arm twisted to his side.

"What are you doing?" Charles said. "Sounds like you're carrying a sack of potatoes upstairs."

"Hang on. Let me get around in front of my visitor and shake him awake."

The man's jacket was bunched up around his neck and

covering the side of his face. His long blond hair reminded me of someone, but I didn't realize who it was until I moved the jacket away from his face.

Liam Mathers eyes stared past me, his unblinking, lifeless eyes. I hadn't had breakfast or it'd be leaving my body about now.

I stepped back, nearly tripped on the edging around the step, and looked around to see if anyone was nearby. I realized the voice I was hearing was Charles. I knelt, tried to catch my breath, and said, "Charles, gotta go. It's Liam, umm, he's dead."

I heard him say, "You sure?"

I dropped the phone. Picked it up off the dew-covered grass, hit *end call*, then punched in 9-1-1. I think that's what I did although I was so shaken, I couldn't swear to it. I managed to tell the emergency operator where I was and that there was a dead body. She said something about me staying where I was and if I was sure the person was dead. I told her I wasn't certain of anything and to send help.

I managed to stand, then slowly walked backward to the edge of the drive, the entire time staring at the lifeless body.

The wailing of police sirens approaching from Center Street jolted me out of my daze. They were followed by the lower-pitched roar of a fire engine's siren heading my way.

A patrol car pulled in the drive. The driver tapped the horn to get me to move out of the center of the driveway. I moved to the back of my drive and leaned against my car. Officer Rodney New was quick to exit his vehicle. He'd been with the force a couple of years, but I didn't know him as well as I did a few of the other officers.

He looked toward the person at the front step, turned to me, and said, "Mr. Landrum, did you call 9-1-1?"

I said I did, and he told me to remain where I was and then he walked over to the body. I doubted my legs would carry me even if I wanted to go anywhere. The officer knelt and moved the jacket away from the corpse's face. He then stood, made a call on his handheld radio, and looked around; I suppose to see if anyone was lurking in the shadows.

A second patrol car pulled in the drive behind New's vehicle. I was glad to see Allen Spencer exit since I knew him much better than I did Officer New. He nodded my direction and headed directly to the front step. One of the city's fire engines pulled off the side of the road and two firefighters who also doubled as EMTs hurried to the gathered police officers. I could've told them there was no need to hurry.

Chief LaMond was next to arrive and parked behind the fire engine at the street. She saw me and held up one finger to indicate she'd be with me shortly, or at least that's what I thought she meant. She then joined her officers and firefighters standing near Liam's body.

A handful of people moved closer to my property line from Bert's parking area next door. Cindy must've seen them, since she said something to Officer New, pointed to the interlopers then to the sides of my house and the front of the yard. Officer New returned to his patrol car and grabbed a roll of yellow police tape from the trunk and began stringing it around my front yard.

Cindy looked in my direction and headed my way. My hands were shaking so badly that I put them in my pocket to try to get them to stop trembling.

I waited for her to make one of her smart aleck remarks she's known for spewing among her friends, but instead, she said, "You okay?"

"No."

"You're shivering. Let's go in the house."

I would've preferred to open my eyes and realize this morning was only a dream, a nightmare.

23

Chief LaMond pointed toward the back yard and asked if I had a key to the back door with me. I did, and she took my elbow and escorted me to the rear entry.

I fumbled twice to unlock the door before Cindy took the key out of my hand, unlocked the door, and pointed to the kitchen table and said, "Sit."

I did and she looked at the empty Mr. Coffee machine on the counter, and said, "Why haven't you made me any coffee?"

Not quite a smart aleck remark, but more like the Cindy I'd come to love.

She didn't wait for my answer. She grabbed the can of coffee from the counter, filled the carafe with water and poured it into Mr. Coffee, then put the coffee into the filter then switched on the machine.

She smiled, patted me on the shoulder, and said, "You tell my hubby I'm this domestic and you'll be spending the rest of your life behind bars, and not the one at Cal's."

I took a deep breath then smiled. She'd achieved her goal.

Cindy waited by Mr. Coffee until the pot had brewed, most likely to give me time to calm, and then poured two cups and placed one in front of me before saying, "Ready to tell me what happened?"

I shared what little I knew about this morning, omitting the call from Mel. I didn't try to avoid telling her about Charles's call since I suspected he would be showing up any moment.

It got more convoluted when I told her about my contacts with Liam and about what Cal had shared last evening about Liam's visit and how he'd asked if I was there. She started to ask if I'd heard anything during the night that was out of the ordinary. I resisted saying anything other than hearing a man getting murdered on my front step.

"Cindy, what killed him?"

"It looks like he was garroted, most likely with a wire. I didn't see anything like it near the body. We'll have to wait for the coroner to make the final determination. And before you ask, I saw no evidence of a hatchet in his back or poison in his veins"

Her humor evaded me.

"Think he was killed out front?"

"That'd be my thought, but again, the coroner will have something to say about it, and also when it happened."

"If he was killed on my front step, it had to be several hours ago," I said.

"Because of the small amount of traffic that would've been driving by in the middle of the night?"

"That," I said, "and that his clothes were wet from the dew. That didn't just happen, did it?"

"Again, the coroner will determine that."

"What I don't understand is why someone didn't see him spayed out on the step and call you all or stop to see if he was okay?"

She shook her head. "You wouldn't believe how many of our citizens spend hours overnight in people's yards or behind buildings sleeping off hangovers. It's one of the unfortunate byproducts of a healthy bar community and our decent weather."

"I suppose—"

The back door flying open interrupted me. Charles, looking like a yellow caution light in his yellow Michigan Wolverines sweatshirt, rushed into the room.

"Chief," he said sounding out of breath, "you wouldn't believe this. Your officers wouldn't let me in the front door."

Cindy sighed and said, "I can't believe they didn't arrest you."

"Why?"

"For being Charles. Now get coffee, take a seat, and don't open your mouth until I ask you a question. Understood?"

"Yes," he said as he got coffee. "I was worried about my friend and that's—"

Cindy waved a hand in his face and said, "Did you miss the part about not opening your mouth?"

"No, I was—"

Her hand went in his face again. He grabbed his cup and took a sip.

Cindy turned to me. "Did you get the impression from talking with Cal that he thought Liam was hinting that he knew who killed Ruby Banes and that's why he was looking for you?"

"Yes."

Charles came close to dropping his cup, leaned toward Cindy, and said, "What?" Then he stared at me. "When did you learn this, Chris? What did—"

Cindy pushed her chair back, stood, and glared at Charles. "One more word, one more word, and I will have to mop your blood off Chris's kitchen floor. Can I make it any clearer?"

Charles leaned back and raised his hand.

Cindy shook her head, stared at Charles, and said, "What?"

"That was clear."

"Good."

This time, instead of Charles, a knock on the back door interrupted Cindy. Detective Adair from the County Sheriff's

Office stepped into the room like he owned it. He looked more like a Gwynn's clothing store model than a detective in his starched-white shirt, gray slacks, navy blazer, and polished shoes. What set the mid-thirty-year-old apart from a model was his unsmiling face.

He nodded to Cindy and said, "Chief," glanced at me with a glimmer of distain and said, "Mr. Landrum." He turned to Charles and said, "Two untimely deaths over here and two appearances by you, Mr. Fowler." He returned looking at Cindy and said, "What do you know about what happened? I briefly talked to your officers out front and got the basics."

Cindy shared what she knew about this morning. I doubted it included anything he hadn't learned out front. She then asked me to tell the Detective what I'd known about Liam including last night's visit to Cal's.

My hands felt numb but at least they'd stopped shaking. I shared my brief discussions with Liam and about receiving the call from Cal yesterday asking if I planned to visit his bar. Charles sat silently sipping coffee. I suspect it was from fear of his blood being spilled on the kitchen floor.

Detective Adair was taking notes and occasionally looked at me and signaled me to continue. I thought I'd covered everything I knew about Liam and stopped talking.

Adair pointed his pen at me and said, "A couple of points. You said this Cal, umm.," he hesitated and looked at his notes before continuing, "Cal Ballew gave Mr. Mather your address."

"Correct."

Adair turned to Charles. "And you, Mr. Fowler, suspected Liam Mathers was Ms. Barnes's killer?"

Charles glanced at Cindy, most likely to see if she'd drawn her firearm, before turning to Adair. "I thought he was. Umm, I don't now."

Adair jotted something in his notebook before looking at me and saying, "And Mr. Ballew thought Mr. Mathers wanted to ask you to set up a meeting with Chief LaMond?"

"Yes."

"To tell her what he knew about Ms. Banes?"

"Correct."

"Do you know where I can reach Mr. Ballew?"

I gave him the name and location of Cal's Bar, looked on my phone's contacts list and recited Cal's cell phone number and his home address."

Adair glanced at each of us and said, "Anything to add?"

I said, "No."

Charles simply shook his head, probably remembering Cindy's threat.

Adair nodded toward Cindy, told her he'd get with her later, stood, and exiting through the back door.

Cindy said, "Guys, anything else you need to share with me?

We said there wasn't.

She stood, leaned down and gave me a hug, and said, "I'm so sorry," before following Adair out the door.

Charles asked if I wanted more coffee. I told him I didn't.

He then said, "We've got to find the killer. Period, no, make that exclamation point."

"We don't know—"

"It's the right thing to do," he interrupted.

"We don't have a way to—"

He interrupted again by saying, "Teddy Roosevelt said, 'Knowing what's right doesn't mean much unless you do what's right.'"

24

The rest of the day had been one long blur. Chief LaMond and Charles had left me in the kitchen staring into my empty coffee cup. Throughout the day, I'd heard noises and people speaking outside the front of the house, but never looked out to see what they were doing. To say I was numb would've been understating the meaning of numb.

Since moving to Folly, I'd stumbled across dead bodies, had come close to being murdered by a soulless killer, and nearly had been decapitated by an airplane tumbling from the sky. Yet, there was something about opening the front door to exit my cottage, my place of safety and peace, to face a lifeless gentleman on my step that smacked my sense of security like I hadn't experienced before. Yes, I was numb.

The ringing phone awakened me the next morning. I

assumed it was the next day since it was starting to get light outside, and I vaguely remembered it getting dark last evening before I fell into a restless sleep. Charles's name appeared on the screen.

"Morning, Charles."

"Did you see them?"

I wasn't ready for playing games with anyone, so instead of beginning with a sarcastic remark or asking if he could ever manage a civil introduction, I said, "Who?"

"Waylon Atwood and Victor Hardin."

I must be awake now since this time I considered uttering a sarcastic remark, but instead said, "What are you talking about?"

"Cranky this morning, aren't we?"

I sighed. "Yes."

"After yesterday, you've earned being cranky. Let me back up. Good morning."

"Thank you. Now, where and when would I have seen them?"

"Yesterday. It slipped my mind until early this morning, but I didn't want to call you at 2:00 a.m. to tell you. When I heard about the body at your front door, I was in such a hurry to get to your place to see if you were okay, I plum forgot seeing them."

"First, thanks for not calling at two. Second, thanks for being concerned about my welfare. And third, I repeat, what are you talking about?"

"By the time I got to your house, the police had stretched

the tape on both sides of your front yard. Remember, I told you and Cindy how they were so rude they wouldn't let me in your front door?"

"I remember."

"Guess who was in Bert's lot and along with a bunch of others leaning against the tape staring at the body on your step?"

"Waylon Atwood and Victor Hardin."

"Yep."

"So?"

"They killed Ruby Banes and Liam. It's as clear as day."

"How do you figure that?"

'Everyone knows a killer often returns to the scene of the crime when the police are there, something about enjoying and reliving their crime."

"Didn't you say there was a bunch of people there who were doing the same thing?"

"Yes."

"Why couldn't the killer be one of them?"

"Chris, Chris, yesterday was a rough one for you, so I'll forgive you for being dense as osmium this morning."

"Osmium?" I said, regretting saying it as soon as it was out of my mouth.

"The densest element on earth. Read about it last night in *National Geographic*. Interesting article, said it—"

Yes, that's why I regretted saying it.

"Why couldn't someone else standing there have been the killer?"

"Have you already forgotten about when we met Waylon and Victor at The Washout how they worked hard to sell the idea that the killer must have known Ruby real good since he managed to get her out where she was hatcheted. Remember how quick they were to say they barely knew her. Deflection, my friend. You also might remember that I told you then they were on my suspect list. Seeing them at your place yesterday, takes them off the suspect list. Yesterday proved they killed her. Don't know why they killed Liam, but they did."

"You might be right."

"I knew you'd see it my way. Want to go with me to tell Cindy?"

I must be dense as osmium since I didn't realize that telling him he might be right was the same as saying he was right. Instead of arguing that point, I said, "Tell her what?"

"You fall asleep again? We've got to tell her about what those killers said at The Washout and that they were at your house yesterday."

"I don't think—"

"If you don't feel like going anywhere today after what you went through yesterday, you can tell her she can come to your house. After yesterday, she'll feel sorry for you and do whatever you ask. I'll meet you there."

That proved he didn't know Cindy as well as I knew her.

"No."

I had never suffered from migraines but was beginning to know what one must feel like.

"No, she wouldn't feel sorry for you? No, you won't call her? Or no, you don't think they killed Ruby and Liam?"

"Yes," I said and tapped *end call.*

Now I definitely know how a migraine feels.

I thought about going back to bed but figured my sleep would be interrupted by Charles calling to ask if I'd changed my mind about anything I'd said "no" to. I fixed another pot of coffee and moved to the recliner in the living room.

A couple of sips later, I noticed that my headache had subsided, and I began thinking about what had happened yesterday and what Charles had said about Waylon and Victor being the killers. He hadn't said anything that would convince me, or for that matter anyone else, about their guilt, but to be honest, it was as good a theory as any I'd heard. They had been arguing about something in the Dog the first time I'd seen them. Could it have been about Ruby?

The answer wasn't as "clear as day" as it was to Charles, so I ventured to Bert's to grab something to eat. This time I'd left through the back door. No, I didn't expect to find another body on the front step, but knew there would be some evidence, if nothing more than police tape to remind me of yesterday.

Fortunately, I didn't see anyone in Bert's who wanted to talk about yesterday and I returned home with two slices of pizza and an ice cream sandwich for dessert. I remained in the kitchen and ate whatever meal you could call it at 3:15 p.m.

25

After getting more sleep than I experienced the previous evening, I 'd been stuck in the house long enough. I needed to stretch my legs and try and enjoy the unseasonably warm day Mother Nature was sharing with us before the cooler, wet days of fall arrived. My hand hesitated as I reached for the front doorknob. I took a deep breath and slowly pulled the door open. The only thing that greeted me was the sun staring me in the face. Any evidence of the horrific event from two mornings ago was gone, all but me reliving the scene in my head. A minute later I was at the coffee urn in Bert's pulling as cup of coffee and deciding I could, okay, should skip the pastry cabinet.

On the way to the exit, I heard Denise, who was working behind the counter, say, "Morning, Chris, only coffee today?"

"Not much of an appetite this morning."

"Got it. Have a good day."

"You too," I said surprised she hadn't asked about the murder that took place fewer than fifty yards from where she was working, I was relieved not having to talk about it.

As I headed toward the center of town, the fresh, morning air had begun to clear my head of negative memories of the other day, so I continued out West Ashley Avenue. A block or so later, I was again reminded that the style of the houses were as eclectic as Folly's population. The decorations in yards and on the houses were as varied as the structures. Some of the houses exhibited traditional beach vibes with shells, dolphins, and lizards, while others looked as if their owners maxed out their credit cards at the Halloween Spirit store.

I was staring at a yard filled with Halloween inflatables while wondering why people enjoyed this holiday so much, when a voice behind me made me jump and turn.

Charles said, "There you are. I've pedaled all over searching for you."

"All over?"

"Well, I would have if I hadn't seen you cross Center Street."

"So, in fact you were following me, waiting for the perfect moment to startle me."

"Putting it like that makes me out to be scarier than those blowup ghosts and pumpkins you're staring at."

"Don't think pumpkins are scary."

"Tell that to Ichabod Crane when the headless horseman hurled one at him."

"Did you track me down to talk about some fictional story?"

"Nope, just left the surf shop heading to the Tides when I saw you. I wanted to see how you were doing."

"Better, thanks for asking. Looking in your empty basket, I'm thinking Dude didn't have deliveries for you."

"None this morning. He asked how you were doing after finding Liam," Charles said as he dismounted from his bike.

"I bet he didn't say it like that."

Charles smiled, cleared his throat, and in his best Dudespeak impression said, "Christer be chill after rad morn?"

"That's more like Dude. Why were you heading to the Tides?"

"Best masquerade party ever, of course."

"It's not until Saturday."

"True, I'm on the setup crew getting the Pavilion Ballroom ready for the event. Gives me a chance to use one of my many talents."

"I had no idea."

He said, "Me either. My first time doing it. If your old bones will let you walk with me, I'll tell you about what it's going to look like at the party. Don't want you to be blown away when you arrive Saturday."

"I never said I was attending."

"I don't know what keeps Barb with you but what I know is a true gentleman would take his lady to the party and be thrilled to do it. Besides, you can't catch a killer without me, so what other plans could you possibly have for Saturday?"

"Tell me about the setup," I said, ignoring his comment about me attending or catching a killer as we headed toward the hotel.

Charles walked beside me while pushing his bike. "There'll be a buffet on one end of the room, the other end is where the band will be. Those tall cocktail tables will be spread around the room, and, of course, the dance floor will be in front of the room."

"Sounds like a typical arrangement, so why do they need your help?"

"Shows how little you know. That's just where stuff will be. A party is nothing without decorations. My job is to hang a hundred masquerade masks along the walls where they're going to be lit with silver or blue lights."

"Sounds like a lot."

"Folly needs something to bring everyone together. What better way than a big party?"

"Have you settled on your costume?"

"Yep, but I'm not telling you. You'll have to come see, another reason for you to be there."

We arrived at the hotel's parking lot and Charles parked his bike near the side entry, turned to me, and said, "You know I'm here if you want to talk about the other morning, but I'm not going to push."

"I know, thanks."

"Besides, we should wait until after the party to talk

about how to catch the killer."

"Don't we need to know who it is first?"

"I figure the killer will be at the party so we can nail down who we need to catch. That's another reason I'll be seeing you Saturday evening."

"Why do you think the killer will be at the party?"

"Deductive reasoning, of course. People who go to masquerade parties hide behind masks. Don't want others to know who they are. So do killers. Well, not wearing masks, but still don't want others to know who they are. That means he'll be there."

I didn't think anything could be accomplished by pointing out that Charles's attempt at deductive reasoning, had enough holes in it to drive a Subaru through. Instead, I said, "Okay."

With that settled, at least in my friend's mind, he pivoted and walked through the hotel's side entrance.

Not ready to see anyone at the hotel, I headed up Center Street to see if Barb was available for lunch. When I reached Barb's Books, my question was answered before entering the store. Even in October, the store had a fair number of customers. Barb was standing in the rear helping a frail-appearing, white-haired lady. The owner looked up, saw me, and nodded toward her office in back of the building. I went through the store and into the office where I grabbed a Diet Coke from the refrigerator and plopped down in her high-tech, ergonomic chair and waited for the popular bookstore owner.

Ten minutes later, Barb came into the room, sat in the chair facing me, and said, "Never thought she would decide on which book she wanted." She sighed, smiled, then looked at me. "It's good to see you. How are you doing, or don't you want to talk about the corpse on your step? That would be the corpse I heard about from a customer I don't know, rather than from the man I've been dating." Her smile remained but I didn't detect much humor.

"You should have sold her both books," I said to avoid talking about the murder.

"I was thinking the same thing. Sally Lee is a firecracker. It's true that dynamite comes in small packages. Hope I'm that feisty at her age...or next year." Barb's expression turned to one of concern through a forced smile. "Now, about the body?"

"I didn't want to worry you. I'm better, simply needed a day or two to process it. Rather not talk about it, if that's okay."

Barb's face softened. She reached for my hand and nodded.

"Thank you." I squeezed her hand and added, "I stopped to see if I could steal you away for lunch, but I see business is busier than I was expecting."

"I'm surprised as well. Thanks for the offer, but I got here late and have had a steady stream of customers."

"Did something happen for you to arrive late."

"I went to Charleston to pick that up." Barb pointed to a black garment bag hanging in the corner.

"What is it?"

"That, my dear man, is a beautiful costume for the masquerade party, that is, if we go. No pressure, of course. I know we haven't talked about it much, but I'd rather have the outfit and not go than not have it and we decided to attend. Otherwise. I'd have to cut eyeholes in my designer sheet to be a pitiful Casper." She smiled and patted me on the arm as she stood to check the store.

"Before stopping by, I talked with Charles about the party. Believe it or not, he's helping with the decorations. To hear him tell it, it will be the event of the year."

"I've heard the same thing."

"If I'm not too late and you've already accepted an invitation from one of the many men you said who've asked you to go with them, would you attend with me?"

She smiled and said, "I would love to. What changed your mind?"

"Life is too short for me to stay in my safe place. Occasionally, I need to be uncomfortable to experience life."

Her smile widened. "Wow, for you that was insightful and deep, but I suspect the real reason for your change of heart was so you could see what was inside that garment bag and what Charles will be wearing."

I shrugged.

She added, "Want me to pick up a costume for you?"

"I appreciate the offer, but I have it covered."

"Then it's a date. Now, I better get back to work."

Barb kissed me on the cheek before heading back into

the store to meet three potential customers who'd arrived while she was in the office. My mind drifted back to the vision of Liam dead on my step and the look on Charles's face after he found Ruby. Yes, life is too short, way too short.

I was in front of First Light's foul weather sanctuary when Preacher Burl stepped out of the doorway and nearly bumped into me.

"Preacher, you in a hurry?"

"Brother Chris, sorry, I didn't see you. I need to pick up some things in Charleston and the time got away from me."

"I won't keep you. Have a safe trip."

"Nonsense, my friends are always more important than any errand I have to run. I was talking with Officer Trula yesterday when she told me what happened at your house. Are you okay?"

"Yes, all things considered."

"You know I'm here if you want or need to talk, day or night"

"Preacher hours?"

"This preacher's help is 24/7 for my flock." He patted my arm as if reading my thoughts. "Especially for those lost sheep."

"Thanks. I don't want to be the reason you get a speeding ticket, so you'd better go."

"Not sure my trusty chariot could accomplish that." Burl's laugh filled the still October air. "You're right though. I need to go. Take care."

26

I opened the closet in my spare bedroom/office and was confronted with ghosts from my past, or as most would call it, my previous business attire. After retiring, I had gleefully donated most of my suits to Goodwill, since I never planned on being in the bureaucratic rat race again. Two suits remained for special occasions when khakis wouldn't suffice: one navy blue, the other one gray. The three-piece gray suit was going to be my costume for tonight's party. Granted, it wasn't a traditional costume, but it was as far as I was willing to go. To complete the bureaucratic administrator look, I added a white dress shirt, a blue and white rep tie with a silver horseshoe tie tack, a retirement gift I'd never worn, and black dress shoes.

I looked at myself in the mirror, smiled because I was thankful that I no longer had to dress like this, and because the suit that hadn't been worn in more than a decade still fit; that is, if I didn't button the coat.

I had ten minutes until I was to pick up Barb, but that wasn't a problem since it took me half that time to drive to her condo. I rang the doorbell and heard her yell for me to come in. I entered and looked around, but my date was nowhere in sight.

I said, "You okay?"

From the bedroom she said, "I know why in classic movies they have maids helping the lady of the house get ready for the ball. Their dresses are not designed for being thrown on and walking out the door."

"Need help?"

"No, I'll be out in a minute, I hope. Have a seat."

I smiled thinking about her getting into a wrestling match with an outfit. Instead of sitting, I moved to the sliding glass door overlooking the ocean. Shadows from the sun were settling low on the horizon giving the ocean an eerie look, appropriate for this time of year.

I was lost in thought when I heard Barb behind me saying, "What do you think?"

I turned to see her looking like she stepped out of a Victorian novel. Her long red dress with gold accents looked as if it was tailor made for her. She was holding up to her face a red and gold eye mask adding more mystery and authenticity to the ensemble.

"You look beautiful. Where did you get it?"

"A theater costume shop in Charleston. I wasn't looking

for anything this elaborate but when I saw it, I knew it was the one. However, if I had known how difficult getting dressed would be, I might have gone for the naughty nurse costume."

"It's perfect. You should consider making it a regular outfit."

"No way, Mr. Landrum. Including the corset, hooped skirt, and bulky dress material, I'm fairly sure it weighs more than I do." She gave me a look going from my feet to the top of my tie, then said, "Speaking of making a change in wardrobe, you look quite handsome."

"There's more a chance of you acting like Scarlett and donning that velvet curtain than me going back to wearing suits. It works for a costume, no shopping required."

"I've something that'll go with your costume," she said then Barb retreated to the bedroom and returned carrying a small box. "Picked this up when I got the dress. I figured if you decided to go, you wouldn't wear a costume."

She handed me the container. I opened it and was amazed to see an eye mask the same shade of gray as my suit. I put it in my breast pocket, so I'd be ready if masks were required.

She smiled and said, "I can't believe how close it matches your suit. I chose it because all the others were black and seemed too much like what the Lone Ranger would wear."

"Shall we go? I'm not sure how long it's going to take to get you in the car wearing that outfit."

"Funny. We can walk. One good thing about the dress being floor length is I'm wearing comfortable flats."

We walked hand-in-hand across the hotel's parking lot to the entrance, where I asked if she wanted to take the elevator rather than the stairs to the meeting rooms. Even in flats, she chose the elevator saying wearing a dress heavier than she was while even walking up one flight of stairs would be a hardship.

The elevator doors opened at the meeting rooms floor where we were greeted by black and silver balloons flanking a large welcome sign telling us we had reached our destination. The event's large lobby had several bar-height cocktail tables decorated with black, silver, and blue tablecloths. Before we reached the entrance to the main party room, we were greeted by Jay wearing a blond wig with long stringy hair, a black butler suit with a dirty white button-down shirt, and green tennis shoes.

"Helllloo," Jay smiled while delivering the drawn-out greeting.

"Riff Raff. I would have recognized you anywhere," Barb said then laughed and patted Jay on the arm.

I'm glad she recognized him because I still had no clue who or what Riff Raff was.

"Welcome to this special night. Let me know if you need anything," Jay said as he escorted us into the large room where a gathering of people were milling about.

The room was even nicer than Charles had described. Different styles of masks were attached to three of the walls and illuminated by blue or silver filters on the lights. The room's fluorescent lights were off and replaced with large silver floor candelabras with black, tapered, battery-powered candles. Numerous cocktail tables were spread throughout the space with silver tablecloths and centerpieces comprised of glass containers holding small fleurs-de-lis, sand dollars, and miniature masks. Members of a band appeared to be finishing setting up on the elevated bandstand in front of an archway of blue, black, and silver balloons. The hotel's staff, along with their volunteer helpers had gone above and beyond making the party Folly's event of the year.

While taking in the sights, I didn't notice Charles heading our direction.

"Dr. Watson, I presume," he said and tipped his hound-stooth Sherlock Holmes hat while holding a pipe in his left hand.

"Wrong, Mr. Holmes. I'm a boring administrator."

Charles turned to Barb, took her hand, and kissed it. "Such a beautiful sight. You should be in better company than with this boring paper pusher."

"Good evening, Charles. I hear you helped with the decorations. They're wonderful."

"I knew such a fine lady would appreciate a fine celebration."

Barb turned to me. "I'm going to the bar and claim a table. I'll let you two fictional characters talk." She kissed me on the cheek and patted Charles on the back.

Charles watched her go, turned to me, and said, "See, she knows we're real detectives."

"You got that from her calling us fictional?"

"Duh, a big yes. She knew our costumes were for fictional characters, so us wearing them made us real."

Barb should have said delusional rather than fictional.

Instead of debating semantics, I said, "Been here long?"

"Long enough to see our top two suspects arrive and lay claim to the table, the one near the band. Speaking of the band, you ever hear the Sweetgrass Basket Band play?"

"Not only never heard them play, I've never heard of them."

"We need to get you out from under that rock you call home. A skink sees more of the world than you do."

"You're comparing me to an amphibian?"

"Nope, to a reptile, but don't get off the subject, our suspects are over there."

I looked across the room to where Charles was pointing with his pipe to see who our suspects might be. Leaning back in a chair was Waylon looking more like Mr. Clean than the Proctor and Gamble mascot. The "suspect" was dressed all in white, had shaved his goatee and was now sporting a gold hoop earring. Sitting next to him was Blackbeard, someone I could only assume to be Victor but would be hard pressed to swear to it, since he'd gone all out to look like the infamous pirate who once sailed nearby waters.

"Brother Chris, Charles." Burl moved up beside us

appearing to be a carpenter with his denim overalls, long-sleeve yellow shirt, work boots, and orange safety goggles.

"Preacher," Charles said, "if I didn't know better, I'd hire you for some renovations."

"If I didn't know you better, I'd say you're playing detective, for a change."

Charles said, "Not just any detective, but the best, until that guy Charles Fowler came along."

"Brother Charles, remind me to tell you what the good book says about pride," Burl said through a wide grin.

He then turned to me, his smile fading and said, "Brother Chris, are you okay?"

"Getting there. Thanks for asking."

Burl turned his attention to the entry and waved someone over.

I turned to see a tall woman dressed in a colorful orange, white, yellow horizontal-patterned blouse with billowy long sleeves, a floor-length matching skirt, and a black mask with orange feathers.

Burl hugged the new arrival and said, "Sister Beth, I love your traditional native American garb. Have you met my friends?"

"Can't say I have." She extended her hand to Charles. "I'm Beth Powell."

"Pleased to meet you. I'm Charles Fowler and this well-dressed man is Chris Landrum."

I extended my hand to shake hers.

"Oh, Folly's famous detectives. Preacher Burl has told me about you."

Rather than acknowledging her comment, Burl waved at someone across the room, excused himself, and headed that direction.

I said, "Not sure what the Preacher told you, but we're neither famous nor detectives."

"Chris is being modest," Charles said. "I'm more interested in your outfit. I'm guessing from what Preacher Burl said, it's authentic."

"I'm a descendant of Osceola of the Seminole Tribe, at least that's what my mother always told me, so my heritage is an important aspect of my life, that and Festus."

She pirouetted and added, "Thus the clothing."

I said, "Festus is your cat?"

Charles glared at me as if I was keeping top secret information from him. Beth's green eyes stared at me in disbelief.

"Yes, but how—"

"Dude Sloan, a friend of mine, told me about meeting you with Liam Mathers and Festus."

Charles's glare intensified and he was about to speak when Beth lowered her head said something under her breath. Her raven black hair draped over her face.

Charles said, "You knew Liam?"

"We dated, but, well, we split up." She looked around the room.

I could tell our conversation was ending, so I said, "We

should let you enjoy the party. It was a pleasure meeting you."

She nodded and headed toward the buffet.

Barb was in an intense conversation with a jester and the queen of hearts. I had no idea who they were in real life.

Charles stared at me and said, "Can't believe you let her walk away. She knew Liam, maybe knew Ruby. She's big and strong enough to have killed them."

"Knowing a victim doesn't make someone a suspect."

"But it helps. Besides, she didn't seem too sad about breaking up with Liam. Besides, she's a cat person."

"Not everyone is as dog obsessed as you are, and from what I've heard, Festus is a neat cat."

"I suppose, cats are good people too."

"On that note, I'll be with my date. If you have other pearls of wisdom or more suspects let me know."

"Good plan, Mr. Watson. We'll divide and conquer."

The Sweetgrass Basket Band was working its way through a Beach Boys medley as I shook my head and walked across the dance floor to spend time with Barb and enjoy how people dressed for the first annual masquerade party.

27

I reached the table as the two people talking to Barb left for the buffet. My date handed me a glass of wine and nodded towards Beth and said, "She's stunning, walks in the room and everyone notices."

"That's Beth Powell, Burl just introduced her to Charles and me. She's a plumber who's been doing work at Hope House."

"Suppose I'm going to have to keep an eye on you." Barb laughed and kissed my cheek.

The band kicked up the tempo and volume with a version of The Isley Bothers' hit "Shout" and several couples merged onto the dance floor, as more guests arrived. It was a wise decision adding tables outside the room for late arrivals or those of us who wanted to get some air or avoid the music that was so loud it vibrated the decorations on the table. Two couples walked over to Barb who introduced me to them, and then she got caught up in small business owner talk with the four.

I was watching the door and saw one of the more unlikely couples walk in. Excusing myself, I made my way across the room to see Junior Richardson and Dude. Junior looked like a lumberjack with his red, plaid long-sleeve shirt, jeans, and Timberland boots. He was minus an ax, probably thought it was in bad taste considering what'd caused Ruby's demise. Dude was wearing a tie-dye T-shirt with a glow in the dark peace sign, green slacks, and loafers. In other words, he came dressed as Dude.

"Christer, me bring Paul B to the ball."

"Evening Dude, what's that on your head?"

"Droopy dog face, from yesteryear." Dude removed the plastic kids' mask off his head and showed it to Junior and me.

I said, "Was that your Halloween mask when you were a kid?"

He nodded and smiled.

Junior, aka Paul Bunyon, looked at me and said, "Nice duds."

"Thanks. It's from my life before Folly collection."

"Mine, too. I had all this in my closet, first time wearing the boots. I bought them years ago when my girlfriend said we should take up hiking. Turned out *we* meant her and a new beau."

"Cal coming over?"

"Don't think so. He told me I needed to get out more and fired me... for tonight. If you'll excuse me, I'll see what they're serving. I can only take my hamburgers so long."

Junior's size cleared a path to the buffet, since a man that large, looking like a lumberjack, doesn't need an ax to move people aside. I watched him go when I noticed a man dressed in a black suit with a red vest, and white face paint that reminded me of a sugar skull walking toward Dude and me. It wasn't until he was a couple of feet away that I noticed a woman trailing him. She was wearing a full-length, black, lace dress with a red flamenco mantilla hair comb attached to a fine black lace veil. Her face paint matched the gentleman's.

"*Buenos noches*," the man said as he shook Dude's hand.

"True be *Dia de los Muertos*," Dude said as he reached around and hugged the woman.

After the hug, the woman looked at me and said, "Evening, Chris."

It wasn't until she spoke that I knew who it was.

"Alyssa, I didn't recognize you," I said and smiled. "I suppose that's the point of a masquerade party."

Alyssa turned toward the gentleman, "Jose this is Chris, he helped me the other day after my fender bender."

"Nice to meet you. I'm Jose Pardo. Thanks for helping Alyssa."

"All I did was pick up a couple of surfboards."

"Newest wave rider," Dude said as he gave Jose a pat on the back.

"Chris, do you surf? I can't get enough of the ocean."

I smiled. "I love the ocean but keep my feet on land."

"No big kahuna, Christer be murder solver."

Jose's gaze narrowed as he said, "You a cop?"

"No."

"Too bad," he said. "Two murders in such a small town is a real downer."

Alyssa said, "I love my new home here, but the killings are scary, especially since Jose knew both victims."

Jose wrapped his arm around Alyssa's waist.

I said, "You knew Ruby and Liam?"

He nodded. "Had a coffee date with Ruby when I first moved here, and I met Liam after Ruby's death. Chris, Dude, if you excuse us, I promised this young lady we'd dance the night away. Nice meeting you."

As Jose and Alyssa headed to the dance floor, I told Dude I'd see him later and started across the room to where Charles had been subtlety trying to get my attention as he appeared in a deep conversation with a bleached blonde, heavyset woman in a full-length, blue dress, and wearing a blue and white Volto masquerade mask. My first impression was she didn't want to be recognized. I was within ten feet of Charles when he stopped the conversation and excused himself to escort me the rest of the way.

"You're never going to believe who I've been talking to. That's Trudy Miller."

"Ruby's roommate?"

"Yep."

Before I could say anything else, Charles introduced me to Trudy. She shook my hand. I was surprised how strong her handshake was, stronger than many men I've encountered. She then glanced down and withdrew her hand.

"Chris, Trudy was saying she's in search of a new roommate, but I saw you and cut her off to get your attention. Please continue, Trudy."

"Like I was telling Charles, I need a roommate. You wouldn't know anyone needing a place to live, would you?"

"Sorry, afraid not. Did your former roommate leave without giving enough notice for you to find a replacement?"

Charles smiled at my question. My private detecting skills were improving.

"Nope, she managed to get killed. Now I'm stuck with rent due and short on time and money."

Charles said, "Wow, Ruby Banes was your roommate?"

"How'd you know? You a physic?"

"Lucky guess. You don't seem that upset about her death."

"Did you know Ruby?"

Charles said, "No."

I shook my head.

Trudy said, "She was well-educated but flighty and immature. Suppose it could've been because she was seven years younger than me." She sighed before continuing, "Made fun of me for focusing on work and not enjoying life." She cleared her throat before adding, "Bet she isn't enjoying life now."

I was surprised and before thinking said, "Seems harsh considering what happened to her."

"Yeah, but life is harsh. Sometimes you're the hatchet other times you're the body it's stuck in." Trudy looked down at her hands squeezing the sides of her floor-length dress before pulling herself up to her full height and looked at Charles then me before adding, "Sorry, I've dedicated my life to helping people as an occupational therapist. I'm normally joking around and cheerful, you can ask anyone at work or my patients. Ruby and I didn't get along and with the financial strain it has put on me, I'm...never mind. Let's just leave it that I'm pissed."

"Stress can bring out the worst in all of us," Charles said. "I'll get us a drink and we can enjoy the music. I'm sure Chris wants to get back to his date."

"It was nice meeting you, Chris. You too, Charles. I'll take a raincheck on that drink. I need to see some people over there." She nodded toward a group across the room.

"The pleasure is all mine," I said, not believing a word of it. Regardless, I doubt she heard me since she had started toward the other side of the room and "Born to Run" was blaring from the speakers.

Charles and I headed to the bar. I needed another drink and saw Barb on the opposite side from the bar motioning for me to get her one as well. I ordered for Barb and me, then Charles ordered before saying, "Ain't no love lost between them, is there? Makes you wonder if Trudy was on the handle end of that hatchet."

The bartender handed me two drinks and said he'd be back with Charles's order.

While we waited, I said, "Virgil thought it might be her because the spouse is always a suspect and a roommate is in a way like a spouse. You're right, she wasn't hiding her dislike for her former housemate."

"When I see Virgil, I'll introduce them. He's not as good a private detective as I am, sometimes you, but he's learning." He took his drink and reminded me it was time for us to divide and conquer.

I turned to take Barb her drink and saw she was talking to the Stone family minus Lugh. Shannon was wearing an elegant green dress, Roisin looked like a fairy with translucent wings, and then there was Desmond, finally embracing what I always secretly referred to him as, Ozzy Osbourne.

I handed Barb her drink and smiled at the Stones.

Shannon returned the smile and said, "Blessed be, Chris, how dapper you look this evening. Seeing Barb's lovely outfit, I thought you might be in a tailcoat and top hat."

Barb lightly tapped Shannon on the arm and said to me, "I was telling Shannon how lovely her dress is. Isn't it stunning with the silver embroidery standing out on the emerald green?"

I said, "The Tree of Life?"

Barb gave me an inquisitive look, probably wondering how I knew that. I didn't tell her my fount of trivia, Charles had told me what The Tree of Life looked like.

Shannon said, "Yes, it's the Celtic Tree of Life. I embroidered it myself more moons ago than I'll admit. It's my favorite dress but I never have a chance to wear it. Tonight was the perfect opportunity."

"I agree," I said then turned to Roisin. "Young lady, you are the prettiest fairy I've ever seen."

She twirled in her light blue dress with shimmering blue-silver fairy wings. A crown of flowers and blue feathers set off the color of her fiery red hair. It was as if one of those old painting of a fairy had come to life in the Tides Hotel.

"Well, businessman, no comments about my attire?"

"Desmond, be nice," Shannon said as she glared at the teen who stood a few inches taller than his mother.

"I was getting to you," I said. "You are the spitting image of a young Ozzy Osbourne. Bite the head off any bats lately?"

"Yuck," Roisin said as Barb elbowed me in the ribs.

Desmond smiled, or what I knew as a smile from my goth friend. He added a dramatic bow with his arms extended. He could have passed for the rocker dressed all in black, a bowler hat, trench coat, combat boots, and black tinted glasses.

"Everyone says I look like the Prince of Darkness, so here I am."

Shannon said, "Barb, Chris, it was so nice seeing you. We'll let you get back to your evening, I'm sure Barb would like to take a spin around the dance floor." Shannon put her arms around both kids and nudged them towards the buffet.

We moved to a corner of the room and watched couples awkwardly trying to dance while trapped in costumes restricting their movements. The buffet line had shortened, and Barb suggested we get some food saying I would need my strength for the dance competition. That would be a dance competition I was first learning about.

We filled our plates with a variety of appetizers ranging from Taco Boy's taquitos to Rita's pimento cheese, and even Loggerhead's crab dip. All the tables in the room were taken so we made our way to the ballroom's lobby and a table near the windows overlooking the Atlantic. Reflections from lights on the Folly Pier gleamed off the ocean, a view made more pleasant in the presence of Barb.

We then focused on the late partygoers coming up the stairs. A gentleman dressed as Zorro reached the top step, looked our direction, and stared at me for an uncomfortable amount of time.

Barb turned away from Zorro and whispered, "Who's that?"

"Don't know, but I'll find out."

I started toward the man when he tipped his hat at me and entered the crowded party room.

I was halfway across the room when from the top of the stairs came the booming voice of Mel Evans. I had anticipated him being dressed in Marine dress blues. The last thing I would've expected was my gruff, obscene, gay friend dressed as conservative Mike Pence. Mel was wearing a dark blue suit, a bright red tie, an American flag lapel pin, and a *Pence for Pres* sticker on his other lapel.

"Hey old man, have I got your vote?" he asked and

grabbed my arm and gave me a politician's two-handed handshake.

"Never," I said and laughed.

That didn't stop him. "You're looking like a stuffy lawyer, so you might be my running mate."

"Are you by yourself?"

"Caldwell was too busy to bother with me or my excellent costume."

"Sorry."

"Never mind me. How are you? Finding that tree-hugging stiff on your porch couldn't have been a good way to start the day?"

"I'm okay. I'm trying not to think about it."

"I'm going to party hearty tonight, but tomorrow I'll be at your house to converse about catching this killer. We've got to get it figured out before you end up on a slab."

"Thanks, I suppose. What time?"

"I'll let your lazy ass sleep in. Be there at 0700."

I was going to protest the hour when the presidential candidate pivoted and left me staring at the back of his suit as he headed to the buffet.

Barb came up behind me, smiled, and said, "Ready to call it a night?"

"You had enough fun for one evening?" I said, hoping she didn't remember the dance contest.

"I was thinking the night's still early, and I have a bottle of wine at the condo."

Yes, I silently cheered, but said, "If you're ready, I could break away."

As we waited for the elevator, I saw Caldwell Ramsey coming up the stairs. I told Barb I wanted to speak to him, and she said she'd wait in the lobby.

Mel is a large man standing at 6'1" but Caldwell towers above him at 6'4", and his choice of costume was to dress as his significant other, Mad Mel. Caldwell had on Mel's leather bomber jacket, camo field pants that were made into shorts years ago, and as a finishing touch, Mel's camouflage fatigue cap with *Semper Fi* on the crown.

His costume failed at that point. Caldwell did something that's not in Mel's repertoire, he smiled and said. "How are you doing? It's been a long time."

"Doing great, I nearly mistook you for Mel, except you're missing his white tennis shoes and scowl."

"Some things can't be replicated." He turned and looked around the area.

"Mel just went into the party. Didn't he know you were coming?"

Caldwell's smile disappeared. "I'm not sure what he's told you, but lately we've not been on the same sheet of music. I want to change that if possible. I've been out of town lining up bands for a couple of venues in Charleston. When I got home, he was already gone. I figure imitation is the best form of flattery, so here I am, with my heart on my sleeve, so to speak."

"Good luck. It's great seeing you. Barb is waiting on me downstairs and you'd better get in there and find Mel."

The band was playing Creedence Clearwater Revival's "Proud Mary" as we left the building.

The night air was brisk on the walk to Barb's condo, but it felt good to get some fresh quiet air away from Folly's first annual masquerade party.

28

I'm a slow learner but wasn't going to be surprised a second time by Mel knocking on the door earlier than normal people considered it polite. I was up, dressed, and drinking coffee while I waited.

I wouldn't have been surprised by a knock, but was surprised when the phone rang, and Mel Evens' name appeared on the screen.

"Morning, Mel."

"Damned glad you didn't say good morning, because is sure as Hades ain't."

"What's wrong?"

"I'm aborting our mission."

"Meaning?"

"Do I have to spell everything out for you damned draft-dodging civilians?"

"Yes."

"Did I knock on your door at 0700?"

"No."

"I ain't coming. Cancelling our powwow."

"Is everything okay?"

"Negatory."

One more attempt at trying to figure out what's wrong and then I may be the one hanging up on one of my friends rather than the other way around.

"You planning on telling me what's wrong?"

"I'll give into your charm at some point and tell you, but this ain't the time. Have a good freakin' day."

The call ended, blowing my chance to hang up on him.

I poured a second cup of coffee and returned to my spot at the kitchen table. Mel had no shortage of idiosyncrasies, but not doing what he said he would do was not one of them. Something was wrong and from what little he'd said, I had no idea what it might be. Should I call Caldwell to see if he knew? With whatever was going on between them, it probably wouldn't be wise to contact Mel's significant other.

I'll give my friend a few hours to, to whatever? Anyway, I'll call him later to see if he's in a sharing mood. If not, I'll incur his wrath, but so what's new? I'm privileged to experience that even when he's in a good mood.

The phone rang again. Could Mel be ready to share?

Charles's name on the screen answered that question.

"Morning," I said, attempting a more civil greeting for the second time this morning.

"Hear about Mel and Caldwell?"

"What about them?"

"Here's an easier question, you on your way to the Dog?"

No, I thought, but said, "Yes."

For the second time in ten minutes, I was hung up on.

Another ten minutes passed, and I was met at the door of the Lost Dog Cafe by Amber who greeted me with the best greeting I'd received this morning, when she said, "Good morning. It's good seeing you."

"Thank you."

"For what?"

"Being civil."

"You're welcome. I assume you'd like coffee when you join Charles who has been looking at his wrist every two minutes and mumbling about what's taking you so long to get here."

"Then I'd prefer whiskey, but better stick with coffee."

"Funny," she said and smacked my arm.

At least she'd started civil.

"About time you got here," Charles said as I pulled out the chair opposite him at the table.

"What about Mel and Caldwell?"

"Gee, no polite 'Good morning,' or 'Thank you for the kind invitation to breakfast.'"

"Nope."

"What happened to manners? Never mind. Where did you and Barb sneak off to last night?"

"Barb had to work today, so we left early," I said, figuring saying it was Barb's idea, the person Charles would refrain from insulting, could get him to move off the topic quicker than any other explanation.

"Well, you missed the excitement. They nearly came to blows. Pow! Pow! Right in the middle of the party."

"Who?"

"Presidential candidate Mike Pence and Mad Mel. Oh, I forgot, you skipped out on your detective job before Caldwell got there dressed as Mel."

"We met Caldwell as we were leaving."

"Good, so you know who he was, or who he pretended to be."

"What happened?"

"Don't know what started it. I was talking to Virgil when the commotion started." He looked at his bare wrist, huffed, then said, "Where is he?"

"Who?"

"Virgil, duh."

I wondered how much better, and calmer, my life would be if I'd thrown my phone in the ocean. My wishful thinking ended when Virgil barreled through the door and headed to our table.

"About time you got here," Charles said.

"Morning, Virgil," I said.

"Stop changing the subject. I was telling you about last night."

"Telling Chris how everyone there loved my creative, and

if I say so myself, stunning Goodwill costume, especially the dandy white fedora?"

Amber set a mug of coffee in front of the new arrival and said, "Virgil, I heard you and your costume were the hit of the masquerade party."

"Miss Amber, the only thing missing at the party was you."

A diner at a table by the door waved her hand in the air, apparently a "polite" request for her check. Amber gave her a fake smile and left to get the check.

"I was telling Chris about the near fight between Mel and Caldwell, that is, I was before you interrupted."

"If I'm not mistaken, Charles, you called and invited me to this gathering."

"Virgil or Charles, would one of you please tell me what happened?"

"Charles, the floor's all yours."

"I didn't hear what started it, but by the time I heard Mike Pence yelling at, never mind, you know who I'm talking about. Anyway, apparently Mel thought Caldwell was making fun of him by dressing up in his clothes and didn't want to leave any doubt by anyone there what he was accusing Caldwell of."

"Christopher, they were on the verge of fisticuffs when Officer Spencer who came as one of those old-time police officers with the long coat, big badge on his chest, and a funny looking police hat. You should have seen him blowing his whistle and—"

Charles interrupted with, "Allen stopped them from hitting each other."

I said, "How did it end?"

"If it was a boxing ring, the referee would've sent each fighter to his corner. In this case, Allen sent them to different sides of the room to cool off. They did, and Mel, the real Mel, stormed out. Caldwell left a few minutes later."

Virgil spread his arms out and said, "The end." He then took a sip of coffee, looked at me, and said, "Did Charles tell you who we figured killed Ruby, and most likely Liam, but we're not sure about him?"

"We hadn't gotten that far. You interrupted the flow by barging in," Charles said.

Virgil said, "Need I remind you, again, that you invited me to this fine dining establishment?"

Charles said, "Trudy did it. I was talking—"

Virgil waved his hand in Charles's face. "Charles?"

"Or it could be Beth."

"What makes you so sure it was Trudy, or perhaps Beth?"

Charles glanced at Virgil who gave him a slight nod and then turned to me. "As I was saying before Virgil interrupted, I was talking to Trudy after you shirked your detective responsibilities and left the party. She was saying how much she didn't like her housemate, nothing new there, but then she started talking about going barhopping a few times with Ruby." He hesitated, took a sip of coffee, and nodded like that explained everything.

I said, "And?"

"Sometimes, you're too dense for your own good. Don't you remember telling me Mel's theory that the killer put poison in Ruby's drink so *she* could get her out of a bar to kill her with the hatchet?"

I looked at Virgil and then Charles before saying, "Your theory is—"

Virgil pointed at Charles and said, "His theory, not mine."

"Charles's theory," I said, "is that Trudy poisoned Ruby during one of those times they were out, and then took her out and killed her with the hatchet?"

"Now you're catching on. First, Trudy didn't like her housemate. Second, she was her housemate and as we all know, the person who lives with the victim, like the spouse, or in this case, housemate, is often the killer. Third, they went to bars together giving Trudy the perfect opportunity to drug her."

I glanced at Virgil who was leaning back in his chair with his arms folded.

"Virgil, I take it that you're not as sold on Trudy as is Charles. You think it's Beth?"

"Yes."

"Why?"

"First, if the two were housemates, why would Trudy have had to poison Ruby at a bar when she could've done it at their apartment?"

"Good point," I said.

"Now to Beth. At the party, Charles told me she knew both victims, said she even dated Liam, one of the dead folks.

That's a big clue in my book. So, after he told me that, I sort of found myself standing beside her." He nodded at Charles. "He taught me that detective maneuver. Anyway, I started telling her how much I liked her indigenous American outfit, she said my costume was outstanding. I started saying something about how horrible the two deaths were, you know, to get her talking about the victims." He took a sip of coffee, turned to Charles, and said, "Are we getting breakfast? I'm famished."

Charles sighed, turned, and caught Amber's eye and motioned her over.

"Amber, Virgil would like something to eat."

"I was wondering if you were ever getting around to ordering. Virgil, what would you like?"

"Thank you for asking, Miss Amber. I believe I'd like an order of French toast."

She turned to me and I said, "The same."

"Surprise, surprise. How about you, Charles?"

"Chris, are you buying?"

"Surprise, surprise," I mumbled, and added, "Sure."

"Then I'll have bacon, eggs, toast, home fries, and a cinnamon roll plus more coffee to go."

Why not throw in caviar and a bottle of champaign, I thought, but said, "You hungry this morning?"

"Didn't have time to eat much at the party. I was working, unlike someone who skedaddled early."

Amber wisely figured we were done ordering and headed to put in our requests.

"Virgil," I said, 'what did she say that made you decide she's the killer?"

"She didn't say much about Ruby more than she'd talked to her a few times at Harris Teeter. Liam is another story. She started in on him hard. Said he seemed nice when they first met. They went out a few times and he treated her well. Then it was like a switch was flicked on or could've been flicked off in her head. Never mind, poor analogy. She stared badmouthing him." He tapped his hand on the table, as if to say, that says it all.

That wouldn't work with Charles, of course, who said, "Examples, Virgil."

Virgil looked at his hand on the table then at Charles. "You know I'm not as great a detective as you, so I might've missed a couple of important things she said, and it was late in the party and I suspected she had a few more drinks than she should have had, so she may not have said things quite right or in order."

Charles repeated, "Examples?"

"Let's see, there was something about him making fun of her claiming she was an Indian, then about a chick being a plumber, then something about her cat Festus. When she got to talking about him and her cat, she, Beth, not Festus, was snarling. I think if Liam had been at the party, she would've killed him all over again."

Our food arrived before Charles had time to demand details about each of those complaints Beth had mentioned.

Over the next half-hour, all that was accomplished was

three meals being consumed. Regardless how many ways Charles asked Virgil, he didn't share anything about his conversation with Beth that he didn't reveal before our food arrived. Charles was unable to remember anything else that pointed to Trudy that he hadn't revealed earlier.

I didn't hear anything that convinced me that either Trudy or Beth had killed Ruby or Liam. Apparently, neither Charles nor Virgil were certain since they didn't demand I call Chief LaMond with the killer's identity.

29

A walk was in order after getting my fill of Charles and Virgil going back and forth on who we, Charles's alleged detective agency, should focus on as the person who killed Ruby Banes and Liam Mathers. October was more than halfway in the history books, but the warm breeze coming off the ocean was not supporting the calendar. Not ready to go home, I left the Dog and headed out West Ashley Avenue to enjoy the day and think about the latest additions to the list of suspects, Trudy Miller and Beth Powell.

Granted, Trudy wasn't a fan of Ruby but was that enough to want her dead? It seemed like the opposite would've been the case. Didn't Trudy need Ruby's share of rent to stay in the apartment? And Beth seemed nice from my contacts with her but according to Virgil she had issues with Liam, and with her size and strength she could have garroted him. Even if Trudy and Beth had a problem with one of the victims, what was the connection with the other victim? Was I missing something?

I glanced around to see where my feet had carried me while my mind was occupied. I was still on West Ashley Avenue a couple of blocks past Loggerheads, so I might as well continue down this road, metaphorically and physically. I smiled to myself thinking how Charles had declared at one time or other that the killer was Waylon, Victor, Jeffery, and Liam. We could safely scratch Liam off the list since he certainly didn't commit suicide on my front step, but did that eliminate him as Ruby's murderer? Jeffery was added to Charles's list because he may have talked with her at Harris Teeter. Waylon and Victor knew Ruby and had been arguing about a woman who could've been Ruby in the Dog. They could as well have been talking about someone other than Ruby. And then, Charles had seen them at Bert's watching my cottage when Liam was found but knowing Folly as I do, half the island could also have been there.

Other than giving myself a headache, I realized my walk had transported me to the entrance of the Folly Beach County Park where I spotted Chief LaMond sitting on the tailgate of her pickup truck.

"Loitering in the park, Chief?"

"Law folk don't loiter, Mr. Citizen. We provide superb community watch services," Cindy said as she patted the tailgate.

I joined her as she grabbed a small Igloo cooler from behind her, pulled out two bottles of water, and handed me one before saying, "You look like you could use some hydration. Don't you know you shouldn't overexert at your age?"

I took a sip, glanced at her, ignored her comment about my age, and said, "What brings you out here?"

"Needed some think time and the four walls of my office were closing in on me. I figured I could come here and get some peace and fresh air."

"Did the change of venue help with whatever you were pondering?"

"No, but no one pestering me was nice, that is until a nosy geezer showed up."

I looked around and said, "Did I run the geezer off?"

"Ha ha," she said, smiled, and elbowed me.

"Anyway, thanks for the water. I've got a question."

"Of course, you do."

"Are you or Detective Adair closer to finding out who killed Ruby and Liam?"

"Nope. In fact, we're not even close to narrowing down a list of suspects."

"How big is your list?"

"Got it narrowed down to everyone on the island, plus, oh yeah, everyone within a few hundred miles of here. That's probably overestimating it, but not by much."

And I thought Charles and I had too many possible suspects.

"No decent leads?"

"Not really. Damned frustrating. We did learn a little more about Liam. Seems he was arrested in Columbia back when he was a student."

"What for?"

"Nothing much. Got himself a DUI charge, but he pleaded down to reckless driving so he could stay on the USC swim team."

"Not exactly the kind of criminal past to get him murdered."

"No. It's the same with Ruby. There's nothing in either of their backgrounds to put them in a high-risk category. Then, that got me wondering if Liam's murder even had anything to do with Ruby's."

"Wouldn't the odds be high for two killings to happen that close together without being connected?"

"Stranger things have happened," Cindy said and shook her head. "Enough about death, let's talk about a boxing match that nearly broke out at a masquerade party."

I assumed she was referring to Mel and Caldwell's "heated discussion."

"Charles and Virgil told me about it this morning."

"You weren't there?"

"Barb and I left before it happened. How'd you hear about it?"

"Officer Spencer told me before I came out here," she said and chuckled. "It would've been quite a sight, faux Mike Pence taking on faux Mad Mel Evans."

"I was supposed to meet Mel this morning, but he

cancelled. I'm calling him later to see what happened. I was glad Allen was there to stop it from escalating." I hopped off the tailgate and added, "I'll leave you to your thoughts and escape from the office."

"Need a lift?"

"Thanks, but I need to walk off this water."

"Good, I wasn't ready to go back to reality. Try not to attract more dead bodies, I'm getting too old for having to save your butt."

On my trek home, I was more focused on the beautiful fall day instead of thinking about murder, suspects, and Mel's domestic issues. The fall light gave the sky a muted glow. It wouldn't be long until the cold, damp winter enveloped the barrier island, regardless, it was still better than being in my home state of Kentucky where October days could be much colder, not to mention what winter would bring.

I approached the house and was surprised to see Roisin Stone sitting on my front step, singing softly, and looking as if she was at home.

"Afternoon, Roisin. What a nice surprise."

"Mr. Chris, welcome home. I thought you could use a pleasant surprise on your porch after the other day." She hopped up and gave me a hug.

"You're right, and I'm honored to have a lovely young lady to greet me when I got here."

"Desmond told me this morning about what happened here the other day. I hadn't heard about it."

"Nor should you have to hear about such bad things.

Your days should be filled with fun adventures. Do you have time for a visit, or do you need to be somewhere?"

"I told Mom where I was going, and it would be a while before I got home.

"Then join me on the porch. I need a drink. Would you like something?"

"Yes please, iced tea if you have any. If you don't, water is okay." Roisin started humming as I walked into the house to get our drinks.

Fortunately, I found a can of tea in the refrigerator, when and how it got there was a mystery. I grabbed a Diet Coke for myself, returning to the porch, handed Rosin her drink, and said, "Did you enjoy the masquerade party?"

"A bunch. It's the first party like that I have ever been to, and Mom let us stay as long as we wanted. We didn't get home until way after my bedtime."

I smiled, and said, "Didn't realize fairies had bedtimes."

She laughed and said, "They probably don't, but in our house, we do, even Desmond. Of course, he always argues that he shouldn't have a bedtime since he's the man of the house." Her smile faded as she looked at her shoes.

Losing her father had to be horrible.

"If you ever need to talk, you know where I am and Preacher Burl is always around," I said and patted her hand.

"Thanks, I can always count on my friends. How are you doing with everything going on?"

"I'm fine, and thank you for asking," I said to the preteen who's far more mature than her age.

"Have you and Mr. Charles figured out who did those horrible things?"

"That's a job for the police. I know they're working hard to figure it out."

"I have more faith in you and Mr. Charles to find the killer. Promise me to be careful. The world cannot lose another good man, and Lugh would be heartbroken if something happened to Charles."

"I promise."

"With that settled, I should head home. Mom wanted me to get some stuff from Bert's."

"Let me give you a ride home."

"No thank you. Walking is my time to commune with nature. Everyone should be so blessed to live in such a magical place." She gave me a quick hug and hopped down the stairs before skipping towards Bert's

"Goodbye, Roisin."

She turned in mid skip and said, "Blessed be, my friend."

I sat on the porch until I realized that I was watching the back of my eyelids more than the traffic. The early morning visit with Charles and Virgil, the walk to the County Park, and late night at the Tides was finally catching up with me. I went into the living room, picked up a magazine, and sat down in hopes of reading an article I'd earmarked earlier, but knew a well-earned nap would win.

30

A knock on the door began the next morning like way too many recently. It was closer to nine o'clock than seven, so I figured it wasn't Mel.

I was right. Burl Costello was standing in front of me with a broad smile and a paper sack from Bert's Market. The short, portly pastor greeted me with, "Good morning, Brother Chris. Did I catch you at a bad time?"

"It's seldom a bad time regardless of when you arrive. How about a cup of coffee?"

"If you insist," he said then smiled.

He followed me into the kitchen, handed me the paper sack, and said, "I know it's not French toast from the Dog, but thought a cinnamon roll from next door might serve in a pinch."

"You're kind. Thank you."

I grabbed two mugs off the counter and poured each of us coffee from my Mr. Coffee machine, then placed his in front of him and took the seat opposite the preacher.

"I'm not that kind. I didn't want to be rude and eat alone. There's one of those gooey delights in there for me as well."

"What has you out and about this morning? I doubt it's simply to bring me breakfast, although I'm not complaining."

"I've known you long enough to know you are excellent at hiding your emotions, especially about things you fear, or your anger." He hesitated, took a bite of his roll and a sip of coffee.

I smiled. "No argument about that."

"I'm projecting what my reaction would be if I opened my door to find a body, a lifeless body on my stoop. I would be traumatized." He shook his head. "My reaction is irrelevant, I'm simply here to enquire about how you are, and to offer pastoral, or in our case, the support of a good friend if there is need. I know I shared this offer with you at the masquerade party, but with so many people present and music exceeding the decibel level of a Harley, I'm not certain everything said was heard or comprehended."

"You don't know how much I appreciate your offer. I admit, I was more traumatized than I would like to let on after finding Mr. Mathers. I've had a few days to absorb the event, and am good, but thank you for your concern, and more for your friendship."

"Then you know, if you ever need anything, I'm available."

That reminded me that I said nearly the same thing to Roisin if she ever needed someone to talk with about the loss of her father.

"I truly appreciate it." To change the subject since he'd already established that I was good at hiding my emotions, I said, "Did you enjoy the party?"

"Better than I expected." He laughed. "Although, I was offered two construction jobs as a result of my carpenter's costume."

"Did you take them?"

"No, but I was able to refer Sister Beth Powell to one of the men. In addition to a carpenter, Brother Lee, one of the men seeking assistance, needed a plumber."

"It sounds like you did a good deed."

"I nearly didn't. If Sister Beth hadn't been at Hope House working on a leaky faucet before going to the party, I probably wouldn't have recognized her at the event. Her native American attire and face mask with the orange feathers disguised her beyond recognition."

"She did look authentic."

He said, "All she lacked as a Seminole was a bow and arrow and a tomahawk."

"Were you still there when Mel and Caldwell had an, umm, animated discussion?"

"Yes, but I missed most of what happened. I was at the

buffet and didn't notice anything wrong until the song the band was playing ended, and I heard raised voices from the other side of the room. By the time I saw who was involved in the, as you called it, animated discussion, it had ended. Didn't you see it?"

"Barb and I had left by then."

"I hope Brother Mel and Brother Caldwell have resolved whatever caused the disagreement."

"Me too. Speaking of attendees at the party, did you talk with Waylon Atwood or Victor Harlan?"

"You asked me about them before. Are you still thinking they had something to do with the two lives lost in recent days?"

"I don't know. I have no real reason to suspect them."

"Hmm. To your question, I didn't speak with them but did notice two men I suspect were the gentlemen in question." He smiled. "Anyone else?"

"How about Zorro, more accurately, the person dressed as Zorro?"

"I saw the individual you're referring to, but we never spoke. He was someone else who had an excellent costume. By excellent, I mean someone dressed as to not be recognized, unlike my feeble attempt appearing as a carpenter, and your effort to appear as a boring bureaucrat."

"Don't you mean, my feeble attempt?"

He smiled, took the last bite of his cinnamon roll, and mumbled. "Your choice of words, Brother Chris."

"More coffee?"

He looked at his watch and said, "Better not. I'm scheduled to meet with one of my flock in fifteen minutes. Being late is not a sin but should be."

"Then I'd better let you get going. Thanks for breakfast and your concern."

31

Cleaning up after Burl left, aka rinsing his coffee cup and throwing away the bag from Bert's, I decided on a second cup of coffee and took it to the living room to finally read an article I'd been trying to for the last couple of days. This time, I was distracted thinking about Burl visiting to check on my wellbeing and knowing my propensity for not showing or discussing my feelings. I've always found it better to silently deal with issues, and not wanting to worry others if something was bothering me. Although, I'll admit, it's comforting knowing I have friends who truly care, brought home by Roisin and Burl literally showing up at my door to check on me, their friend.

As I thumbed through the magazine, my thoughts drifted away from the printed page to something Burl had mentioned. He had commented on Beth's costume at the masquerade party, saying that the only thing to make it more authentic was a bow and arrow and a tomahawk. Hatchets and tomahawks are so similar that I've believed the two words were often used interchangeably.

From what I've seen in documentaries, indigenous Americans were more likely to favor ancient remedies and weapons, either to heal or harm. If Beth was caught up in her ancestry, it would make sense that she could also embrace that knowledge to know how to poison a person with wolfsbane or inflict a fatal blow with a tomahawk or hatchet. And as Virgil observed, she would have the strength to garrot Liam. I also realized I was making these assumptions and don't know if Beth even knew Ruby. If she didn't, why kill her?

I put aside the magazine, once again having failed to pay attention to anything in it. My thoughts were on the two deaths. Achieving absolutely nothing, it'd be a good time to head to Cal's to get my mind on something more cheerful. Listening to the old crooner regaling me about the 'good ole days' and seeing how Junior enjoyed the masquerade party seemed more enjoyable than anything I could do here.

I was greeted by Vern Gosdin singing "Set 'Em Up Joe" from the antique Wurlitzer. Cal was arranging two pumpkins and a foot-high ceramic ghost on the far end of the bar when he spotted me.

He pushed back his Stetson and said, "Look what the coyotes dragged in."

"Set 'Em Up Joe," I said as I tipped my Tilley to the owner.

"Yeah, like I've never heard that before, pard." He handed me a glass of wine.

"First time hearing it from me," I said and raised the glass. "I suspect you'll forgive me."

"Don't I always?"

I nodded and said, "Did Junior survive his time off the other night?"

"He showed up yesterday, but his engine was running on no sleep. He's doing better today."

Junior walked out of the kitchen. "You telling Chris about me thinking I was still a twenty-year-old?"

"Didn't say a word, son." Cal cleaned a glass with a pumpkin-colored dish towel with a silhouette of a bat on it, while not making eye contact with Junior.

I smiled at Junior and said, "Is it safe to say you had a good time at the masquerade party."

"Too good, haven't been out in so long I done forgot what it's like not being on this side of the bar. Ended up closing the party down with Bride of Frankenstein then we went to Charleston to have an early breakfast at Waffle House." Junior shook his head. "I'm not as young as I once was."

"Who is? At least it sounds like you had a good time."

Cal cleared his throat and said, "Can my not-so-young son get you anything from the kitchen?" The tone in Cal's voice made me think he wanted to share something with me in private.

"I'd love one of your famous burgers."

Junior yelled into the vacant kitchen, "Hamburger for the young man at the bar." He laughed then followed his order into the kitchen.

Cal looked around the room then took a step closer to me.

"Chris, I'm sorry, so sorry." Cal's eyes looked out from under the brim of the Stetson.

"Sorry for what?"

"Giving that young man your address and how horrible it must have been for you to—"

"Not your fault. You had no way of knowing what would happen."

"Kind of you to say, but we both know it was my fault, at least where he was and not what happened. I never would've brought that horror to anyone, let alone you. Again, sorry."

"You had no idea." I put my hand up finishing the topic.

He slowly nodded and gazed toward the kitchen.

"I'll see what's taking Junior so long with your burger." He pointed to a vacant table near the dance floor and added, "Grab that table and I'll bring your food."

A couple of minutes later, Cal set the burger in front of me and left to check on the few other patrons.

I was enjoying the meal and listening to the sad sentiments of Patsy Cline's "She's Got You" when Cal returned with another glass of wine, grabbed my empty plate, nodded to someone entering the building, then headed to the kitchen.

I turned and saw Jeffery Fuller walking to the bar.

"Afternoon, Jeffery, let me buy you a drink."

He saw me, changed direction, and headed to my table. "Thanks, I'd have to turn in my man card if I refused a free round." Jeffery pulled out the chair across from me, while looking around the room. "Not too busy in here."

"The good thing about off season is you seldom have to wait long in a restaurant."

As if on cue, Cal arrived to see what the new arrival wanted and said, "Name your poison, pard."

"Budweiser."

I said, "Put it on my tab."

Cal quickly grabbed the beer from the cooler, returned and placed it in front of Jeffery. Cal smiled at me and said, "You don't know what to do without your partner here, the one you're always buying drinks for."

I laughed and said, "Charles isn't the only one I lavish my wealth on."

"If I had known you were lavishing wealth, I would've ordered an international brew instead of domestic." Jeffery said with a smile.

"Top shelf next round, my friend," Cal said and tipped his Stetson. "I need to bus a table and punch in more songs."

"Haven't seen you around lately," I said to Jeffery. "Been keeping busy?"

"Got a job working off island so I spend most of my days the other side of Charleston. How about you? Come across more fender benders?"

I smiled, "Nope, just yours. I went to the masquerade party the other night and here today."

"Have a good time?"

"Yes, sorry you missed it."

"Like I said, I've been off island recently."

"So, you're back to shopping at Harris Teeter and not Bert's for your breakfast of champions."

"Wow, you really listen to what people say. Wish more people did." Jeffery smiled then turned serious. "Speaking of Harris Teeter, the other night there was a lady in there raising a stink. She was making a scene about deserving her roommates last paycheck. What made it amusing was it was so out of character for her."

"Sounds like Trudy Miller. You know her?"

"How'd you know who it was?" He then took a drink of beer, finishing it, and flagged Cal down for another.

"She was Ruby Banes's roommate and Ruby worked at Harris Teeter, so it was a lucky guess."

Cal returned, looking at my half-full glass, and handed the beer to Jeffery.

"Lucky guess, hogwash," Cal said. He pointed at me while looking at Jeffery. "Chris and his buddy Charles are the best darn detectives around."

"Detectives? I thought you were a retiree."

"Cal's being dramatic; Charles and I have been involved in a couple of issues throughout the years, but I'm no detective."

"Wish I was not a singer the way you're not a detective,"

Cal said. "Hell, I'd have had more number one hits than George Jones."

Jeffery leaned toward me and said, "To answer your question, I know Trudy. She's an occupational therapist. My work's rough on my back, so I had to use her services about six months ago, even gave her a ride home one afternoon when her car was in the shop."

"That was nice," I said and took another sip. "The world could use more people helping each other."

"True. Crime's rising at an alarming rate. The world's a strange place."

Cal was pushing more selections into the jukebox and was singing along with Roger Miller's "Chug-a-Lug."

Jeffery watched Cal's duet with Roger, laughed, and said, "On that bright note, I'm heading out. Thanks for the drink. Next time it's on me."

I remained at the table for another hour listening to Cal sing along with numerous songs he had lined up. It wasn't until a large group arrived that I decided to call it a day.

Junior walked out to help his dad with the new group. I handed Junior money for my tab, waved bye to Cal, and walked out into the chilly October day. As the door shut, I heard the intro of Tanya Tucker's "Delta Dawn."

32

The next day I headed to Bert's to grab a newspaper. As I crossed the small parking lot adjacent to the store, Officer Allen Spencer exited the building and headed to his patrol car backed into a space in the lot.

"Afternoon, Chris," he said as he placed the paper sack holding his purchases in the back seat of his vehicle, then leaned against the car and waited for me to respond.

To not disappoint, I said, "Going to or from work?"

He smiled and said, "Neither, I'm in the middle of a double."

"How many of those have you worked lately? It seems like a lot."

"Remember when we first met?"

"Hard to forget. I'd just stumbled across a body at Lighthouse Inlet. Then here comes you and, umm, what was his name?"

"Officer Robins, I've already forgotten his first name." Allen laughed and added, "I remember he was as enthusiastic as a sloth and carried the weight of a baby elephant."

I chuckled. "Yeah, that's the one. What ever happened to him?"

"Last I heard he was working security for one of those warehouse complexes in North Charleston, but that was a few years ago."

"I hope he gets to ride around on something motorized."

Allen smiled and said, "He wouldn't have taken the job if he had to walk more than a few feet to do whatever he had to do. Anyway, back to my point; I was thin in those days, not to mention a hell of a lot younger."

And looked like a twelve-year-old, I thought, but didn't say it. I nodded.

"I could work doubles all week and it never bothered me. Now, well, let's say they're much tougher."

"We could both do a lot more of most everything back in those days than we can now."

"You're not kidding. Know what I appreciated about you then?"

"Seems you thought I was a murderer."

He laughed. "That was Officer Robins's theory. What I remember was you treating me with respect. Many others acted like I was a school crossing guard rather than a real cop."

"From what I can tell, you were then, and still are, a professional law enforcement officer."

"Thanks. I'm glad I ran into you. I wanted to tell you a theory I've been—"

His radio clacked something. He took it off his belt, smiled, and said, "They caught me again." He walked around his vehicle and responded to the message.

I couldn't hear most of what was being said but caught the words East Hudson and a number that seemed slightly familiar, but I couldn't place why.

Allen returned from the call and said, "Break's over. Good talking with you."

He pulled out of the parking lot and turned toward Center Street, and I continued to Bert's.

On my way home, the air was filled with the distinct sound of the siren from one of the city's fire engines on Center Street. Roughly ten minutes later my phone rang. Charles's name was on the screen.

"Afternoon."

"Where are you?"

"At home."

"Get your rear in gear and head to Lowlife."

"Why would I want—"

"Get over here," he said and hung up.

After hearing numerous commands from Charles over the years, I knew there was something more important than meeting him at Lowlife Bar for a drink or a meal. I made the short four-block walk to the popular dining spot.

There was a clue as to why I'd been summoned when I saw one of the city's patrol cars blocking off East Hudson fifty yards past Lowlife. On the far side of the patrol car, the city's fire engine that I'd heard earlier was parked in the center of the blocked-off street. I had to wait before crossing the street to let an ambulance coming from off island turn on East Hudson. Officer Trula Bishop was quick to move her patrol car from blocking the road to let the ambulance through.

Charles was in front of Lowlife talking to Brian Ross, a friend who works at the bar. They saw me approaching and Brian said, "Hey, Chris."

I nodded.

He said, "I need to get back to work. I'll leave it to Charles to fill you in," and headed inside.

"Charles, what's going on?"

"Don't know, but figured with all this happening, you'd want to be here."

He wasn't wrong, but he'd never hear it from me.

"Did Brian have any idea?"

"Not really. Said he didn't notice anything until the emergency vehicles started arriving. They blocked the road and seemed to pay attention to something going on up there on this side of the road." He pointed toward a patrol car and a fire vehicle a couple of houses past Lowlife.

I then did something that Charles had perfected over the years when I said, "Let's see what Trula knows."

He glanced over at me as we went from Lowlife's front

parking area to the adjacent lot and said, "Ain't I supposed to be saying that?"

I rest my case.

We nudged our way closer to the front of Trula's patrol vehicle that she'd again used to block the street after she'd let the ambulance through. She was standing by the driver's door, saw us inching closer to her vehicle, rolled her eyes, looked toward the other emergency vehicles behind her, then came our way.

Before she could say anything, Charles said, "What's going on?"

"Fellas, don't make me regret telling you this."

"Absolutely not," Charles said without knowing what he was talking about.

She again looked in the direction of the gathering of official vehicles and said, "I know very little. I've been stuck here since our guys arrived. Haven't made it to the apartment building yet. I do know one of our guys was shot."

I now remembered why the address I heard the dispatcher telling Allen Spencer sounded familiar. It was Ruby Banes's apartment building. I made a silent prayer that I was wrong about who'd been injured, then said, "Was it Officer Spencer?"

Trula looked at the road near her feet and slowly nodded.

Charles jerked around toward me. "How did you know?"

I ignored him and said to Officer Bishop, "Is he going to be okay?"

"Mr. Chris," she said and glanced back in the direction of

the apartment building, "I don't know but get the impression it's touch and go."

Chief LaMond's official pickup truck pulled behind Trula's vehicle and tapped its horn. Trula rushed to move her vehicle off the street. Cindy's didn't waste any time rushing past where we were standing. She was followed by the ambulance and then a patrol car.

The three vehicles turned on Center Street and then sped toward Charleston and I assumed the nearest hospital.

My prayer was that they'd get there in time to save my friend.

33

One of Folly's newest officers I only knew by sight pulled in beside Trula's vehicle. She met him when he exited his patrol car and they huddled together for a minute before Trula moved her vehicle out of the road and to the space the ambulance had vacated, and the new arrival blocked the street with his vehicle. Instead of joining the other officials, Trula came back toward Charles and me and motioned us to go behind Lowlife where she met us on the side of East Huron, the street running parallel to the one with all the activity.

"Why don't you guys wait here and if I get a chance, I'll let you know what I find out?"

I thanked her and she left to join a couple of other officers who were scouring the ground near a small storage building or garage that was behind Ruby Banes's apartment building. Another officer was stringing crime scene tape around the building and attaching it to trees and a large shrub that anchored the back corners of the yard. Trula assisted with the tape.

Charles put his arm around my shoulders and said, "I don't know Allen as well as you do, but I know he's strong. He'll be fine."

I wish I had that much confidence but appreciated Charles's attempt to comfort me.

I realized I was exhausted, most likely from stress rather than from doing too much and looked around for somewhere to sit. There was a rusty metal bench at the edge of the field adjacent to Lowlife and I slowly walked over and flopped down on it. Charles followed me.

"What do you think happened?" he said.

I told him about talking with Allen in Bert's lot when he got the call about something happening at the apartment building we were staring at. I had to tell him twice that Allen hadn't said what the call was about, and that still didn't convince him that I didn't know more than what I'd already said.

He said, "Why didn't you ask him what was—"

I interrupted, "Enough. I didn't and don't know."

"Okay, okay. I'm trying to find out what's going on. It has to be something to do with the murders, doesn't it?"

"It'd be too big a coincidence if it didn't, but I have no idea what it could be."

"Maybe the killer was going after Trudy, Ruby's roommate."

"That's possible."

"I think it's more than possible. What if—"

Officer Bishop was walking our way, so I put up my hand for Charles to stop talking. Trula looked back toward the yellow tape then motioned us to follow her across the street out of sight of anyone at the crime scene.

I said, "Any word on Allen's condition?"

"Nothing yet."

Charles, having the patience of a chipmunk, said, "Well, what happened?"

Trula took a small notebook out of her back pocket, flipped through a few pages, and said, "A Trudy Miller called us to report that she'd gotten home from work at Roper Hospital to find her apartment door ajar with what she described as crowbar marks at the lock. Don't know if it was a crowbar or not, but something was used to force the door open."

Charles said, "What'd they steal?"

"Mr. Charles, did I mention anything was stolen?"

"Umm, no."

"Officer Spencer was dispatched to the scene of the 9-1-1 call."

"Chris heard that," Charles said, once again interrupting Trula.

She looked at me and I gave her a thirty-second summary

of what I'd heard while talking with Officer Spencer then encouraged her to continue.

She gave Charles a look that I interpreted to mean don't interrupt. I silently wished her luck with that.

"Officer Spencer clearly arrived at the scene since his cruiser is parked in front of the building. This is where it gets confusing."

Charles said, "Why?"

He received another irritated look before Trula continued, "If Miller is to be believed, he never made it to the apartment. Officer New was second to respond. He went to the apartment and talked with Miller. Officer New had seen Allen's cruiser out front so he began checking the property to see if he could find him." She hesitated and shook her head. "He found Allen behind that storage building over there then called for backup, the fire vehicles with their EMTs, and an ambulance. Officer New then started CPR. Allen had two wounds, one to the chest, the other to his thigh."

"Did he say what condition Allen was in when he arrived?"

Trula looked at the storage building and whispered, "Bad."

"I'm sorry. I know you and Allen were close."

"Yeah."

I saw a new arrival at the crime scene and from this distance, it appeared to be Detective Adair.

"Was Adair called?"

Trula looked over her shoulder toward the apartment

building. "Yes, the chief speculated that the incident is related to the two deaths."

"I know you need to get back, but before you go, did you learn anything about what happened? Do you think Allen saw someone? Or if not, why was he by the storage building?"

"He'd pulled his service weapon, so he must've seen someone suspicious. He didn't have a chance to discharge his firearm, so I'd say he was ambushed. How, I have no idea. But that's me speculating. Sorry, Chris, I know you go way back with Allen."

Trula slowly walked back toward the cordoned off area.

Before she got to the tape, she answered her phone, stopped, listened, then lowered the phone to her side. She then looked back to where Charles and I were standing.

She turned and returned to us and with tears rolling down the side of her face said, "He didn't make it."

34

Logic told me that I'd walked home from where Charles and I listened to Officer Trula Bishop break the tragic news, but for the life of me, I didn't remember how or when I got from there to the recliner in my living room. How could I have forgotten the walk past restaurants, shops, visitors and locals, past music filling the air from restaurants?

Had I fallen asleep in my chair and had a bad dream, no, a nightmare? Would Allen laugh when I told him about it? Would Charles make fun of me when I told him?

Who was I kidding? My head throbbed, my stomach tied in knots. It was no dream when Trula had said, "He didn't make it." My friend for more than a dozen years was gone, never to laugh at me again when I did or said something stupid, never to assist me again when I needed help. True,

Allen and I weren't close friends, we'd never hung out together, never shared deep dark secrets, but I knew he was always there if I needed anything, and he'd shared that he knew I was there for him if need be.

The next thing I remembered was looking at the clock revealing it was 2:30 a.m. Had I been asleep for hours? Why was I still in the recliner?

I slowly moved to the bedroom and flopped on the bed. I was fully dressed, but didn't care. The rest of the night, or technically morning, I stared at the ceiling, glanced at the unlit lamp on the bedside table, and looked out the window at the darkness that reflected how I felt.

The phone startled me awake, the phone that was beside me in the bed, although I had no idea how it got there. Charles's name appeared on the screen.

"Yes," I said, as I looked at the clock showing 9:00 a.m.

"Yes? No 'Good morning,' or no smart remark?"

"Sorry," I said although not certain I meant it.

"That's okay, I understand. How are you?"

"How do you think I am?"

"Sorry, it was a stupid question. You up to meeting me to get something to eat or do you want me to bring you something?"

"Not really."

"You sure?"

"Yes, but thanks for asking."

"You'll let me know if you need anything?"

"Sure."

"Umm, okay. Talk to you later."

For the next twenty-four hours, I moped around the house, fought the urge to kick furniture, and, truth be known, did little other than feel sorry for myself. I didn't want to see anyone, talk to anyone, or do anything that took more energy than pacing from room to room.

Word of Allen's death spread rapidly. My phone rang more times than it ever had. I received two more calls from Charles, two from Barb, plus one each from Cal, Amber, Mel, Jay, Dude, Virgil, Chief LaMond, and Shannon Stone who said Roisin asked her to call since she didn't want to bother me. I tried not to be rude to the wonderful people who were enquiring about me, but I still didn't want to talk to anyone longer than a moment or two.

The next day, I realized I couldn't remain isolated and continue asking myself countless times why. Why did Allen have to die? Why did someone feel the need to kill him? Why? Why? Why?

Late that afternoon, I realized the question I'd constantly been asking myself had morphed from *why* to *who*? It was still a question I didn't know the answer to, but it was one that could be answered, as opposed to why Allen had to leave this world long before his time.

Another question was what I was going to eat. During my self-inflicted isolation, I'd eaten everything edible from the kitchen, plus a couple of cookies I found in the back of the cabinet that had outlived their shelf life by years. A walk to Loggerhead's should allow me to stretch muscles in my legs I hadn't used for three days, and it allowed me to take deep breaths of the cooler air that had moved through the area fewer than two weeks before Halloween.

Because of the weather, most of the diners who would normally be on the deck filled the interior tables. I took a seat at the bar, where Reggie, the bartender, was quick to me and asked if I wanted a glass of red wine. I said not this time and went with a Diet Coke.

Before Reggie returned with my drink, Officer Bishop entered and looked around the restaurant. I gave her the best smile I could muster and patted the empty seat beside me. Before sitting, she hugged my shoulder.

"Mr. Chris, thought I saw you coming up here. Wanted to come check how you're doing?"

"Let's just say I've been better. How about you?"

"If I've had three worse days in my life, I couldn't tell you when. I didn't know Allen as long as you did, and seldom saw him off the job, but we got close. He treated me like a professional law enforcement official and never hinted he had anything against me being a female, a black female. Afraid I can't say that about everyone."

"He was a great guy. Any idea who did it?"

She shook her head.

Reggie set my drink in front of me and asked Trula what she wanted. She told him she'd have the same thing I was having, then Reggie asked if I wanted anything to eat. I asked him to give me a few minutes.

Trula watched him go and said, "We know little more

than we did when I saw you there. About all anyone figures is most likely it was the person who killed Ruby Banes and Liam Mathers."

"Because of the break-in at Ruby and Trudy's apartment?"

"Yeah, but that's not much to go on, is it?"

"Doesn't seem like it, but I'll tell you what I know. I'm going to ... never mind."

She glanced at my hands balled into fists, then looked me in the face. "I'm not going to ask you if you're thinking about trying to figure out who killed Allen. Know why?"

I shrugged.

"Because I don't want you to lie to me. But do me a favor."

"What?"

"I lost a friend three days ago. I ain't ready to lose another one."

I didn't want to lie to Trula either, so I said, "What are the plans for his funeral?"

"Day after tomorrow. The funeral procession will begin in the Tides parking lot at 10:00 a.m. and go up Center Street. The Chief wanted everyone on Folly to have a chance to say goodbye to Mr. Allen. It'll then go to the Holy Cross Cemetery on James Island. His parents flew in day before yesterday. They've requested a graveside ceremony and nothing at the funeral home."

"Thank you."

Trula looked at her watch and said, "I need to get going."

"Before you go, let me ask a question."

She smiled and nodded as she put a couple of dollars on the bar for her drink.

Reggie returned and asked if we were ready to order. That reminded me why I'd walked to Loggerhead's in the first place and said a cheeseburger. Trula said she was okay with the soft drink.

The bartender headed to the kitchen with my order, and I said, "Do you know if Beth Powell is on anyone's radar as a suspect?"

Trula's smile turned to a glare, before saying, "Not that I've heard. Why?"

"Something I heard made me think she could be a possible suspect."

"Why don't you tell me what and I'll pass it along to the Chief?"

"It may be nothing and you and the Chief may already know this, but Ms. Powell claims to be a Seminole Indian. She was in full regalia at the Halloween party. Preacher Burl was teasing, saying all she needed was a bow and arrow and tomahawk. A tomahawk is a lot like a hatchet."

"That's it?"

"Said it may not be anything. Add to that, I'd heard she dated Liam then split with him."

"Okay, she may have had reason to be pissed with Liam, but enough to kill him?"

I shrugged.

"I'm no detective, but it still doesn't make sense."

"I—"

She waved a hand in my face and said, "I'll pass it along. That's all I can do."

She was right and I knew it.

"Thank you."

What I didn't say was, there's no way I'll rest until I learn who killed Allen, and I suppose Ruby and Liam.

35

Allen Spencer's farewell to Folly Beach was to begin in less than an hour. A glance out the window told me the weather gods were in the same mood as I was as well as most of the community. The sky was as gray as I felt, and a light rain did nothing to improve my spirits.

I had agreed to meet Charles in front of Mr. John's Beach Store so we could respectfully observe the motorcade pass through the figurative center of Folly. My friend was already there when I arrived fifteen minutes prior to the announced time for the sad event. Not only was Charles there, but so was Virgil Debonnet, who appeared in animated conversation with Charles. They were two of what must've been a couple hundred others lining both sides of Center Street. Some were holding umbrellas, but most were without anything covering their heads as the light rain continued.

"Good morning, Christopher," Virgil said as he stuck out his hand to shake mine. He wore a lightweight navy-blue jacket, gray slacks, and a white dress shirt with frayed cuffs peeking out from under his jacket sleeves. His ever-present sunglasses covered his eyes. "Charles said it'd be acceptable if I rode with you to the cemetery. The weather isn't cooperating for me to take my scooter."

"You're always welcome to ride with us," I said as we shook hands.

Virgil said, "Is Barb coming?"

"Think she's getting a cold. With this weather, I told her she should stay inside."

"She listened to you?"

I smiled and said, "This time."

Charles still hadn't said anything, rare for my best friend, so I turned to him and said, "You okay?"

"No," he said and wiped some of the light rain off the shoulders of his jacket, a jacket not displaying any college name or mascot. His outerwear was partially zipped but I didn't see any words or logos on the sweatshirt he had on under the jacket.

I thought I knew what he meant with his one-word response, and said, "It's a terribly sad day for our community."

"Truer words have never been spoken," Virgil said.

Charles limited his response to, "Yeah."

"Christopher, you know Chester Carr, don't you?"

I'd met Chester five years ago when Charles and I joined a walking group to get exercise and help another friend learn more about someone in the group who was attempting to blackmail him. But that's a story for another time. Chester was in his mid-nineties and had lived on Folly much of his life.

"I've known him several years. Why?"

"I was talking with him last evening. He was standing in front of his house and I, oh well, none of that's important. Know what he told me?"

Charles must've detected a bit of trivia was going to be revealed. He moved closer to Virgil, and said, "What?"

"Officer Spencer is the first Folly Beach police officer to lose his life in the line of duty."

I didn't know that for certain but wasn't surprised since he was the first I'd heard about. Charles said he already knew it.

"Chester also said that Allen was his favorite person on the job. Said a couple of years back he thought he had a peeping Tom, or I suppose it could've been a Tomette, anyway, that's neither here nor there. Chester told his suspicions to Spencer. For the next few weeks, Allen made extra patrols by his house and down the alley between his house and Coconut Joe's to make sure no one was snooping in his back yard."

That didn't surprise me since I knew Allen had done similar things for others.

Virgil started to say something else, when he noticed the crowd along the street that must've doubled since I arrived fifteen minutes earlier had suddenly gotten quiet.

We looked toward the Tides and noticed the funeral procession had begun moving toward us.

The Folly Beach Department of Public Safety aerial ladder fire engine was pulled onto West Cooper Avenue beside City Hall in a mirror image of a James Island aerial truck on East Cooper. Their ladders were extended seventy-five feet into the air with a huge American flag draped between the ladders. Black buntings were draped across the entrance to City Hall. I couldn't see all of them, but the businesses I could see had closed and their employees were standing silently in front of their stores. Dude was on the top step to his surf shop. His head was bowed, and he held an American Flag over his head. Across the street from where we were standing, I noticed Shannon, her two children, and Lugh. I barely recognized Desmond who was dressed in black slacks, no surprise, but wearing a white polo shirt.

Following the slow-moving hearse and a funeral car, Chief LaMond's official vehicle led four other Folly Beach patrol vehicles, and then a line of police cars from various departments that must've numbered a hundred followed. The only sounds I heard were the vehicles' engines.

We stood silent and still until most of the police vehicles passed and then we rushed to the house to get my car to follow the procession.

"This is touching," Virgil said from the back seat as we

pulled in behind the police going to the same place we were.

The procession was moving faster than it had been through town, but below the posted speed limit.

Charles looked out the side window and said, "Chris, you know what this means, don't you?"

"I don't know what it means to you but I'm 100% certain what I'm going to do."

Virgil leaned between the two front seats and said, "You're going to catch whoever did this horrific act to Officer Allen Spencer."

I smacked my hand on the steering wheel. "If it's the last thing I do."

Charles turned from looking out the side window, stared at me, and said, "Me too."

"That makes three of us," Virgil said and hit his hand on the console between the front seats.

I thought about it for at least the thousandth time, but didn't say, "Any idea how we're going to do that?"

Roughly five miles up Folly Road, we turned right on Fort Johnson Road, and in another couple of miles came to a halt, most likely so the long line of vehicles in front of us could maneuver their way onto the cemetery property a mile or so ahead of us and found a place to park.

"Christopher, I am confident you, umm, we will catch the evil doer, but was wondering how we would make that happen?"

Charles chimed in with, "Good question. Chris, what is—"

"Guys, this isn't the time to talk about that. We'll soon be saying our last goodbyes to Allen. That's where my head and heart are."

The entrance to the cemetery at the traffic circle where Fort Johnson Road intersects with Harbor View Road was now in sight. A couple of minutes later, we entered the cemetery's property where two police officers were waving for us to take a left at the first road and park behind the cars that entered ahead of us. Mourners were walking back toward where we'd entered the property.

"That's okay," Charles said as he exited the car, "we'll figure it out on the way home."

I nodded and began following the group in front of us. The rain had stopped by the time we exited the car. The ground was still wet, and we all walked on the edge of the road to keep our shoes dry as possible.

It didn't take a detective to see where we were going. Allen's mahogany casket with an American flag draped over it rested on a structure with railings on either side. Three chairs were facing the casket and a semi-circle of uniformed police officers stood three deep behind Chief LaMond and a man and woman I assumed to be Allen's parents in the chairs. His parents appeared to be in their mid-sixties, the man a little overweight, and with gray hair, the woman petite with hair matching the color of her black dress. Neither looked anywhere but at the ground in front of them. Cindy wore her dress uniform, only the second time I'd seen her wearing it. She, like all the other police officers present, wore a black mourning band on her badge. Larry, Cindy's husband, stood directly behind her with his hands resting on her shoulders.

We stood to the left of the assembled officers and waited for those who arrived after we did to gather.

Virgil leaned toward Charles and me and nodded toward the casket before saying, "That's a CLS."

Mr. Trivia Charles, to no surprise, said, "What's a CLS?"

Virgil looked around exhibiting a look on his face showing regret for telling us it was a CLS. He then turned to Charles and whispered, "It stands for casket lowering system."

"Why do you know that?"

I subtlety elbowed Charles, who then mumbled, "Sorry."

The service began and to be honest, the entire time it was going on, I wasn't paying attention. I spent that time recalling memories I had spending time with Allen over the years; about how we had bemoaned being newcomers to Folly, and then years later, complained about newcomers disrespecting our way of life, littering our yards, and partying until all hours of the morning. I also recalled our friendly debates about surfing, how he thought it was the greatest thing since air conditioning, how I put it in the same category as being in a field of biting, irritating no-see-ums.

I hadn't realized the service had ended until Charles patted me on the shoulder and asked if I was ready to go. I also hadn't realized that tears were streaming down my cheeks. Goodbye, Allen.

36

We weren't the last to leave the service but most of the attendees had already made it to their vehicles. As on the trip over, we were behind a line of cars, but this time traveling back Fort Johnson Road toward Folly Road. Unlike on the drive over, the vehicles seemed to divide at the intersection with half turning toward Charleston, the other half toward Folly.

As we reached the intersection Charles finally spoke, "If you turn right, we can get lunch at Casa Fiesta before we head home."

"If it's all the same, I'd rather go home."

"It's my treat."

"Raincheck." My eyes never left the road.

Charles patted my arm, "Sure, just thought—"

"I know, thanks but—"

"No need to explain," Virgil interrupted from the back seat. "We'll get through this. Besides, Charles, I have a taste for some Woody's pizza. Christopher can drop us off there."

The rest of the drive back was in silence. I stopped on Center Street in front of Woody's Pizza, Virgil thanked me for the lift and hopped out. Charles remained seated, turned toward me, and said, "I know this isn't easy and it's something none of us ever wanted to go through. I'm not going to push but know you can call me anytime."

"I know."

Charles stepped out, leaned back into the car, and added, "Don't be like your good buddy and bottle those feelings up. As you've told me more than once, it ain't healthy."

I gave him a halfhearted smile and said, "Yes, Dr. Fowler."

It wasn't until both of my friends had entered the restaurant, that I pulled back onto the road and headed home, the only place I wanted to be. I pulled into the drive, turned off the ignition, and stared at my cottage. My head was spinning as I thought about today's events, and what had occurred over the last few weeks in my community. I slammed my hands on the steering wheel, then leaned back and closed my eyes.

I wasn't sure how long I sat there before going into the house. The rain was gone but the overcast day was not helping my mood. Even the house seemed darker than usual, dark and without warmth. After changing out of my funeral attire, I was tempted to climb into bed, but fought the urge.

Instead, I went to the kitchen, grabbed a Diet Coke and a note pad I kept for my seldom followed grocery list.

I took the drink and pad to the living room and plopped down in the recliner. Across the top of the first sheet in the note pad, I wrote Ruby, Liam, and Allen. Below each name, I added the cause of death, then on the next line I'd planned to list what the victims had in common. I quickly realized the answer was they had nothing in common; at least, nothing I was aware of. Ruby worked at Harris Teeter and I'm certain the other two shopped there, but that wasn't a connection. I shop there and had never met her. Allen, of course, because of his job would have been privy to information about the other two murders but from what he and Cindy had shared, the investigation was going nowhere. Looking at the mostly blank page, I realized the list was more worthless than the grocery list I used the pad for. The other thing I realized was that I was hungry.

I reached for the car door to drive to a restaurant when I looked to the sky. It was still overcast, but no more rain was forecast, so perhaps a walk to Planet Follywood would do me far more good than driving.

I was less than a block from the restaurant when a van pulled up next to me.

"Brother Chris, need a lift?"

I pointed to the mural on the side of the restaurant and said, "Preacher, I was headed to Planet Follywood. Want to join me?"

"I'd love to, but I'm meeting one of my flock members in a few minutes."

"Then, I don't want to slow you down."

"Was planning to call you later today, so I'm glad I saw you. I've decided to cancel the Hope House Halloween Party."

"Why?"

"Three tragic deaths, Brother Chris. Tragic deaths in our wonderful community. My flock needs my pastoral guidance and attention both individually and in small groups. This is not a time for levity."

"I hate to hear about the cancellation but understand."

"Perhaps hosting an uplifting Thanksgiving event next month could be something for Hope House to do."

"That's an excellent idea. The community is lucky to have you."

"Have a pleasant lunch. You know my door is always open."

I entered Planet Follywood's side door, and the bartender told me to sit wherever I wanted. Officer Trula Bishop was at the table overlooking Center Street. She looked up, saw me, and waved me over.

"Mr. Chris, come keep me company."

"It would be my pleasure."

After joining her at the table, she pointed to a carved pumpkin sitting on the windowsill and said, "Did you know the tradition of carving jack-o'-lanterns began in Ireland where they used large turnips, potatoes, or beets? Immigrants brought the tradition to America."

"I admit, I didn't know that. Did Charles tell you?"

She chuckled. "No, but I have no doubt he knows it. I read it in the *Folly Current*. With Halloween around the corner, I figured you needed to know that bit of trivia."

"It's hard to believe I've lived all these Halloweens without knowing about it," I said and realized this was the first time I'd seen her out of uniform. She was wearing a purple sweater and jeans. I added, "No uniform?"

"Went home and changed after the service. I wanted to fly under the radar the rest of the day."

"I understand. Is the chief working?"

"No. Matter of fact, none of our folks are. The Sheriff's Office sent over officers to handle calls that come in this afternoon giving us a chance to grieve."

"That's nice of them. I know it's appreciated."

"I was sitting at home staring at the wall, getting more depressed by the minute, when I told myself to get up and out." She held out both arms to her sides. "So, here I am."

"I was doing the same. Charles and Virgil wanted me to go to lunch with them as soon as the service was over. I simply couldn't."

"If you want to be alone, I won't be insulted."

"No way," I said and smiled. "How would I have learned about the history of pumpkin carving if it wasn't for you?" I turned serious. "Besides, I think talking might be the best thing for me."

"Before you came in, I was going over everything Allen and I had been talking about lately. The good, bad, and ugly."

"Tell me something good."

"Allen bought a new surfboard a week or so ago." She added, "Said he was going to start surfing again, like he did years ago. Said he was going to out surf the king of all surfers, Dude Sloan. That was the only thing that lightened his mood."

"Mood?"

"Well not really mood, he told me how tired he'd been lately with all the double shifts and horrible things happening on and off the island. Something about I should enjoy being young and still in tip-top shape." She smiled. "Does this chunky body look in tip-top shape? Besides, he was only two years older than me."

There's no way I was going to agree with her about her *chunky* body, so I said, "Allen mentioned that to me, the part about being tired, not me being in shape." I smiled. "Or me being young."

Trula giggled and waved to the bartender to get his attention. He came over, introduced himself as Chuck, and then apologized for the delay, something about getting sidetracked filling drink orders. Trula ordered a beer and the Southern Po' Boy, and I went with a Diet Coke and the Dagwood Club.

Trula watched Chuck head to the kitchen then said,

"Think everything was getting to Allen and with no answers about the deaths making it worse."

"It was about three weeks ago when he mentioned to me how tired he felt. He also made a fleeting comment about a hit and run, but I never heard anything else about it."

"Was September twenty-fourth. Allen was first on the scene. Apparently, the victim was visiting someone off Sol Legare Road when he was hit and killed."

"Was the driver caught?"

"No. We were given a vague description of a pickup truck, but the witness didn't actually see the vehicle near where the person was hit. 'In the vicinity,' she said. Not much to go on."

Chuck arrived carrying drinks and our meals quicker than expected.

He set the items in front of us and said, "Told the cook to put your meals at the front of the line since I had you waiting so long. Need anything else?"

Trula said, "Thanks, that'll do for now."

We each took a bite and I said, "It's strange that I never heard anything about the accident that happened that close to the island."

"Two days later, Miss Ruby was murdered in such a bizarre manner that her death sucked all the talk about anything else out of nearly everyone."

I nodded and said, "You're right, I suppose. Who ever heard of someone getting poisoned then having a hatchet added to her back? A hit and run is as tragic but doesn't hold a candle to the weirdness of Ruby's death."

"That reminds me of something I wanted to tell you about Allen's murder."

"What?"

"The day he was, umm, killed, I told you that two rounds hit him."

"I remember."

"The coroner said the first round killed him. If it's any consolation, he said Allen was probably dead before hitting the ground. He didn't suffer. The second round was, how shall I say it, umm, overkill."

37

The next morning, after two cups of coffee and finishing a large Danish I'd bought and started last evening, I found myself sitting in the living room trying to make sense out of what'd happened the past three weeks. I was failing miserably. Sure, Ruby Banes's death was horrible, but it had nothing to do with me other than my best friend stumbling upon her body. I got sucked into looking for clues about who might've caused her death because of my friendship with Charles. Finding Liam Mathers's body on my front step as the cliché says, hit me close to home, literally. Yet, I barely knew the victim. Then, when I thought I couldn't be more deeply affected after seeing the body on my doorstep, Allen Spencer's death hit me harder than a sledgehammer. The more I thought about it, the less sense it made.

Another cup of coffee later, I began replaying yesterday's bittersweet conversation with Trula about Allen Spencer. Until yesterday, we had never talked about how Allen had affected each of us. While she hadn't known him nearly as long as I had, she'd accumulated positive and often humorous anecdotes regarding my friend. I hated that it took his death to get us talking about Allen but was glad we had the opportunity.

She also said something that at the time hadn't meant anything to me; something that could possibly lead to the identity of the person or persons responsible for the three deaths. If only I could remember what.

A knock on the door interrupted me from trying to figure out what she'd shared.

I was greeted on the other side of the door by Dude in one of his many long-sleeve, tie-dyed, T-shirts with a large, glow-in-the-dark peace symbol on the front, a purple witch hat, and his Australian Terrier, Pluto on a rhinestone-studded leash wearing a small version of Dude's purple hat.

"Yo, Christer, be acceptin' guests?"

"Only those accompanied by adorable canines."

"Pluto, knew you be lucky," he said to his companion and followed me into the living room.

"If you're trick or treating, I don't have any candy or dog treats."

"Not be trick or treatin'. That be illegal. Only be in the spirit of Halloween."

"Then, would you like coffee?"

"That be cool. Pluto hankerin' for water."

"I think I can find a bowl of water for him," I said and headed to the kitchen followed by my short and shorter witchy visitors.

Dude plopped down in one of the kitchen chairs and leaned back like he lived there. Pluto seemed more like a visitor and sat beside Dude and watched me get the coffee and fill a soup bowl with water.

"What brings you out this morning?"

"Pluto be emotional support animal. Figured you be needing his services."

"That's thoughtful. Thank you," I said then bent down and rubbed Pluto's back.

He licked my hand and gave a low whimper.

Dude smiled. "See, he be supporting." His smile faded, he took a sip of coffee, and said, "Topic two. Me be figuring on killings. Think killer be Jose Pardo, yep, be Jose."

"What makes you think that?"

Dude tapped the side of his head and said, "*Moi* remember at mask party he say he knew Ruby B. and Liam M."

"You're right. I remember Alyssa saying that at the party. Other than knowing both victims, any other reason you think he's the killer?"

"Gut feeling. At party, Alyssa let feline out of bag when say Jose knew them. Jose admitted it, then found reason to go truckin' out of there. *Mucho* suspicious."

"That's a good point."

Dude looked at his watch, glanced at Pluto, and said, "Be telling Chief LaMond?"

"I'll think about it."

"Good, me be heading to surf shop. Surfers a waitin'. Want to borrow Pluto?"

"Thanks for the offer, but he already has me feeling better." I knelt and rubbed the *emotional support animal*'s back. "I appreciate you bringing him over."

Two more pats on Pluto's back and one handshake for Dude, my word-challenged friend and his canine headed to the surf shop, and I headed back to the kitchen to try to remember what I'd been thinking about when my visitors arrived. I started to pour another cup of coffee, realized I'd already had more than I would be comfortable consuming, and that when Dude said Jose had trucked on after it was mentioned that he knew both Ruby and Liam it reminded me of what Trula Bishop had said that I hadn't paid much attention to at the time. Unless I was mistaken, it didn't have anything to do with Jose being the killer.

I called Trula and asked if she had a few minutes to talk. She was at work, but said that even an underpaid, lowly, city cop had to eat and suggested something from the deli inside Bert's Market would meet her discerning taste and she'd be available in fifteen minutes. I took the hint and said I'd meet her there.

Ten minutes later, her patrol car pulled into the small lot beside Bert's. I met her at the store's entry where she said, "You missed me, didn't you?"

"Yes. I haven't seen you since way back yesterday."

"Enough warm-and-fuzzy, I'm starved."

Ten more minutes later, we were seated in her patrol car with her wolfing down a roast beef ranchero sub and me a four cheese melt panini.

"Chris, I know you didn't call to have the pleasure of watching me stuff down lunch. What gives?"

"Yesterday you mentioned someone seeing a pickup truck leaving the scene of that hit and run a couple of days before Ruby Banes was killed."

"Finally, someone pays attention to what I'm saying. If I wasn't already married, I'd have my handcuffs on you and dragging you to Preacher Burl to hitch us before you could turn me down. Anyway, what about it?"

"Our server interrupted before you finished. Was there anything else about it?"

"Not much. She wasn't certain if it was involved in the accident, only that it was just past where the person was hit. She was sure it was a GMC pickup truck. The only reason she knew that was because her son has one like it."

"She mention color?"

"Her son's truck is red."

"You know what I meant."

She smiled. "It was green."

"Don't suppose she got the license number?"

"If she did, we'd already know whose vehicle it was and if the driver had seen anything that'd help us."

"And if the front of it had damage."

"That too."

"Did she see the driver?"

"It was late, dark, and no, she didn't see enough to know if the driver was male or female, black, white, or cyan, much less able to identify the person. Now it's my turn. Why the questions?"

"I'm not sure. Something you said last night got me thinking about the three killings."

"Are you thinking the hit and run is somehow connected to what happened to Banes, Mathers, and Allen?"

I shrugged. "Could be."

"Care to share how?"

"I would if I knew."

"I'm not going to try to force you to tell me what you're thinking, but you owe it to Allen and the others to share if there's anything that could help us catch the person or persons responsible for the deaths. Is that clear enough?"

"It is."

"Good, and remember, it's our job to catch bad guys or gals, it's not your job. Now I've got to get back to work."

"Thanks for taking time to meet me."

She nodded and said, "One more question, whose job is it to catch the killer or killers?"

I sighed. "The police."

"Good, don't forget it. Now, get out of here and let me get going." She patted me on the arm, not unlike the pats I'd given Pluto.

Instead of walking fifty yards to the house, I took the

longer walk to the Fishing Pier and sat on a bench near the far end of the structure. It was one of my favorite places to clear my mind of clutter, think in a peaceful environment, or according to Charles, take a nap while pretending to think.

I don't know why I didn't pursue what Trula had said yesterday about a truck being seen near the scene of the hit and run. What she'd just told me, reinforced a glimmer of a thought I had last evening. Jeffrey Fuller has a green, GMC pickup truck. Did that mean anything? Wouldn't there be numerous vehicles in the area that fit that description?

But add to that, hadn't Jeffery claimed he didn't know Ruby Banes when I'd first asked him? He'd also shared that he got his breakfast in the evening at Harris Teeter because of his work schedule and Ruby would've been there at the same time. Was it possible that he didn't know her? Sure, but hadn't his story changed when he told Charles days later that he'd talked to her a few times in the grocery?

Even if it had been his truck near the scene of the hit and run, and even if he'd either been confused or intentionally misled me about not knowing Ruby, what could that possibly have to do with her murder? Could Jeffery have poisoned Ruby and then stabbed her with the hatchet? Of course, but so could countless others.

Assuming Jeffery killed Ruby, what reason would he have had to kill Liam? Add to that, what reason would he have had to break into the apartment Ruby had shared with Trudy Miller?

Trula was right. It was the job of the police to solve the

murders and catch the person or persons responsible. Yes, it was, I repeated to myself, but not very convincingly.

38

Should I call Chief LaMond and tell her my theory about Jeffery? What would I tell her? Do I have proof he murdered three people plus the hit and run victim? No. Do I have enough circumstantial evidence to convince her to act on my suspicions? Probably not. Yet in the past, I'd taken more harebrained theories to her, and she'd taken me seriously, at least enough not to laugh or try to have me committed. Would this be one of those times? There's one way to find out.

Before I called her, it'd be wise to discuss it with Charles for a couple of reasons. First, he often, okay, occasionally has valuable insight into what I share with him. And second, if I go to the police without him knowing, I'd be subjecting myself to hours of grief for not bouncing whatever it is off him first.

Instead of sharing my theory over the phone, I'd rather we talk in person, and would prefer doing it in a more private setting than in a restaurant or bar. Besides, I'd like to get out of the house and with the temperature being warm for late-October, the walk to Charles's apartment would do me good.

The walk gave me time to put my thoughts into some semblance of order, although I realized while I had a theory about why Jeffery had killed Ruby, I had no idea why he would've killed Liam or Allen. Perhaps Charles could shed light on Liam's death.

Perhaps Charles could shed light on Liam's death if he'd answered the door when I knocked twice and then knocked louder two more times. He didn't. His car was in front of his unit so he must not have travelled far, so why not peek in a few of the island's restaurants and bars to see if he happened to be there? As I headed back to Center Street, I smiled thinking that Charles often took that approach when he was trying to find me, often walking, and looking in businesses rather than calling my phone. I was learning valuable private detective techniques from the person I generously call a faux private detective.

My far-from-efficient search revealed that he wasn't in The Washout, Planet Follywood, Woody's, or the Crab Shack. If he wasn't in Cal's, I was going to concede failure and call his cell phone.

Before crossing the street to Cal's, I saw Jeffery's green pickup truck or one nearly identical parked a half-block past my destination. Was I ready to see the person I was convinced had been responsible for the deaths of four people or should I skip Cal's and call Charles?

The decision was made for me when Cal Junior walked around the corner of his dad's bar, saw me reach his side of the street, waved, and said, "Hey, Chris. Good to see you. Let me play doorman and bring some class to this fine establishment." He gave a slight bow before opening the door and motioning me in.

Tom T. Hall's "Grandma Whistled" playing on the jukebox, the din of the nearly full bar, and the smell of burgers greeted me as I entered and looked around. I saw several people I recognized but none were named Charles. I pivoted to leave when I noticed Jeffery Fuller, one person I didn't particularly want to see, seated at a table along the far wall.

He saw me, stood, and waved me over. It was too late to pretend I didn't notice, so I smiled and headed to his table and said, "Hey, Jeffery."

"You look lost."

"Lost, no. I was looking for Charles Fowler. Has he been in tonight?"

"Haven't seen him. Guess I'll have to do. Have a seat?"

Cal arrived, set a glass of red wine in front of me, and asked if I wanted something to eat. I thanked him for the drink and that I didn't need any food. I also asked if he'd seen Charles.

"No, pard. If I do, I'll send him your way. Would stay and talk, but I'm as busy as a stump-tailed bull in fly season. Don't know why, but I'll take it."

Jeffery watched Cal stop at the next table to see if the group there needed anything, then said, "Stump-tailed bull in fly season."

I smiled and said, "Cal's from Texas."

"Oh," he said as he glanced back at Cal, then turned to me. "Learn any more about the person who killed those people?"

I took a sip of wine and wondered how much I should say to the potential killer.

"No, how about you?"

"I figure it was someone from outside the area. Probably a drifter, now long gone."

"Why think that?"

"I figured you'd know." He laughed and continued, "Everyone I talk to says you're a better detective than the cops."

I smiled, took another sip, and said, "I have confidence the police will catch the killer. Why do you think it was a drifter?"

"That black cat burned into the handle of that hatchet, ax, or whatever killed the lady. Must've been one of those Satanists, devil worshipers, or something like that. Doubt he wanted to stay around. That's why I think he's long gone. Don't you agree?"

I started to say I didn't know, when I remembered Cindy telling me that the police were holding back information about the cat and the lettering on the hatchet. Only the killer and a few others she trusted would know about them.

Does that mean my thought about Jeffery was right? While it still wasn't proof, was it was enough to share with the police?

"Chris, I said, don't you agree?"

"Sorry, my mind was wandering," I said and gave him my best faux smile. "Happens to us old guys, you know."

He glared at me, then smiled, looked at my near-empty wine glass, and said, "I owe you a drink. Let me get you another wine."

I started to protest but wasn't quick enough. He'd already hopped up and weaved his way through the increasingly crowded bar, giving me time to focus on what he'd said and if it was enough to tell Cindy. No doubt it reinforced my theory about Jeffery's truck being involved in the hit and run. I should've called the chief instead of going on my futile search for Charles.

Another, more immediate, thought popped into my head. According to the most viable theory about why the killer, Jeffery, poisoned Ruby Banes, it was so he could get her into his vehicle and take her to where he ended her life. Was Jeffery doing the same thing now? He's gone to get me a glass of wine and has been gone long enough to spike it with something to disable me. Was I being paranoid, or was I in danger? Where was Jeffery?

Three customers were standing in front of the bar blocking my view of anyone buying drinks. I stood and saw Jeffery standing near the end of the bar and holding my wine. Why was he still there? Shouldn't he be returning? Was he putting something in the glass? Was he intending me to be his next victim?

One of my favorite songs "He'll Have to Go" was playing, but it wasn't doing anything to help reduce my anxiety and growing fear. What do I do? I could exit Cal's as quickly as possible without having to face Jeffery. That might prevent a dangerous encounter, but how would that help me keep the promise I'd made to myself, the promise to do everything possible to find the person who ended Allen Spencer's life. A riskier approach would be to call Cindy and ask her to come to Cal's so I could present her with a glass of potentially poisoned wine and the fact that Jeffery knew about the markings on the hatchet.

I didn't have time to consider my alternatives since Jeffery was setting my wine in front of me, smiling, and saying he was sorry it took so long, something about having to wait for several others to order before Cal got to him.

It wouldn't be wise to tell him I didn't believe him.

Instead, I said, "Gotta go to the restroom. I'll be back."

Cal's restrooms were tiny by most restaurant standards, so I was fortunate I was the only person in the men's room. I quickly tapped Cindy's number in the phone and preyed she'd answer rather than getting her answering machine.

"What are you going to say to ruin my delightful dinner with my wonderful hubby?"

"Where are you?"

"No 'I'm terribly sorry for interrupting. You can call me tomorrow.'"

"Cindy, where are you?"

"Okay, okay, Mr. Cranky. We're at the Crab House, the one on Wappoo Creek, why?

"I'm at Cal's. How quickly can you get here?"

"Why would I interrupt eating this tasty Alaskan snow crab with Carolina grits then savoring dessert?"

I sighed then said, "To catch the person who killed two of your citizens and one of your officers."

"You serious?"

"Yes."

"Be there in twenty minutes."

"Please hurry," I said to the dead phone.

I hope that's all that's dead tonight, I thought to myself as I headed back to the table. My next thought was *How do I keep from drinking the wine?*

39

Jeffery smiled and said, "Thought you snuck out on me."

"Sorry, there was a line."

He stood and said, "My turn," before heading toward the restroom.

Now's my chance. I grabbed the new glass and rushed to the bar. Cal looked at me, handed a beer to the man standing in front of him, and said, "Something wrong with your wine?"

"Don't have time to talk. Get me another one, take this, and put it behind the bar. Make sure no one touches it and don't pour it out."

"Chris, is something wrong?"

"Please hurry," I said and looked toward the restroom.

Cal must've figured he wasn't going to get anything else

out of me. He poured another glass, gave it to me, and put the other glass under the bar. I thanked him and rushed back to the table before Jeffery returned. I glanced at my watch. Fifteen more minutes to stall before the calvary arrives.

I finished my first glass of wine, set it aside, took a sip out of the new glass, as Jeffery returned to the table.

He said, "What were we talking about?"

I took a large drink from the new glass and said, "You thought the person who killed the three people was a devil worshiper because of the engravings on the handle of the hatchet that killed Ruby Banes."

"You agree, don't you?"

"That's a possibility."

"You don't believe it, do you?"

"I didn't say that. It's as good a guess as anything else."

His gaze narrowed as he said, "I hear you're a good friend of the police chief. What does she think?"

"Don't know," I said, then took another drink before continuing, "She doesn't say much to me about—"

"Hold that thought. Got something to show you," he said, stood and pointed to the door.

"Where're we going?"

"It's in the truck. You'll be interested." He leaned closer and whispered, "It has to do with Ruby's death. The Chief will want to see it."

"What about our drinks?" I said, hopefully to discourage him from us going outside.

"We'll only be gone a second. We'll leave them here, no one will take our table."

It'd look suspicious if I pushed harder to keep us in the building. Since it would be ten or more minutes before Cindy arrived, I didn't want to spook him into leaving before she got here.

As soon as we got outside, he looked at me and said, "You're looking pale, you okay?"

What were the symptoms of wolfsbane poisoning that Cindy had shared? She'd joked that they were things some people over here experienced most Saturdays. Seems like they were lightheadedness, fainting, confusion, and something I couldn't remember.

"Feeling a little lightheaded," I said assuming he'd used the same poison on me that he slipped into Ruby's drink.

We slowly walked to his truck, I lowered my head and shook it like I was close to fainting. He opened the passenger door and said I should sit while he got something out of the rear compartment.

I slid into the front passenger's seat while he went around the truck and opened the rear door, moved a couple of items around, then closed the door. I couldn't see what he was doing until he opened the front driver's side door and hopped in.

Seven or eight more minutes to stall before Cindy showed.

I turned to Jeffery and said, "What do you want to show me?"

He didn't answer, but it didn't take a detective to see it was the pistol he had pointed at my side.

"Chris, you're looking sick. Think I need to take you home."

"What's going on?"

He stared at me as he turned on the ignition, put the truck in gear, glanced in the rearview mirror, pulled onto the street, and sped away from the place where Folly's chief of police was going to meet me.

"You knew it was me," he said as he turned on Center Street and then left on East Ashley Avenue.

"Knew what?"

"Don't play dumb, it's not a good look on you. I saw how you were looking at me at the masquerade party."

"I didn't see you there," I said and wondered what would happen if I opened and jumped out the door with him doing thirty-five miles-per-hour.

"Sure you did. I was Zorro, and I saw you staring at me. One thing I've learned about you is you're a damned good detective. Too good." He glanced at me. "Feeling sick?" He then smiled. "Now you know how Ruby felt, that is, before she felt a stabbing pain in her back."

"Why?"

"Why should I tell you anything?"

"Why not? What do you have to lose? You poisoned my wine, didn't you? I'm dead anyway, so why not tell me?"

"Bad luck."

"Whose?"

"Three of us, Ruby, that kid on Sol Legare Road, and me."

"The hit and run victim?"

"I knew you figured it out. I should've done this days ago. I foolishly told your buddy I knew Ruby. That was my first mistake."

I thought his first mistake was killing Ruby but didn't want to point that out and irritate him more than he already was. He thought he'd poisoned me, so hopefully I'll be able to use that to my advantage.

"What did knowing her have to do with the hit and run?"

"She talked to me that night. She was working, I was getting food for the next day. I also may have had a few beers. Anyway, she was getting off work as I was leaving Harris Teeter. I saw her getting on her scooter but didn't think anything of it." He shook his head, but the handgun pointed at me didn't waiver. "The kid stepped right in front of me, or I think he did. I was in crude terms *drunk as a skunk*. Don't know what really happened. Don't matter, I hit him, killed him. Wouldn't have done him any good if I stopped, so I didn't."

"Did Ruby see it happen?"

"Said she didn't, but I know she was behind me when I left the store's parking lot. How could I take a chance that she did and was lying to me?"

I shook my head and slowly said, "When did she say she didn't see what happened?"

"Next night at Rita's. She thought I bumped into her by accident, but I followed her there from work, came in after her, and acted surprised to see her. She was too gullible for her own good. I slipped something in her drink just like I did yours. How're you feeling, by the way?"

"Sick, dizzy," I said.

He chuckled and said, "It'll get worse."

"Then what happened?"

"Seems like you'd be more concerned with what'll happen next to you, but hey, that's just me. Said she wasn't feeling too good and I, being a perfect gentleman, offered to take her home. You know the rest, Mr. Detective."

"Why...umm, why kill Liam?"

"That boy was smarter than he looked. In fact, he was even a better detective than you are. I'm not certain I know how, but he figured I was responsible for Ruby's death. I said he was smart, but maybe I was wrong. Know what he did?"

"I'm feeling sick, where're we going?"

"Almost there. Don't worry, it won't matter to you. Don't you want to know what Liam did?"

I nodded.

"Had the nerve to come to me on the street, said he knew what I'd done. I'd only talked to the guy a time or two, so I asked what he was talking about. He said I killed Ruby and said for a couple thousand bucks, he'd forget about it. I didn't figure he could've possibly have known that and laughed at him, figuring that'd be all there was to it."

"So why kill him?"

"Started thinking I may've been too quick to sluff him off, to laugh at him," he said then pulled the truck into a parallel parking space in front of the washout section of Folly. Since I'd been in the truck, I'd only seen two vehicles pass us going the other direction, and headlights from one or two behind us. And this was one of the darkest and least populated stretches along the road. "Sorry for the interruption. Here we are, but back to Liam. After I laughed at him, he said I'd regret it. I followed him to your house. At the time, I didn't know why he would be visiting you, that was before I heard so much about you being as nosy as you are and how you meddle in police business. Anyway, for work, I carry a spool of wire in here. It came in handy when I caught up with him at your house. He never saw me coming. I suppose you know what happened next. How're you feeling now?"

I leaned against the side of the door and said, "Bad. Think I'm going to pass out."

"Well, crap. I'd planned to walk you across the street to that field over there and well, let you die where it'd be a couple of days before anyone found you. Now that you're too lazy to walk, I'll have to dump you out here and push you down those steps to the beach. Don't worry, some early-morning surfer will find you. It'll ruin his day, but he'll call someone to come haul your body away."

I doubted I had much longer to find a way out of this. I wondered what the odds were on someone stopping and asking if we needed help? Even better, how about the odds on the police stopping to see why we were here?

How much longer could I stall before he realized I wasn't dying as quickly as he thought I should be?

"Jeffery," I said as I closed my eyes and nodded like I was having trouble staying alert. "Two more questions?"

"Damn, you've earned your reputation. What?"

"Why the hatchet? Were you trying to make Ruby's death look like she was killed, like you said at Cal's, by a devil worshiper?"

He laughed and said, "Want to hear something funny?"

Anything to postpone what he had in mind for me. I slurred, "Yes."

"I bought that hatchet two years ago at a yard sale. Paid three bucks for it. I hadn't even noticed the cat and lettering on it until I took it out of the toolbox in the back of the truck. That was when I decided it'd be a good way to end Ruby's life since I underestimated the amount of poisoning it'd take to kill her. Didn't make that mistake with you. Anyway, I bet that's still throwing the cops for a loop looking for a witch, a warlock, a nut case, or some other weird believer to blame the death on." He looked in the rearview mirror then in the windshield, and said, "Okay, time's up. You just stay leaning against the door while I come around to help you out."

Two thoughts came to me. First, I remembered what Trula Bishop had told me about it being up to the police to catch the killer. And now, Chief LaMond was probably arriving at Cal's looking for me. Second, what do I do now?

40

I'm certain the sky had been darker, but I couldn't remember when. The nearest house was several hundred yards down the road and even farther the other direction. I'd remembered a vehicle or two behind us, but none were in sight.

My only hope was to somehow fake being unconscious and surprise Jeffery when he was least expecting it. Of course, there were problems with that plan. He was taller than I was, appeared much stronger, not to mention, being my junior by twenty years.

I was trying to figure out my escape, when he opened the door that I was leaning against. I nearly fell out of the truck.

He smiled, and said, "Sorry. I almost forgot, you said you had two questions and you only asked one. Wouldn't want you to think I was rude." His chuckle turned to a laugh. "A killer, yes, but not rude."

I saw no humor in his comment, but since I didn't have a viable plan to escape, I said, "Why did you break into Trudy's apartment?"

"I'd love to tell you, but to be honest, it's sort of a long story, and I'm afraid you wouldn't be around to hear the end of it. Now, before you drop dead, lean more this way so I can pull you out of the truck. Wouldn't want you to hurt yourself falling out."

I leaned on the door handle and slowly put my right foot on the running board while looking for a way to swing my body behind his torso and clamp my arms around his neck. I didn't think he would figure I was well enough to do that, but he still didn't turn enough for me to get behind him. He jerked me the rest of the way out of the truck, and I landed hard on the sandy area between the road and the steps leading to the walkway over the dunes and down to the beach.

"Damn, am I going to have to drag you up those stairs? Can't you get up?"

I didn't say anything, so he began pulling me. My best option was to let him get me to the top of the seven steps leading to the landing and then to the steps down to the beach. If I could catch him off guard, there was a chance I could push him down the stairs. A slim chance, but at least, a chance.

I was afraid he was going to break my back while trying

to drag me up the steps, so I faked leaning on my side and pulling up the wooden steps with my arms and pushing with my legs. The painful trip up the steps took forever, but I, with help from Jeffery made it to the landing where I collapsed.

Still no traffic.

"Change of plans," he said. "You're useless, so I'm going to have to push you off the top of the stairs. Sorry if anything breaks on your way down, but that should be okay since you won't feel it." He then dragged me across the landing until we were near the stairs leading to the beach. "One more thing, I want to apologize for killing your cop friend. It was his fault, you know. He saw me outside Trudy's building and started chasing me. I had to shoot him, don't you know? Sorry."

Jeffery then made a mistake that I hoped he'd be sorry for. He turned away from me and scanned the beach to see if anyone was nearby. He started to turn back to me when I rammed my foot into the back of his calf. He shouted a profanity. His leg buckled and he tumbled headfirst down the steps.

I didn't wait to see if or how badly he was injured. I took one look at him, said, "That's for Allen," and pushed up from the landing and ran as fast as my aging legs would carry me down the stairs toward the road. I was thankful it was as dark as it was. I couldn't see where I was going and knew if Jeffery had managed to get up unscathed, he'd have a difficult time finding me in the dark.

It was pitch dark until it wasn't. I was startled when the headlights from a vehicle that'd been parked fifty or so yards behind us in the sand along the street came on blinding me. I put my hand over my eyes enough to block out much of the light and hurried in the direction of the strange car.

The driver's door opened, someone stepped out, and said, "How long's it been, Chris?"

"Mel?"

"Who else would be out here in the middle of nowhere saving your bony butt? So, how long's it been since I saved you the last time?"

I wasn't ready for a quiz but couldn't have been happier seeing Mad Mel. "Don't recall, now again, what're you doing out here?"

"Following you and your friend. Speaking of him, what'd you do with him?"

"I'll answer you after you help me round him up before he gets in his truck and leaves."

"Point the way."

I did. We found Jeffery still at the bottom of the steps. He had managed to sit up and was gripping his left leg while mumbling something about it being broken. I, and I doubt Mel, had any sympathy for him. Mel lifted the disabled killer while I fished through the nearby sand and found his weapon.

"I ain't carrying this sand-covered criminal in my pristine Camaro. Get his keys and I'll stuff him in the back of his truck so you can take him wherever you want to. I'll follow in case I need to save you again."

Mel, good to his word, stuffed Jeffery in the back of his

truck, removed Jeffery's belt, and looped it around his wrists and tightened it to the point of Jeffery uttering another profanity. Mel smiled.

On the way to town, I called Cindy and apologized for not being at Cal's when she arrived and said I'd explain everything if she'd meet us in front of her office.

"You sure you'll be there this time? Remember I gave up a wonderful meal trying to chase you down."

I promised her I would be there. And I was. While I didn't provide her with a *wonderful meal*, I told her a story that she said made her year. I know it made mine.

Cindy took possession of Jeffery Fuller, escorted him into the fire station downstairs from her office and left Mel and me sitting in his *pristine Camaro* where I once again asked him what he was doing parked behind Jeffery's truck.

"Was coming to Folly to tell you the good news. Caldwell and I have worked out our differences. Knew you were worried, and I wanted you to be one of the first to know. I also figured you'd buy me a beer to celebrate."

"That's great, congratulations."

"I was headed to your house but thought you might be out and about since you have trouble staying at home. I figured you'd be at Cal's or Loggerhead's and went by Cal's first. Guess who I surveilled walking out of there? You looked like you were staggering drunk. That wasn't like you, so I decided to follow in case you needed me to save your butt, save it again."

"I didn't see you behind us."

"That's because I was a Marine. We're trained to be sneaky. Anyway, I parked and saw him lugging you up the steps and was about ready to come save you. Did I mention, save you again?"

"Several times. And I appreciate it."

41

I t'd been two days since my near-fatal encounter with Jeffery Fuller and my body still complained as I slowly maneuvered my way out of bed. Catching a killer is a young man's game, and as Chief LaMond has repeatedly reminded me, a job for law enforcement. Working through the pain in my back was my first task of the day, so I shuffled to the kitchen to fix coffee. I grabbed a bag of powdered donuts, waited for Mr. Coffee to do its thing, and plopped down in one of the kitchen chairs.

My thoughts were filled with relief that my little island would again return to normal with no killer stalking its citizens. The depressing and powerful feeling of loss was still at the forefront. I was having a difficult time accepting that Allen Spencer would no longer be part of my life. Even when

I'd handed Jeffery off to Cindy, I half expected Allen to be there to assist.

The phone ringing forced me out of my thoughts. I glanced at the caller ID and was surprised to see Cal's name.

"Morning, Cal."

"Hey, stranger, Happy Halloween. Calling to make sure you're coming to tonight's party?"

"Are costumes required?"

"Not unless you're itchin' to wear one."

"Not this year."

"Is that like not this year, not last year, not next year?"

"Exactly."

"Got it. See you there."

The phone went dead, and I was once again reminded how nearly everyone I knew was adopting Charles's phone etiquette.

I was pouring a second cup of coffee when a knock on the front door provided the second sound to interrupt my morning. This time it was my best friend.

"Morning, Charles." I stepped back so he could enter.

"Don't want to bother you but wanted to stop by for a minute to make sure you're okay."

"I'm sore, but otherwise okay. Want coffee?"

"Nah, already had enough."

"I'm surprised I haven't heard from you earlier."

"After you called the other day and told me what happened with Jeffery, I figured I wouldn't bother you since you obviously didn't need my help."

"Don't be like that. I couldn't risk your life, not after Allen's, umm, death."

"What, you think I'd be any better off if I lost my best friend?"

"But you didn't."

"I understand Allen's murder affected you a bunch, so I'll overlook you going rogue on me. Don't let it happen again. Remember, I'm the brains behind this outfit."

I didn't remind him that he'd always claimed that was my contribution to his detective agency, nor that I'd told him I was looking for him when I was taken by Jeffery. I said, "Deal, next time I go after a hit and runner, poisoner, hatchet hacker, garroter, shooter you'll be my first call."

"That's better. Will I see your smiling face at Cal's party?"

"He called right before you got here and reminded me it was tonight. I'll be there."

"Good. I'll be anxious to see your costume."

"You know—"

He laughed, said he had to make two deliveries for Dude, and left.

At least some things don't change. My friends will always be there for me, and they have no concept how people off this island handle phone calls.

I spent the rest of the morning and afternoon resting and trying to keep my mind off Jeffery, Allen, and the other untimely deaths. The weather turned dreary as I left for the party. A light mist began falling and the evening couldn't have felt more like Halloween. As I approached Cal's front door, which was draped with a string of orange LED lights, I saw a large werewolf growling and snarling at me. Since it was standing vertical and six-foot tall, I figured it contained a person and I wasn't in much danger, but it did get my attention.

A voice behind me made me jump and pivot, coming face to face with Chief LaMond. Instead of her usual attire, she was dressed as a zombie with tattered clothes and a bloody gash across her face.

"You look lovely, but I don't think you needed to dress so formally for Cal's."

"Smart ass," she said through blood running down her cheek. "Larry and I are on our way to Charleston for our annual Ghouls and Gals party. I saw you and figured I'd catch you up before you went in."

"Everyone would love to see you dressed up. Why not come in for a few minutes?"

"Nope, need to get away with my hubby for some down time, but wanted to let you know what Jeffery had to say after you deposited him at the fire station."

"He confess to everything he told me?"

"You may not believe this, but yes." She shook her head. "The dummy refused a lawyer and wrote down everything from the hit and run, to the other three deaths, and abducting one senior citizen."

"Did he say why he waited so long after Ruby's death to break into Trudy's apartment?"

"Matter of fact, he did. He talked to Trudy at the

masquerade party, well more like Trudy talked to him. She asked if he knew anyone needing a place to stay to help pay the rent on her apartment."

"He broke in to see if he'd be interested in renting the room?"

She rolled her zombie eyes and said, "No, during their conversation, Trudy mentioned having all of Ruby's things boxed up taking up space in the apartment. She told him that the only thing of much value was her cell phone."

"Did I miss the reason for him breaking in?"

"The mention of the phone had Jeffery thinking that Ruby may've taken a picture of his truck after the hit and run. He looked for a phone when he killed her but couldn't find it. As he put it, finding the phone became an obsession, he had to get it. He broke in and was going through Ruby's stuff when he heard someone coming up the steps. He hid in the closet but instead of the newcomer, who happened to be Trudy, entering the apartment, she stayed in the corridor and called us before heading out front to wait for help to arrive. Jeffery rushed out of the apartment when Officer Spencer arrived and saw him running through the back yard. You know the rest." Cindy paused and held her breath, eyes closed.

"Did he say anything else?"

"Believe it or not, he apologized for killing Officer Spencer. Said Allen didn't deserve that fate." She sighed. "Like the others did?"

"Thanks for letting me know. Sure you don't want to come in?"

"Nope, got ghouls to dance with in Charleston." She started for her vehicle, paused, turned back to me, and said, "One more thing. Allen was figuring this all out. This morning, I was going through his effects from the coroner's office." She slowly shook her head. "I couldn't do it when I got them the other day. Anyway, I found his notebook. He'd written that Ruby's death was related to the hit and run, and Liam must've known about it, but Allen couldn't put his finger on how." She hesitated before saying, "Chris, his last entry was about you."

"About me, why?"

"He considered you a friend." She smiled and said, "Hell if I know why. Anyway, it said, 'Talk to Chris and tell him about my theory and warn him.' That was all."

Was that what Allen had started to tell me when he got the call about the break in? I'll never know.

"Sorry, it has to be hard for you."

"It's hard for all of us to lose such a good man."

I gave Cindy a tight hug. She leaned in and hugged back. We stood there for a minute before she stepped back and said, "Zombies don't cry," and wiped her face before adding, "Larry is waiting. Happy Halloween, Chris. Try and stay out of trouble, I'm dead tired of murder."

"You look it."

She slapped my arm and turned away. I think she mumbled, "Smart ass."

I watched as she walked to her car. When she opened the passenger door, I saw Larry dressed as Frankenstein, green makeup, and all. He waved when he saw me looking. I turned and walked into Cal's.

42

Cal always went to extremes with Christmas decorations. Walking through the door I realized his Halloween décor might outshine the Yuletide. A look around revealed glowing jack-o-lanterns, bats hanging from the ceiling, animated witches, and ghosts along two of the walls. Every table featured a glowing cauldron or an old-fashioned lantern. Strands of orange lights like those around the front door were strung above and around the bar. The jukebox was playing the theme song from *The Addams Family* television series.

Before I could make my way to the bar, Barb, dressed in an orange sweater and long black skirt, walked up beside me, placed a kiss on the cheek, and said, "How are you doing?"

"Better, you look festive."

"I love this sweater but with the color I can only wear it on Halloween, otherwise risk being called a pumpkin."

"Or a candy corn." I said, laughed, and received a smack on my arm.

"Mr. Comedian, why don't you get us a drink and meet me over there with Trudy and Beth?" She nodded toward a table where the two ladies were seated.

I watched Barb make her way back towards the table and noticed that Beth had brought Festus, that is, unless there was another cat on Folly the size of a Labrador Retriever.

Beth, and I assumed Trudy, were talking when Barb arrived at the table. They turned and smiled at her and the three seemed to be friends. I made my way up to the bar, where Junior was pulling beers from the cooler and handing them to the line of patrons.

He saw me standing off to the side and said, "Welcome to Cal's Halloween to Remember."

"I had no idea your dad enjoyed Halloween this much. The amount of décor comes close to what he does at Christmas."

"He didn't until he found out that it's my favorite holiday. To my surprise, he went all out."

"You, talking about me behind my back?" Cal said as he came up behind me and put his hand on my shoulder. His Stetson had a jack-o-lantern pin with illuminated eyes and his rhinestone jacket had a bat on the lapel.

I smiled, turned to shake the crooner's hand, and said, "Nope, not behind your back. We're in front of you."

"Cute. Happy Halloween pard, glad you're still around to enjoy it."

"Me, too."

"You never can tell about a person." He shook his head. "Everyone wears a mask of some sort. Jeffery had us fooled, except for you, that is."

"The decorations look great, and you have a good crowd. Let's focus on that."

"They're all here to hear my rendition of "Monster Mash." It'll be the highlight of the night."

"No doubt," I said not knowing if he was teasing about the song. "I'd better get this drink over to Barb before she finds another fellow."

Cal tipped his Stetson toward the ladies, and said, "Never keep a pretty lady waiting."

I was halfway across the room when I noticed a dark presence near the small stage. Desmond was standing beside Roisin. Next to her was Lugh licking the face of Pluto happily perched in Dude's arms. I detoured over to the Wiccans, the surfer, and their canine companions.

Roisin gave me a hug while being careful not to spill the two drinks I was carrying.

"Mr. Chris, so happy to see you."

"It's good to see you too, and you as well, Desmond."

Desmond said, "Heard you caught another bad guy, this one with the help of that old Camaro dude, Mad Melvin."

I laughed at Mel being called old and Melvin, details I wouldn't share with him.

Dude said, "Christer be hero."

"Not a hero, stupid and lucky," I said.

"Not a good combination; someone your age should be wiser," Desmond said and offered one of his smirks.

Roisin looked up at her brother and said, "Desmond, be nice."

"Roisin, it's fine. He's joking." I said and smiled at Desmond. His smirk got wider as he nodded.

"Lugh was telling Pluto goodbye," Roisin said. "Mom let us come over for a little while but wanted us home before things got wild in here, something about it being a bar."

"That's understandable, and good advice."

Desmond took a step toward Lugh, grabbed his collar, and said, "We witches need to fly, can't be late collecting souls or stirring cauldrons."

"Desmond, you are impossible. Why does Mom let you out of the house?"

Dude said, "Dark Prince be joking," then patted Lugh's head as the large dog gave Pluto a final lick.

Roisin looked at her brother and said, "If your girlfriend was here, you wouldn't be such a buffoon."

Desmond said, "You don't even know what buffoon means."

She glared at Desmond and said, "Yes, I do, it means you."

With that, Desmond let out a big "Shhh," pointed to the jukebox as Credence Clearwater Revival's "Bad Moon Rising" filled the room, hooked the leash on Lugh's collar, and started toward the door.

Roisin smiled after getting in the last word with her brother, the buffoon. She gave me a small curtsy and followed Desmond and Lugh. After going about five feet away, she turned to me and said, "Tell Mr. Charles I said hi, and that life is too short to be mad at his best friend."

I wondered how she knew about Charles's anger with me, although when it came to Roisin, nothing should surprise me.

After the Stones left, Dude turned to talk to someone who made a comment about Pluto's fancy collar. I headed to Barb who had been waiting patiently for me and her drink.

She took her drink and said, "Chris, you know Trudy and Beth, and this is Festus."

"Yes, we met at the masquerade party, except for Festus."

"Unfortunately, I didn't meet them there," Barb said. "We've been having a pleasant conversation and I got to meet Festus."

I said, "It's good to see you both again and to meet such a beautiful cat."

Trudy walked around the table and shook my hand. Unlike the first time we met, her grip was softer as was the look in her eyes.

"Chris, thank you for finding out who killed Ruby and that sweet officer. We can all breathe easier."

"Don't forget Liam." Beth spoke for the first time, her smile darkened by the sad look in her eyes.

"I was lucky. Somehow, I put the pieces together and managed not to get myself killed in the process."

Barb reached over and squeezed my arm. I turned towards her and placed a quick kiss on her cheek, knowing later we'd be having a conversation about my meddling in things that didn't concern me or that could get me killed.

I turned to Trudy, "You look more at ease than you did at the party."

"I'm nearly back to my old self. Not only is the murderer of my roommate off the street, I have a new roommate, this time, one I have much in common with."

"That's wonderful. Who?"

"That would be Festus and me," Beth said. "Met Trudy at the masquerade party, and we connected. She loves cats and this way I can still maintain my business and save money to eventually buy a house. It's a win for everyone."

"That's great."

"Oh, there's Preacher Burl." Beth said as she picked up Festus and left to meet Burl in the center of the room.

She said something to the preacher and pointed over to us. They headed our way as "Witchy Woman" by the Eagles played. Apparently, Cal had loaded every Halloween-themed song he could find on his normally country-centered machine.

Burl's sweater was appropriate for the event since it featured an orange carved pumpkin with a smiley face and battery-powered LED lights in the eyes and mouth.

"Brother Chris, Sister Barb, and of course Sister Trudy,

Happy Halloween. Who wants to be the first to comment on my holiday sweater?"

I said, "I didn't realize Halloween had an ugly sweater contest?"

"I suppose I asked for that. Anyway, Brother Chris, I'm thrilled to see you are still on this side of the grass. Like I've told you before, I am in no hurry to preach your eulogy."

"I'm thrilled to be here."

Burl took my arm and steered me away from the table. We moved out of earshot of the others. Burl leaned close and said, "Brother Charles is outside keeping company with that toothy werewolf. May I suggest you go talk to him?"

"What's he doing out there?"

"He wouldn't say."

I nodded and weaved my way among the ever-growing crowd, with some dressed in everyday attire, and others in costumes. As I walked out the door, Charlie Daniels was telling the story of the Devil who went to Georgia. The October air hit me, and my body shivered as I looked for my friend. He was standing beside the road and watching the werewolf that'd greeted me when I arrived. The beast was heading toward Center Street.

"Charles, who was that?"

"Don't know. Why?"

"Call me odd, but I think it's strange seeing a tall werewolf on the sidewalk."

Charles smiled and said, "It's Folly."

I know a dead end when I arrive at one, so I said, "You okay? Come in and join the fun."

His smile faded. He looked at the sidewalk then at me before saying, "Couldn't go inside yet... I, umm." He stepped closer and gave me a tight hug.

Were those tears in his eyes or water from the light rain? I stood frozen and shocked since that was something he'd never done.

"Charles—"

"Damnit, you should've known better, going off on your own hunting a killer. I could've lost my best friend." He took a step back and wiped his face, adding, "Damn rainwater."

"Sorry."

"Promise me you'll never do anything like that again."

"Never, next time you can be the victim," I said, hoping to bring a smile to his face.

He chuckled, slapped me on the back, and pointed to the door. "You going to keep me out here all night or buy me a beer?"

We made our way into the bar where Charles saw Pluto and went to talk to him and possibly Dude, while I got our drinks.

Cal handed me wine and a beer for Charles before I ordered. He tipped his hat and said, "On the house."

I made it back to Charles who'd finished talking with Pluto and Dude when Waylon and Victor walked through the door, saw Charles and me, then headed our way.

I said, "Waylon, Victor, it's good seeing you."

Waylon smiled and said, "It's good knowing we're off your suspect list for killing those folks."

"Why would you think you were on a list?" Charles said and took his beer from my hand.

"We show up to town and then three people get killed. I'd have me on a list." Victor slapped Waylon on the back. "If not me, certainly this bald-headed freak."

The bald freak said, "We wanted to tell you both how much we love your island, and we'll be back."

"You're leaving?"

"Our construction work is seasonal and now moves to southern Florida and then Texas."

Charles said, "Safe travels."

"Thanks, we're going to close this place down tonight and head out in the morning."

The music tempo changed, and I recognized Louis Armstrong singing something about skeletons in a closet. I looked over to Barb and saw she didn't appear to be missing me since there was a group of people around her. Charles left to talk with Junior who was behind the bar.

My attention was drawn to the door as Mel walked in holding hands with Caldwell. I smiled and waved at the two men and went to greet them.

"Great seeing you both."

Caldwell let go of Mel's hand and grasped my hand with both of his. "Wonderful to be here and so thankful you're okay."

"I'm only okay because of Mel. If it wasn't for him, we may not be having this conversation."

"Yeah, I saved your life again. Amazing how many times I've had to do that for a draft dodger."

"Thank you again for being there, nice to know I have friends who will go out of their way to help."

"After I saved you and got the killer to the cops, I started contemplating how short life is and how in an instant it could be gone. Chris, it shook this old Marine knowing how silly people can be and worry about such unimportant things."

Self-reflection wasn't a phrase I'd ever associate with Mel, so I was speechless.

Fortunately, Caldwell wasn't, and said, "I was at home when Mel got back and for the first time in a long time, I saw the man I fell in love with. We'd talked earlier and realized we needed and wanted each other."

"It's not going to be all roses, but now we know what each wants and we'll go from there."

"That is the best news I've heard in a long time."

Mel cleared his throat and said, "Enough touchy-feely crap, let's get this party started." He and Caldwell headed to the bar.

Louis Armstrong continued his spooky tunes with "Jeepers Creepers" and I was surprised how many people got up to dance. I'll never understand the fun of this holiday. I leaned against the wall and watched everyone when a couple caught my eye, Alyssa and Jose. When he saw me, he grabbed Alyssa's hand and walked my way.

Jose said, "You okay? We heard about the abduction."

Alyssa said, "I was telling Jose how shocking it was to learn it was Jeffery Fuller. He seemed so nice after our fender bender."

I said, "It crossed my mind how he'd been so gracious and not wanting to involve the police. After everything was over it struck me. Jeffery didn't want to call attention to his truck or himself after that hit and run when there could have been some evidence of the accident on the vehicle, and he didn't know in addition to Ruby who may've seen his vehicle that night."

"You never know about people," Jose said and wrapped his arm around Alyssa's waist. "I'm grateful you were there with Alyssa when they collided." He looked toward the bar and added, "I need to get this pretty lady a burger and beer. Again, glad you are among the living."

A voice behind me got my attention.

"This is some pumpkins."

"Virgil, didn't see you there, what about pumpkins?"

"Oh, Christopher, I am falling short in teaching you Victorian jargon. The phrase *some pumpkins* is slang for something that is terrific or impressive. Also, it's appropriate with today being Halloween."

"Thanks for the lesson," I said, while failing to mention that I probably will have forgotten it by tomorrow.

"You're fortunate to be here if what I've heard is true.

Going off fighting evildoers on your own, leaving Charles and me out of it." He shook his head.

"*Damfino*, he wants all the glory, the boy's getting too big for his britches," Charles said as he walked up beside Virgil and tipped his beer bottle in my direction.

I said, "Not true, and what's *damfino*?"

"It means *damn if I know*. Virgil taught it to me yesterday when we were discussing your near-death experience."

"He's a quick study, Christopher, a worldly man." Virgil and Charles broke out laughing and I couldn't help but join in.

Our attention was directed to the small stage as Cal reached the microphone and tapped it twice. Junior turned off the jukebox midway through "Purple People Eater" and I for one was not disappointed.

"Evening Halloweeners," Cal said, "Can I have your attention? Preacher Burl, will you join me on stage?"

Burl had the deer in the headlights look, before clearing his throat. "It's bad enough you get me up there Christmas. I'm happy down here."

Cal straightened to his full height, and said, "Please come forth, preacher man."

Burl sighed, stepped on the elevated stage, looked around the room, and then at Cal who had a smile on his face.

Cal said, "I know this is a party, but we're missing one of our own. I, and I know you, would be honored if Preacher Burl said a few words." He then stepped back and motioned Burl to the fist-sized antique silver microphone.

"It would be my pleasure. Thank you, Brother Cal, for the opportunity. Most of us in this room knew Officer Allen Spencer and all the great things he did for our community, both on and off the job. Brother Allen never put himself above anyone else. He treated everyone fairly, listened to what they had to say, and even those he arrested he treated with respect. Brother Allen was a good man who will be missed. Let's have a moment of silence to reflect and remember him."

Silence filled the room. The only sounds heard were a few sniffles and the clearing of a throat. Burl whispered, "Amen."

Cal returned to the microphone. "Thanks, Preacher. Now to what you all have been waiting for, my version of 'Monster Mash.'" Cal strummed his guitar and sang the best and possibly craziest version of the Halloween classic. Many customers joined in. I was not one of them. I made my way across the room with Charles and Virgil to stand beside Barb and watch the wonderful, if not a bit kooky citizens of Folly sing and dance along to Cal's singing.

What a Halloween, I thought, in more ways than one.

ABOUT THE AUTHOR

Bill Noel is the best-selling author of twenty-four novels in the popular Folly Beach Mystery series. The award-winning novelist is also a fine arts photographer and lives in Louisville, Kentucky, with his wife, Susan, and his off-kilter imagination.

Angelica Cruz is the award-winning coauthor of *Sea Fog: A Folly Beach Halloween Mystery and Pretty Paper: A Folly Beach Christmas Mystery*. Ms. Cruz lives near Elizabethtown, Kentucky, with her husband Hector, two dogs, a bird, two cats, and four chickens.

Learn more about the series and the author by visiting www. billnoel.com.

BILL NOEL'S
FOLLY
BEACH
SOUTH CAROLINA

1 Rita's
2 Dude's surf shop *
3 Sand Dollar
4 Haunted House *
5 Loggerhead's
6 Snapper Jacks
7 St. James Gate
8 Surf Bar
9 Cal's
10 Mr. John's Beach Store
11 Landrum Gallery/Barb's Books *
12 The Crab Shack
13 City Hall/Public Safety
14 Sean Aker, Attorney *

15 Planet Follywood
16 Woody's Pizza
17 The Washout
18 Post Office
19 Pewter Hardware *
20 Lost Dog Cafe
21 Bert's Market
22 The Edge *

* From my imagination to yours.

Printed in the USA
CPSIA information can be obtained
at www.ICGtesting.com
LVHW021243281023
762436LV00010B/709